THE ONCE YELLOW HOUSE

Gemma Amor

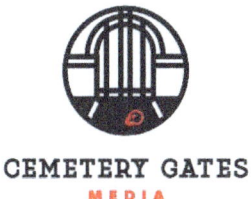

CEMETERY GATES
MEDIA

The Once Yellow House
Published by Cemetery Gates Media
Binghamton, New York

Copyright © 2023
by Gemma Amor

All rights reserved. Without limiting the rights under the copyright reserved above, no part of this publication may be reproduced, stored in, or introduced into a retrieval system, or transmitted in any form or by any means (electronic, mechanical, photocopying, recording, or otherwise) without prior written permission.

ISBN: 9798386489762

For more information about this book and other Cemetery Gates Media publications, visit us at:

cemeterygatesmedia.com
twitter.com/cemeterygatesm
instagram.com/cemeterygatesm

Cover Art & Design: Gemma Amor

For you.

You know who you are.

I don't.

"You have a mystery service ahead, and will soon enough realise what is expected of you."

—Hilma af Klint

"Yellow, if steadily gazed at in any geometrical form, has a disturbing influence, and reveals in the colour an insistent, aggressive character."

—W. Kandinsky

FOREWORD

For as long as I can remember, I've been drawn to works of epistolary fiction. It's a subgenre that lends itself quite naturally to horror as it presents the events unfolding throughout the narrative as honest and factual. There's something so deliciously unnerving about reading material that feels like you're reading something you shouldn't be. It feels inherently forbidden, as if what you're reading is taboo, or off-limits.

That's exactly how I felt while reading Amor's *The Once Yellow House*. When Gemma first approached me to write the introduction for this book, I was, of course, honored. I have been a devoted fan of Gemma's work since I first read *Dear Laura* upon its initial publication in 2019. I think what attracted me initially to Gemma's fiction was how heartfelt it seemed. More to the point, because of her honesty and the care she takes when crafting characters and sentences, her fiction seemed slightly dangerous to read, as if the pages could unfurl and swallow you whole at any moment. That kind of danger—that uncanny feeling of unease when reading a book—is exactly what I look for when I search for compelling horror fiction.

When Gemma told me that she was writing a piece told entirely in the epistolary format, I was immediately intrigued. Gemma and I had already been on an Epistolary Horror panel together at StokerCon in 2021 where we were able to analyse the sub-genre and explore why it remains so fascinating to readers. As I began reading *The Once Yellow House*, I found myself instantly unsettled. It felt so decidedly uncomfortable to read—in the best way, of course. Gemma has crafted a dangerously compelling narrative where information is fed to the reader bit by bit. Moreover, there's something so delightfully troubling about the work and the way in which the events are presented. The book is a complex puzzle that must be solved by the reader.

I think that's another reason why I admire the epistolary format so much—it's an engaging sub-genre that forces the reader to become an active participant in the narrative's events. We, as the reader, become somewhat complicit in the horrors that are unfolding before us. We consequently become a character in the book's narrative whether we want to or not. As I previously mentioned—reading Gemma's fiction feels somewhat dangerous, as if we're reading something we shouldn't have access to. I would argue that's what makes Gemma such a brilliant voice in epistolary horror. There's something about the way in which the information is presented in this book that makes it seem like we have private access to something unusual and decidedly bizarre. It feels prohibited, as if an authority figure were about to snatch the book from our hands and scold us for reading the contents at any moment.

In fact, as I write this introduction, I'm reminded of how horror has been unfairly maligned by the mainstream. Horror, in general, feels forbidden sometimes. We are told we should be ashamed to read horror, that it's not a 'legitimate' literary genre. You can imagine my outrage when I'm told such ludicrous things by others. If ever there were substantial proof that horror has literary merit, it's because of authors like Gemma who are confidently operating in the field and producing high quality work with such tenderness and care.

I say this with the utmost certainty: *The Once Yellow House* is probably my favorite work of Gemma's to date. Not only is it a testament to her remarkable talent as one of our finest contemporary horror writers, but the book skilfully illustrates how the epistolary format remains one of the most effective sub-genres of horror.

That said, there's something uniquely dangerous about this book. I urge you to continue reading to find out why…

Eric LaRocca
Boston, MA
November 2022

A QUICK NOTE FROM THE AUTHOR

This is a strange book. For me, at least. Strange not just for the format I decided upon after a lot of humming and haa-ing, but for some of the concepts and imagery that popped up as I wrote. I have long wanted to explore the relationship between art and love, art and horror, and art and spirituality, but I did not expect some of the other things that arose while exploring those themes. The more research I did, the more these individual elements flourished and intertwined. Science and geometry in nature, mathematical principles and coincidences, the wondrous way that colours work, the interconnect between organised religion and symbolism and then some other, darker themes. Like control. Like abuse of power. Like love, but a corrupted form of love, love that binds people together whilst not necessarily making them happy.

And with that (as is becoming habit before I let you dive in) I would like to point out that there are a couple of themes in this book that some readers may wish to be cognisant of before they start reading. Domestic violence and relational abuse, references to baby loss, and some inferences of sexual exploitation and abuse, to be clear.

My due diligence done, it only remains for me to thank you, once again, dearest reader, for your continued support. This is my eleventh book (my fourth for Cemetery Gates Media, who hold my eternal gratitude), and I really hope you like it.

And the colour yellow.

Gemma
March 2023

A NOTE FROM THE EDITOR

The following account of what has become known as the Yellow Massacre of 2020, in which three hundred and forty-seven members of a secretive society known as 'The Retinue' were brutally slaughtered at a property registered to married couple Hope (missing and wanted for questioning) and Thomas (believed deceased) Gloucester, has been collated from a variety of sources.

These sources include: entries and sketches from the alleged personal scrapbook/diary of Hope Gloucester herself, intelligent verbatim transcriptions (cleaned) of a recorded conversation that took place (exact date unknown) between Hope and an anonymous participant (for the purposes of this book we have referred to her as 'Kate'), emails between Kate and our editor, and other sources including pertinent web articles, letters to local news publications and extra references we have deemed relevant.

As forensic work to precisely I.D. the extensive human remains found at the property (known locally as the 'Once Yellow House') continues in the aftermath of the tragedy, there is still much mystery, obfuscation and misreporting surrounding the tragic and bloody event. In particular, the precise role played by Hope and Thomas Gloucester in the so-called massacre.

Thomas Gloucester in particular is an enigmatic figure around which many conflicting stories circulate: we found numerous references to him in various online social media groups as a 'Leader, 'Father', 'God' and other flattering honorifics. Digging into his multiple internet personas and behaviours threatens to take even the most rational of explorers down a deep, dark rabbit hole, for he was a prolific 'online' individual who maintained a number of distinct and separate characters, alt accounts and burner profiles. Beyond the internet, whispers (as of yet unsubstantiated) of familial abuse predate Gloucester's tenure as leader of the Retinue. These whispers conflict with the image he presented at large to his wide circle of colleagues, friends and peers in the years before he moved with Hope to the Once Yellow House. That image was polished, professional, and to all intents and purposes, Thomas was a loving husband, stable partner and reliable friend to those who knew him.

Conversely, little is known of Thomas' artist wife Hope, who largely kept to herself and did not seem to engage with any online activity beyond occasional emails. Her presence on social media platforms is non-existent, and as a self-employed creative she did not have a large circle of friends or colleagues with whom she interacted, like her husband. Those acquaintances we have been able to track down remain tight-lipped and ultimately unhelpful when it comes to providing more insight into her character for the purposes of this book. What we do know is that Hope struggled at school, was diagnosed with dyslexia at the age of ten, and emigrated to the United States from Bristol, in the UK, when she was eighteen years old. Beyond that, she has been a murky character in a slowly unfolding horror story that has gripped many of us for some time. Murky until, we hope, now.

It is for this reason—to shed light on a confusing and divisive incident—that we are publishing this collection of materials. We thought long and hard about whether doing so before conferring with the relevant authorities was the right course of action, however, we believe it is. The obliteration of the Retinue during the Yellow Massacre has, without a doubt, become one of the most compelling unsolved mysteries of the decade, if not century. To date, no one individual or organisation has been charged with the perpetration of any crime. The families of those involved in the massacre remain in the dark as to why their loved ones died in such a brutal and unexpected fashion. This darkness has been perpetuated by heavy censorship of any reporting on the incident.

It would be too easy to think of this manuscript as simple exploitation of a poorly documented tragedy, but we do not view it that way. We view it as an attempt to shine a light into the dark.

Regardless of your thoughts on our motivations as publisher, what follows is a collection of somewhat surreal first-hand accounts of a catastrophe that seems to be part truth, part rumour, part fantasy, and one might even suggest: part performance art. The exact formulae of these potent ingredients will only ever be determined by those who were there on the 19th of November 2020, which we were not.

This book is a limited-edition small print run. We have elected to donate all earnings from the sale of this publication to the Yellow House Charitable Organisation, founded by an anonymous benefactor to help those who have left fundamentalist groups and cults to start a new life in safety.

Readers will note: we have taken a few liberties with the presentation to make your experience a little less chaotic. All timestamps have been removed from audio transcriptions, for ease of reading. Images are annotated where possible.

The cover art is by Hope Gloucester herself, taken from an original work of art as discovered in her scrapbook.
All liability falls at the feet of the publisher.

Brhel & Sullivan
Cemetery Gates Media
March 2023

1.

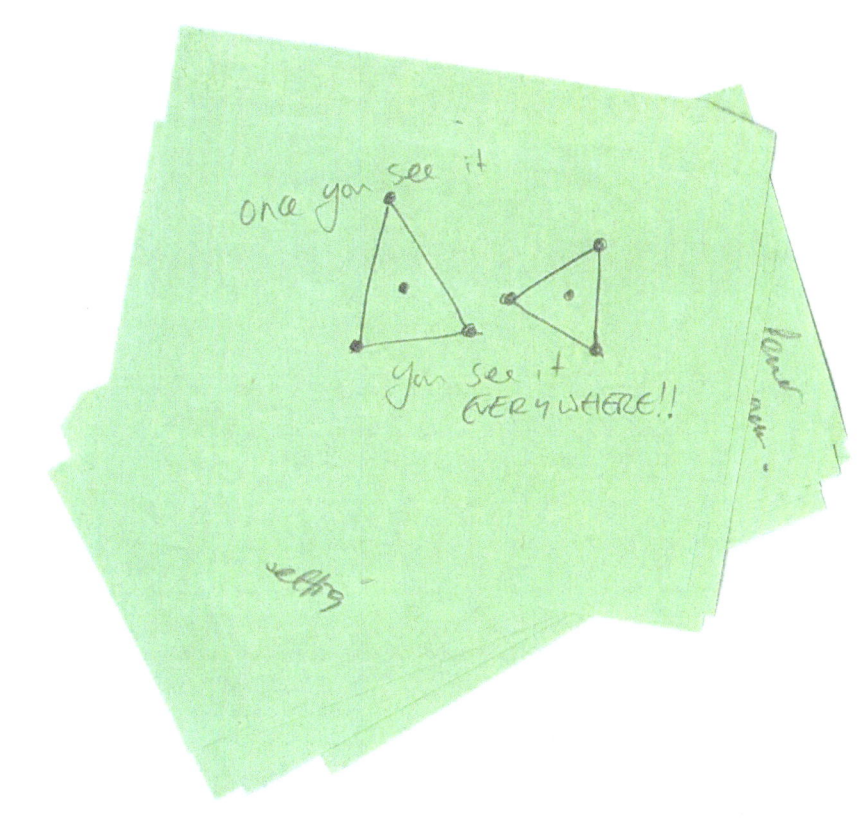

13

2.

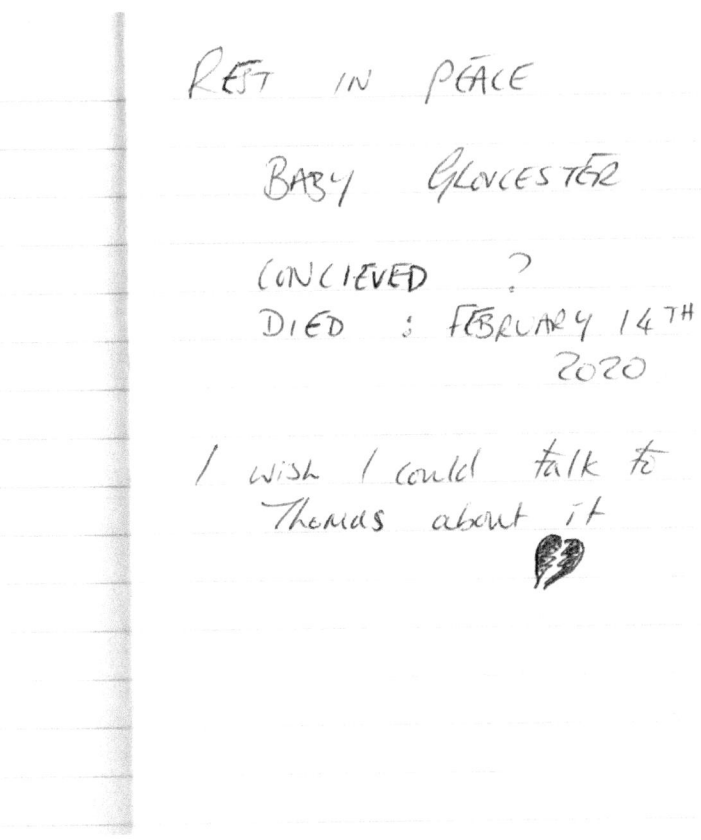

Scanned excerpt of a note found in Hope Gloucester's diary/scrapbook, dated February 14th, 2020[1]

---

[1] *Hope rarely speaks of this event in her diary again, despite the obvious trauma associated with baby loss. It is noticeable that this sad occurrence takes place (on Valentine's Day) only a few weeks before Hope and Thomas relocate to the Once Yellow House. One would assume the miscarriage added significantly to Hope's mental burden and the noticeable stress of moving house.*

3.

Diary Entry, personal diary of Hope Gloucester
October 15th, 2020 (1)

Today, when I went in to see to Thomas, I found not a man lying in bed, as I expected (hoped), but a length of something long, limp and *textured*, instead. It looked a lot like seaweed, draped across the covers.

It sang. Yes, *sang* to me, in this weird, high-pitched buzz that made my nose bleed.

It is not the first time I've found something alien in place of my husband waiting for me in our bedroom. I have become somewhat used to Thomas cycling through different identities, but that is largely because each of those identities was always, up until now, demonstrably human. Arms, legs, ears, fingers and toes, human speech, that sort of thing. Not the man I married, but still the same species as me, which counted for something.

Four days ago, that began to change.

When I went to check on him first thing, as I always do (and I'll admit, a part of me wonders and sometimes even hopes that maybe he has died during the night) Thomas was twisted into a shape like a pretzel. His head down by his belly, his shoulders contorted above him, arms and legs intertwined like someone had manipulated strands of wet dough together. I knew I should have felt terrified, but instead I felt numb. I could see one wide, staring eye amongst the plaits of flesh, looking at me in panic. The rest of his face and his mouth were gagged by a kneecap that was long and pliable, like warm toffee. It was a wonder he had not smothered himself to death before I got to him.

I hastily untangled his limbs (they were cold and sticky) as if it was the most normal thing in the world, biting the insides of my cheeks hard and tasting my own blood as a way of keeping myself grounded in some form of reality. Then I took myself off to the bathroom, where I retched and heaved without vomiting for nearly an hour.

Later that afternoon, I went back in to give him his meds, although I'm beginning to suspect this continued adherence to his medication schedule is a futile routine that is more for my sake than his. It would be fine if the patient were normal, but Thomas is no longer normal, is he? He is something else entirely.

Anyway, I entered the bedroom, pills in hand, ready to try again, ready to be a good wife and nurse, ready to give him his bed bath, only to find him writhing and thrashing about with a squealing horse's head perched atop his body instead of a human head. I sketched it later. It helped me to process what had happened.

I think about it now, and I wish, wish, *wish* I could feel some abiding sense of horror or disgust or anything approximating a logical emotional response, but I can't. I mostly feel numb inside (not a new sensation, I have been numb for a long time, but still), even as I remember how his equine features *whinnied* at me from the bed, grotesque, shrieking, while his tiny, weak-by-comparison human neck and starved body, unable to support the weight of the stallion's skull, which lay like a boulder upon a stack of pillows, floundered atop the sheets. He was struggling to get away from himself, I could tell, his form wrestling with transformation, and he started defecating and soaking the bed with stinking hot backwards-centaur/man-horse piss (I didn't make paint pigment out of it, perhaps I should have) before collapsing, suddenly, completely, into a pile of ash-like substance out of which bright yellow stamens grew, wavering and reaching for the scant light coming in through the bedroom window. Those stamens were coated in beads of a tacky, sticky glue that was impossible to wash out of the bedding afterwards. I had to burn the duvet and fitted sheets and pillowcases and pillows and ask the Retinue to get me a brand new bed set, but that is just part of living with Thomas.

At this point, I know anyone looking in on my life would be seriously questioning why I have not left. I should be questioning that too, and my own sanity, for these are not normal things to be seeing. I keep thinking about that, whether all of this is a real experience or whether perhaps I'm simply trapped in my own mind, and then I think about why I stay, and all I can come up with is that love, when all is said and done, is a two-handled suitcase.

And on realising that, I get up, get dressed, and start making breakfast for Thomas.

I think I have lived with uncertainty long enough now that the transformation of Thomas has become a part of me, ingrained like wood stain leaching in between all the growth rings and knotholes of my soul. The stain has sunk deep, like my sense of duty and obligation. I now function in an automatic state the same way my Uncle Lenny, who was a functioning alcoholic, managed to hold down a job and perform at family occasions. On the inside, he was rotting, like me. Outwardly, he would smile, nod, ask how my day was, and never listen to the reply. His eyes watered a lot, his smile never wavered, I remember that.

And yet. Ingrained despair and servitude isn't so bad, all things considered. Even if it does come with significant risks to my own life. Adrenaline is a lot like the demon drink: I think you become dependent on it after a while. You get used to that heightened state until you find you *need* a little risk, a little danger, in order to function. In order to get out of bed, put one foot in front of the other. And the way I have started to look at it: if I'm at risk of losing my life, at least I know I'm alive, right?

It's obvious that I'm lying to myself. It's not the adrenaline I am dependent on.

It is him. It always has been.

Despite everything.

Sounds arse-about-face, but I know what I mean.

Anyway. Safe to say, Thomas is no longer the Thomas I knew. A silly, goofy, moody, complicated man who used to tickle the back of my neck lightly with his fingertips, wrap his hands around my throat and pretend to squeeze when he was angry, buy me flowers when I was sad, criticise my every waking thought, action and movement to my face whilst praising me to the skies behind my back, plan adventures with me around the world whilst trapping me in a life of endlessly folding laundry and ironing shirts, talk shit about my appearance but secretly stroke my hair while I slept, make fun of me in public in his adamantly *I-don't-mean-it-or-do-I* voice, write love letters that melted the recurring doubts clean away with a few well-chosen words, cook steak for me when I felt tired...those things are like strange, idiosyncratic customs of a bygone era. It is all in the past, now, who he used to be. Who *we* used to be. What remains is a multitude of things that I cannot even begin to wrap my head around. Every time I go into that bedroom to see him, I never know. Whether or not I will make it out alive. I don't ever let my guard down around him, but then, I never did. Ever. Which is, perhaps, a miserable state to have been in for a large chunk of my adult life: fight or flight, freeze or fawn. Miserable, but practical.

All par for the course when you're married to a burgeoning demiurge.

I think his transformations are escalating. He can't seem to settle on a distinct form for very long. He cycles through varying manifestations in an increasingly chaotic way.

When he isn't cycling, he is on his phone. Scroll scroll tap tap tap, face all frowny and jowly as he stares down, eyes lit up by the glowing oblong of doom. Who is he talking to, still? Sometimes when he is sleeping I look for the phone, thinking I'll unlock it and find out what he's up to, but he manages to hide it, fuck knows where. I never see it charging, or plugged in. Regardless, it reappears, and he treats it like a slim black lifeline, a lifeline that connects him to a world outside the Once Yellow House. A world which I suspect no longer exists, and I wouldn't have much need for it anyway, beyond food and medical supplies. My world is now the rotting, mould-splattered walls around us, the splintering boards beneath my feet, the sounds that come out of Thomas' room when I approach.

I feel very alone.

But then, I always have.

Original sketch, scanned from Hope Gloucester's scrapbook/diary, dated October 15th, 2020.

4.

Email: Once Yellow Kate
Weds, Nov 9, 2022, 03:24 am
iwasonceyellowtoo@gmail.com

To cemeterygatesmedia@gmail.com

Joe,

I have found her. Don't ask me how. But I found Hope Gloucester's new address. She doesn't live in the States anymore. That is as much as I am comfortable sharing, for the moment. I have a flight booked in a few hours. My intention is to find her and make her talk. I will record the conversation and send you the files. What you do with them after that is up to you. I don't trust any of the major news outlets to do the story justice. Matter of fact I don't much trust anyone these days, but this is a story that cannot stay buried.

    I won't lie to you, I am nervous. I've been looking for Hope since the day it happened, almost two years now. I haven't slept or eaten a great deal since. How am I supposed to sleep after the things I've seen? I have so many questions I am hoping she has the answers to. If she agrees to talk to me. I don't mind if she doesn't. I don't plan on going anywhere until she tells me what I need to know. If I have to camp on her doorstep and stalk her every movement until she relents, I'll do that. I'm hardly a stranger to camping.

    For the purposes of our correspondence, you can continue to refer to me as Kate. I could tell you my real name, but that would be stupid. My name isn't important anyway. Knowing it doesn't change what happened. It doesn't bring back all those dead people. It doesn't alter the truth in any way. It just embellishes it, unnecessarily.

    If you can send me the money for the flights, I would appreciate it. I'll forward the details separately.

    I will keep you updated.

    Regards,
    Once Yellow Kate

5.

Special Report
Source: CrimeHound.com

November 26, 2020 6:12 AM EDT
Last Updated 3 hours ago

347 Confirmed Dead or Missing in Grisly Yellow Cult Catastrophe

By Brian Boston

Authorities and residents of the small village of Lestershire in New York State are still reeling from the discovery of nearly 350 deceased adults and children at a property known unofficially by locals as the 'Once Yellow House,' a formerly unassuming, ordinary bungalow situated on the edge of the Sunshire estate—not far from notable local tourist attraction the Sunshire Chateau. The bungalow no longer exists; it, too, was destroyed in the event.

The victims were suspected members of a secretive, cult-like group known as 'The Retinue', about which very little is known. Rumours persist amongst locals and online, however: the Retinue wore distinctive yellow robes, aspired to self-sufficiency, and worshipped a specific deity they referred to as 'The Great God Thomas'. They seemed to hold geometric symbolism in high regard, and many strange markings have been found around the property on trees, rocks, and graffitied onto abandoned buildings nearby. They also believed fervently in an apocalyptic event called the 'End Days', and bore all the markings of a doomsday cult, according to the testimony of locals, and experts on the subject matter.

The Retinue's tenure was tragically short-lived, even by the standards of a cult. The men, women and children who made up the organisation formed an intense connection seemingly out of nowhere, and, according to one disgruntled local, 'descended like a plague of locusts' over a period of mere weeks, gathering in large numbers around the Once Yellow House upon the alleged invitation of self-appointed cult leaders Hope and Thomas Gloucester, to whom the property is still registered. The bungalow itself, as mentioned before, has since been razed to the ground in what is quickly becoming the largest incident of unexplained death and trauma in the modern history of the state. Only the charred foundations remain, which may be a source of relief for local authorities who do not wish for the site to become an unofficial pilgrimage point for disaster tourists drawn by the allure of tragedy and violence.

As for the alleged massacre itself, the precise details of the event are still to be established by authorities. No official statements have as yet been issued, despite mounting pressure from press and the public alike.

Police were first alerted to the scene when residents of Lestershire began to report strange anomalies in the weather and environment late in the afternoon of November 19th, 2020. Dozens of reports were subsequently made of freakish storms, strange 'rainbow' lights in the sky, and mysterious booming noises that sounded like explosions. Concerned citizens were told that although these occurrences indeed sounded peculiar, they were not worthy of urgent investigation by law enforcement.

However, when multiple reports of body parts falling from the sky started to flood emergency switchboards, Lestershire's police department had no choice but to investigate. When they did, they found themselves wholly unprepared for the scene of devastation they encountered.

Upon arrival, law enforcement found catastrophically damaged human remains strewn across a wide radius, seemingly flung from the epicentre of a large explosion that left scorch marks in the ground spanning a diameter of almost thirty yards. Amongst the heavily mutilated bodies, the corpses of thousands of birds lay, thought to have been caught in the blast radius. Beyond this, a number of freshly dug, unmarked graves were discovered. These are thought to have predated the explosion. Forensic experts are still excavating the site.

Reliable sources indicate that prior to the event, the large camp that sprang up around the bungalow had incorporated almost two hundred temporary structures, a large canvas and pole meeting hall that doubled as a makeshift temple, and extensive allotments, from which the members of the Retinue presumably hoped to source their food.

Military personnel have been working hard to secure the area from the eyes of the public and the media, and are assisting local authorities with the grim task of processing remains.

In the meantime, family members of those identified are gradually being contacted in an ongoing effort from local law enforcement, aided by the FBI, to reunite the lost members of the Retinue with their loved ones. The cause of death for named victims has apparently been cited on official documentation as 'accidental' owing to an 'unexplained explosive event', but this has not been confirmed explicitly and no further details have as yet been made public, despite gathering concern and outrage over the secrecy surrounding the massacre.

'The social and cultural implications for this catastrophe will be far reaching,' warns Brock Coker, an author who specialises in cult activity. Coker has written several well-regarded books on historical cult catastrophes. 'Groups like this usually appear in response to a perceived lack, by which I mean: people gather together in large numbers in order to find something they think is missing from their everyday lives. Although little is known of the practices and ethos of the Retinue, it would not surprise me to find any rhetoric they were endorsing to be simply that: a sound-byted disguise for underlying truths which often, in these cases, include abuse, monetary ambition, exploitation of the vulnerable, sexual coercion, and in some scenarios, outright slavery. The more information made available about this terrible event, the better, so we can continue to learn from our societal mistakes and stop these sorts of things from happening again.'

Investigations remain ongoing. There is a confidential helpline in place for the families of those affected and for anyone who may possess further information they wish to share anonymously. Please call 1-607-555-5662. Your call will not be recorded and will be carried out in complete privacy.

6.

Diary Entry, personal diary of Hope Gloucester
October 15th, 2020 (2)

Sketching the man-horse gave me an idea. I think I shall start painting every single one of Thomas' manifestations. I have the new paints and easel he gave me, and a stack of small canvases that I originally set aside for a series of landscapes, triptychs, but I think it makes more sense to use them to document his many forms. I shall keep them up in the attic, make a sort of gallery up there, so I don't have to look at them all day while the oils dry. It will help me to sort things out in my mind, I hope. I'll make it a part of my daily routine. Thomas always liked posing for me, before. It made him feel wanted, I think. Admired. He's always needed the admiration of others. I don't think he got much validation, as a child.

    I've been thinking a lot about the relationship between art and the supernatural. I remember reading about Hilma af Klint, a surrealist artist, mystic and medium active in Sweden in the 20th century. She painted geometric shapes, patterns, lines and other surreal motifs years before Kadinsky became renowned for it. She also believed her art was guided by some higher power. She held seances and communed with ghosts and entities as part of the creative process. Her most famous body of work, a series entitled *Paintings for the Temple*[2], was her attempt to guide herself through these colluding worlds and realities by using her innate creativity to translate some of the feelings she had while communicating with

---

[2] Ed. note: *Paintings for the Temple* are a fascinating collection of works including a beautiful image (title: Altarpiece, n̊1) comprised of an equilateral triangle divided into multiple rows of color (yellow being prevalent), tipped by a golden circle. One source (Serpentine Pavilion) interprets this painting as being 'inspired by Egyptian imagery', and goes on to note that in Theosophical and Anthroposophical spiritualist theory, each of the spectrum of colors has symbolic meaning. Furthermore, the triangle is mentioned as an ancient symbol that crosses the gap between the physical and spiritual world like a bridge, and is supposed to point towards enlightenment. Another painting in this series goes on to invert the imagery of Altarpiece, n̊1, with the triangle pointing down into the earth instead of at the sky, but with the sun still topside, balanced on the base. One cannot help but notice, as Hope Gloucester evidently did, an emerging pattern of geometry interlocking with artistic expression solely in relation to religious and spiritual fervour that is compelling and surely warrants further study and examination— more than we have time for in this publication.

whatever unearthly power she thought she'd built a connection with. I think I can get behind that sentiment, without being too much of a copycat. Klint also worked without an audience, preferring to isolate herself away from any artistic community or circle, and banned people from showing her work until she had been dead for twenty years. Which gets me thinking, in turn, about the performative nature of some paintings- are they painted to be merely seen, or because the artist wants to explore something else other than an eventual onlooker's reaction to it? I don't mean that in a contrary way, I just think there is something exciting, almost, illicit, about a private collection of really fucking weird portraits hiding in my attic. Portraits never intended to see the light of day. Who am I documenting these faces for? Me, and me alone. Or maybe for Thomas. Isn't that enough?

I'll paint him, then.

It'll be just like old times, I'm sure.

Meanwhile, I've promised myself I'll never fall in love again.

7.

Audio Transcript
File name: Once_Yellow_House_Transcription_01
Audio length: 00:05:07
Date recorded: Unknown
Date transcribed: 12/22/2022

Kate: I am recording this introduction for my own sake, really. I kind of need to warm up, I guess. Maybe it'll give context for anyone eventually listening to this. I'm hoping you'll have everything transcribed professionally, in which case this introduction won't be necessary, but if not, at least do me the courtesy of listening. To the whole thing, I mean. I understand you'll come at it with a certain amount of scepticism. That's fair. This…situation. It's a lot. I struggle with it every day. What I've seen. What I've been through. But that's why recording it will help. It leaves an evidence trail. An audio affirmation. That I'm not crazy. You can choose to believe the things you'll hear, or not. I don't care. I tried, that's the main thing. I tried to find some answers.

You can probably tell from the engine noise, I'm driving at the moment. It's not an automatic, and I'm not used to driving stick, especially on icy roads like these. I'm in the middle of nowhere, as literally as a person could mean that. The road is this long, narrow winding country road in the Scottish Highlands. They call it a B-road, I think. Cute. All the names here for things are cute. Anyway, I'm on my way to the house of Hope Gloucester. Or at least, I hope I am. I don't actually know for sure that she lives at the address I dug up. I'm really hoping this doesn't turn out to be a wasted trip. But the drive is nice, so that's something, at least. And I always wanted to see Scotland, so there's that. Thanks for paying for my flight by the way, and the car rental. This might be the only opportunity I'll ever have to travel, so I may as well make the most of it, huh?

It's funny how there's no other traffic out here. It's a coastal route, and there's this large bay to one side of me. There's an island in it, a small one, a little ways out. A tree in the middle, I think it's a tree. Only one. Kinda looks like a cherry tree, in bloom, but that can't be right, because it's winter and all the other trees lost their leaves. *[sigh]* It's pretty out here, though. It snowed recently. This rental car has these snow tires on, and there's grit on the roads. The tops of the hills nearby are white. Just how I always imagined Scotland would be. Cold and beautiful and lonely. I can see why she chose to run here. I haven't seen another person for hours.

Everything seems so small, too. I just now passed through this tiny place called Laide. *[laughs]* It had a cemetery and a large campsite, and literally nothing else. Oh, this, like, minute gas station, I guess. The gas stations here are adorable, they're so old fashioned and quaint. Like cardboard models or miniatures or something. They call it 'petrol', not gas...oh, shit, is this still the right way? Do I turn off here or…

[pause]

No it's fine, just a bit further.

[sigh]

I don't know if you can tell from my voice and how I'm babbling on, but I'm nervous. I feel like I've been building up to this day for a very long time. I'm also having flashbacks and finding it hard to deal with those. I don't think it helps that I wore my yellow tunic, so Hope will know right away who I am. Putting this thing on makes me anxious. Like, it brings back memories I don't want. And it makes me ashamed, I guess. Yeah. But, needs must. There were so many of us at the Once Yellow House, I wouldn't be surprised if Hope doesn't remember my face. Or know what I was to Thomas. *I* don't even know what I was to him, not really. Kinda hard to put a label on a relationship where you're fucking a new god.

It doesn't matter. She'll recognise the yellow tunic.

Anyway, I think I'm almost there. I…yeah, I can see her house up ahead, just off-road. *[Laughs]* Shit, that has to be it. I should have known. *[Laughs]* It's a cottage, old, stone, you know the drill. And I think it used to be painted white, like all the others around here, but guess what? She's painted it yellow since she moved in. Bright, cadmium yellow.

[Laughs]

She's a fucking idiot.

[The recording cuts here after several seconds of engine noise.]

8.

Audio Transcript
File name: Once_Yellow_House_Transcription_02
Audio length: 00:04:27
Date recorded: Unknown
Date transcribed: 12/22/2022

[Recording starts again. Muffled noises indicate the recording device is concealed. Fabric and rustling. A dog is barking from inside the house]

Hope: Quiet down!
Kate: I am sorry for interrupting you, I-
Hope: Yes, because I have such a busy life, with a jam-packed schedule. What do you want? Now that you've found me. *[Dog barking escalates]* Shut up, dog!

[Pause]

Kate: I know I'm disturbing you, I just-
Hope: Spit it out, would you? Whatever it is, I hope it's worth upsetting my dog like this.
Kate: I just want to talk, Hope.
Hope: About that day? *[Laughter]* You know they call it 'The Yellow Massacre'. The media have to find a catchy name for everything, don't they? Are you sure you're not a journalist?
Kate: It was a massacre. What else would you call it? Hundreds of people were ripped apart, Hope.
Hope: Where did you get that yellow tunic from? Did you steal it from the site? Huh. Smart. Knowing I'd see it and not be able to shut the door in your face.
Kate: It's mine.
Hope: You do look a little familiar, I'll give you that. And the tunic certainly fits you well. Still. It doesn't mean I have to talk to you.
Kate: *[Sigh]* They're still piecing together body parts to try and identify them, did you know that? There was...they found entrails hanging from the branches of nearby pine trees. A man who lived three miles away discovered a decapitated head in his backyard. It just landed there, like a football, fell clean out of the sky.
Hope: Is that so?

Kate: I lost everything that day, Hope. I came here to-

[Renewed frenzied dog barking]

Hope: Shut *UP*, Chester! *[Pause]* You came here to what?

Kate: I saw things I'll never be able to reconcile that day. I still can't sleep through the night. A man exploded, right in front of my eyes. I saw a small child eat the nose off his mother's face. She was laughing as he did it. *Laughing.* I heard the cartilage grind between his teeth. I...*[Long shaky breath]* They called it rapture, but it was a massacre, by every definition of the word.

[Brief pause of seven seconds]

Hope: I'm just not sure it needs to be sensationalised, is all. We don't need to go over it all again.

Kate: You don't think the mindless slaughter of hundreds of innocent victims should be sensationalised? What should, if not that?

Hope: Why don't you tell me? And what makes you think they were all innocent? By who's definition?

Kate: You don't think maybe you're desensitised, and that's the problem?

Hope: *[Laugh]* You are a ballsy thing, aren't you? Standing on my doorstep, unannounced, decked out in acolyte yellow, berating me about something you understand absolutely nothing about. Even if you were there, at the camp. I don't know why you're trying to appeal to my human decency. That yellow tunic tells me everything I need to know about you. Hats off to you for getting out alive, though. I didn't think anyone else had made it.

[Pause of ten seconds]

Kate: I sometimes wish I hadn't.
Hope: Yes well, you're not alone in that. Survivor's guilt, they call it. Point is, you don't need me to regurgitate it all. I'm not the most reliable of witnesses, am I?

[Pause]

Hope: Unless you're recording this, that is. Yes, that would make more sense. An ulterior motive.

Kate: *[Rustling]* You don't seem sad at all, Hope. There's no...You don't think...about all those people? It doesn't keep you awake at night like it does me?

Hope: No. They came of their own free will. It isn't my place to feel sad for them. What good would it do?

Kate: Nobody deserves to die like that. Like they did.

Hope: I don't disagree with you. But you have to understand, I used up all my sad on Thomas. On what happened to him. I didn't have much left after he'd done with me.

Kate: I suppose I can understand that.

[Pause]

Hope: So are you going to come in, or dither out here all day? It's too fucking cold to have this conversation with the door open.

Kate: Yeah, I'd like to come in, and talk some more. If you're okay with that.

Hope: Will you go away if I don't say yes?

Kate: No.

Hope: *[Laugh]* Well, I suppose...*[Sigh]* Like I said, it's not like I have anything better to do. At some point I need to walk the dog but...you may as well come in. Be warned, it's almost as cold in here as it is outside.

Kate: It's cold everywhere in Scotland, from what I can tell.

[Muffled noises as the two pass into the house and move to a room later identified as the kitchen. Chairs scrape. Recording ends.]

9.

Diary Entry, personal diary of Hope Gloucester
October 20th, 2020

Today when I went to see Thomas, he had red hair, and he spoke to me in French. I changed his head bandage and he kept yelling '*Putain! Putain!*' Over and over, with increasing violence. It means whore, I think. Not the Russian dictator dude, which makes a lot more sense. Even without understanding what insults he was hurling at me, I understood enough from his tone that he was being abusive, so I told him to stop, using my very best school french (*Arrete*, at least, that's what I hope the word is, because that's what I kept saying to him), and then I asked him his name, his non-Thomas name. He said it was Theodore, and then his eyes started glowing red. I dropped the glass of water I was trying to give him, and backed away. It landed on his legs, spilling all over the bedding. I knew I had to clean it up, so I tried to ignore the physiological changes and go about my business, stripping the covers down, tucking in new ones, knowing that otherwise, I would have to go back in there twice in one morning, and that is never very good for my nerves, or mental health.

I noticed, while the covers were off, that he has a bed sore that's broken open again on his left side. I could smell it from where I stood. Still can, if I think about it. He also has an angry case of cellulitis attacking his lower legs, but I've managed to stay on top of that, for the moment. We have antibiotics, which sort of work when he is human, and I keep his legs (when he has them) raised on a stack of pillows to mitigate the swelling. I also change his bandages down there as often as he'll let me.

I knew I needed to clean the new wound, disinfect the site and replace the dressing. I was not overly excited by this prospect, because getting up close and personal with Thomas is risky business, these days, but I couldn't let him rot, could I?

So I tried washing the bed sore and redressing it, but every time I touched the affected area, Theodore roared at me in more French, cursing and swearing and rattling off phrases I couldn't understand at hyperspeed, slapping and hitting me whenever I came close, and I couldn't help it. I lost my temper. I was trying to help him, and being abused like that felt like one misery too far, for me, so I took him sharply by the shoulders and shook him, just once, a nasty, violent shake to bring him out of his mood, and it seemed to work, for a second. He went quite still, and then looked at me almost as if waking up.

Then he opened his mouth. A rat, slimy with spittle, crawled out of it. Then another, and another. Soon, the room was full of rats. They swarmed. I didn't know what to do. Mimi, who was watching from the doorway as she normally does, went berserk, diving into them, chasing them as they scurried for all four corners of the room, grabbing one and throwing it against the wall where I think it broke its back, for it landed on the floor and went still, apart from legs that twitched.

After the rats, butterflies erupted from him, and he started laughing in this weird voice I've never heard before, chomping down on the insects as they escaped, mashing the bright yellow wings between his lips and teeth, and more butterflies just kept spilling out, and he would lash out and grab fistfuls of them, stuffing them into his mouth and crushing them in his palms and rubbing them on his face, and I couldn't take it anymore.

I ran. I ran out of the house and through the Retinue camp and along the road before anyone could stop me, going until I was out of breath. When I stopped, eventually, there was no-one around. I breathed fresh air for the first time in days. Then I realised Mimi wasn't with me. She was probably still chasing rats.

If not for her, I might have just kept on walking then, and never looked back.

I did go back though, eventually. I always do, I always have, although I don't know how much longer I can do this, in all honesty. Whatever Thomas is, I don't quite know how to love it, not now. I'm trying, but all our parameters have changed, which means the love has, too. He is monstrous, and pathetic, and terrifying, and disgusting and piteous all at once. I feel like my soul is being ripped to pieces the longer I stay here, but every time I think, *that's it, I'll leave, I'll take Mimi and just go,* the house does something to make me stay. I know it is the house, because of course it is. It always has been. It is not a house, not really. It's more of a gateway to something I don't fully understand. A realm of weird that is ripping my husband apart, atom by atom, and repurposing him into this awful carousel of entities that make me sick, every single one of them, to my stomach.

Doesn't stop me painting them.

Today's portrait: a man with red hair and red eyes, spewing rats and butterflies[3].

---

[3] *We can assume that all Hope's paintings were destroyed in the same event that reduced the Once Yellow House to ash.*

10.

Sun Bulletin October 31st, 2020
Letter to the Editor[4]

Dear Editor,

As a long-term resident of the once fine and pleasant Village of Lestershire within the Town of Union, I feel compelled to write to you in anger about the makeshift eyesore encampment that's sprung up on the outskirts of town at the property known as the Once Yellow House (formerly, I believe, the residence of an employee of the Sunshire Estate called Mackenzie, from Scotland originally, but that's hardly important.)

The house itself has long been a source of discontent for the local community, not just for its shocking state of disrepair but for the activities rumoured to have taken place there while it was unoccupied- drugs, sex, and God knows what else. I had hoped, with the advent of a new owner, that things would improve, the house and its surrounding land would get a makeover, and our concerns would be met.

However, this has not been the case. Instead we are now subjected to this rag-tag new 'community' of outsiders who have set up camp on the land next to the house and call themselves (rather self-importantly if you ask me) 'The Retinue.'

I don't need to tell you the impact such an enormous and rapid influx of strangers has had on the community of Union, and on the wider area of Sunshire Hill and Lestershire at large. It has been profound. Every day more and more members of the 'Retinue' pitch up, and their arrival has put a significant strain on our resources, our peace of mind and general sense of wellbeing. Crime rates have risen noticeably, and litter, vermin and chaos abound. Not to mention the influx of people presenting a wild potential disease risk to a popu-

---

[4] *This snippet is one of a few local newspaper clippings found loose in Hope's diary. It is interesting that despite being largely disconnected from the outside world, some physical media made it through. The snippet is heavily crumpled and paint spattered, so the newspaper may have been used to clean paint brushes, hence it slipped through the imposed communication ban Thomas subtly enforced on Hope.*

lation already struggling with the spread of so-called 'deadly virus' and the economic fallout of this so-called 'pandemic'.

This used to be a peaceful, uneventful town. I know I'm not alone in feeling perturbed and threatened by the sight of so many yellow robes walking down the street whenever I leave my house or run an errand. I can't help but wonder why Mayor Lester, in his infinite wisdom, is ignoring these squatters and not taking any action to move them along. What is he afraid of, exactly? At what point do we put a stop to this? Are we now to be plagued by a whole new canvas village on our doorstep? I think not. My hard-earned taxpayer's dollars would be better spent on fixing the roads and on other public services rather than clearing up the trash and damage these immoral, misguided vagrants are leaving in their wake.

Mark Zielewicz

11.

Audio Transcript
File name: Once_Yellow_House_Transcription_03
Audio length: 00:03:27
Date recorded: Unknown
Date transcribed: 12/22/2022

[Recording resumes]

Hope: Where do you want me to start? I assume you want to get right on with it. Considering you've travelled such a long way, that is.

Kate: Wherever you feel comfortable.

Hope: Comfortable? I haven't been comfortable for years. *'My life was attacked at the very root.'*

Kate: What?

Hope: Nothing. *[Laughs]* It's something Van Gogh once said. The artist.

Kate: I know who Van Gogh is.

Hope: You'd be surprised at how many people don't.

Kate: Okay. *[Pause]* You...could start at the beginning, I guess? From when you and Thomas bought The Once Yellow House.

Hope: No. I'd rather not.

Kate: Oh. Okay then. From before then, maybe. Where did you live before?

Hope: No.

Kate: No?

Hope: No. I can't start there. That wouldn't make sense.

Kate: What would you prEfer to start with?

Hope: Yellow. I think I'll start with the color yellow.

Kate: *[inaudible 00:27]*

Hope: Of course. Use that chair over there, you can take the books off it.

Kate: Thank you. It was heavy.

Hope: Is it for me? I do hope so.

Kate: Of course. I could hardly come aLL this way without a peace offering, could I?

Hope: A peace Offering, or a bribe?

Kate: Whatever. Whiskey is a lot cheaper here than it is back home.

Hope: You have some manners, at least. I can appreciate that. I accept your offering. As you can see, my circumstances don't allow for such luxuries, or my budget. Not that I drink much anyway, not anymore. But sometimes, on a cold winter's day like this, I think about it. Whiskey and snow go well together, they really do.

Kate: I was worried the roads would be closed.

Hope: Not yet. Maybe soon, although they're pretty good with snow ploughs and gritting around here. The locals have this strange co-operative where they maintain the roads and land without much input from the council. Everybody knows everybody's business out here, that's the downside. Still, they seem to be capable of keeping their noses out of my affairs, and that's all I care about. They know how to keep secrets, I think.

Kate: I don't like secrets. I think they hide too much evil. Too much intent. Secrets are like...blueprints for misdeeds. At least, my mom used to tell me that.

Hope: Yes, well, that doesn't surprise me. You look the type. Wide-eyed. Too honest by far. Righteously oriented.

Kate: Is there such a thing as too honest?

Hope: You tell me. I've never been much for hiding who I am. Which reminds me. Before we get into it...

[Chair scraping, footsteps, sound of distant drawer opening, closing, returning footsteps, chair scraping again. Something is placed on the table.]

Kate: What is this?

Hope: My sketchbook. Journal. Diary. Whatever. I've always kept a diary, for doodles. Random thoughts. Part of the creative process, note making. Scribbling. It'll come in handy, now, I expect. My memory is not what it used to be. After the event...I think large chunks of it all got burned away, somehow.

Kate: Yeah, I get that. I'm the same. Sometimes I remember things and I don't know if it's a true memory, or something I dreamed.

Hope: That's why I kept this, even though I should probably have burned it, I know. I just had this feeling that sooner or later, someone would find me. Ask me about Thomas. About the house. I thought it would be a journalist. I suppose I should be happy that it's you.

Kate: I spent a long time looking for you.

Hope: I admire your resilience. I made sure I was hard to find.

[Pause of eleven seconds]

Hope: Noone else has ever seen this, you know. My diary.
Kate: Why are you showing it to me now?
Hope: I don't know. Maybe it's the yellow tunic. Maybe I'm tired of carrying all this shit alone. I really couldn't say.

[Pause]

Kate: Whenever you're ready, Hope.
Hope: If I'm going to do this, I may as well treat myself to some lubrication. Want one?

[Sound of a cork being unplugged, of a glass being filled with whiskey.]

Kate: No thank you. It's…ten in the morning.
Hope: It's happy hour somewhere in the world, I always used to say. *[Sound of bottle being re-corked]* There, now this is cosy, isn't it? [Chuckles] The look on your face is positively prudish.

[Pause]

Kate: Any time, Hope. I'm listening.
Hope: Fine. *[Sigh]* Where to begin. I said I would start with yellow, didn't I?
Kate: You did.
Hope: Yes. Yellow. That seems as good a place as any.

12.

Diary Entry, personal Diary of Hope Gloucester
March 15th, 2020[5]

Notes on Yellow

I've been thinking a lot about the colour yellow lately. I think yellow has always been my favourite. As a child, I remember I was cocooned by it. Mum hung yellow curtains in my nursery, which I can recall vividly to this day. They had paintbrushes on them with streaks of blue and red coming from the paintbrush tips in a repeating pattern. My bedding was yellow too. So were the walls. As a teenager, I found that yellow suited me. Someone told me it complimented my hair and eyes. I wore it a lot.

Yellow was also one of Vincent van Gogh's favourite colours. For a while he lived in a building called the Yellow House. I have a postcard of his painting of the property on my bedroom wall. Van Gogh wanted to turn it into an artist's retreat, but couldn't drag his 'friends' away from the bright lights of Paris to come live and work with him there. I have a feeling other artists found him to be too intense, in real life. They seemed happy enough to correspond, send each other paintings, keep him at friendly, manageable distance. I think he was a profoundly lonely man. You can see it in his work. Brushstrokes, the pressure, the colour choices. An expulsion of loneliness, on canvas. Even his own brother got periodically tired of him. He must have felt like such a pariah, so often.

I can relate. I have always felt lonely.

In the end, Van Gogh was evicted from the Yellow House after he cut off most of his ear, walked to a nearby brothel, and handed it to a prostitute. A little time after that, he wandered into a wheat field and shot himself in the chest. He wrote to his brother beforehand, told him 'my life is attacked at the very root'. His last paintings were largely of wheatfields, and there is a notable absence of yellow.

---

[5] Editor's note: Hope's diary entries are, for the purposes of authenticity, presented here in the order they were found written in her scrapbook, NOT chronologically. We feel that rearranging the order of her diary entries might misrepresent certain aspects of her working mindset at the time of writing. For this reason we recommend keeping a diligent eye on the date of each entry. She jumped around a lot with her entries, and seemed to write on the empty pages that appealed to her at the time, not in a linear, front-to-back way.

My own fascination with yellow has been encouraged by my love of impressionism. I truly believe that of all the impressionists, Van Gogh understood the colour best. He used cadmium yellow, but only when he could afford it, for he was poor and it was expensive to make, prepared either by heating metallic cadmium with sulphur, or by the precipitation of insoluble cadmium sulphide. Manufacturing the pigment came with risks: it gives off a gas, hydrogen sulphide, which is both poisonous and stinks like rotting matter. Cadmium sulphide occurs naturally as the mineral greenockite[6], which looks like a hexagonal crystal made from solidified honey or earwax, something crafted by worker bees or sticky hands. It comes from Scotland, amongst other places.

Before Van Gogh's use of cadmium yellow, chrome yellow was all the rage. More affordable for a struggling artist, it contained toxic lead. The pigment offered good coverage, but tended to darken and oxidise after being exposed to the air. That is why some of the master's paintings now seem muted and brown. Brown is a sad colour, when all is said and done.

When artists of the time realised the vibrancy of their work would not survive with chrome yellow, they defected to cadmium, Van Gogh included. The irony being that cadmium yellow is also, by nature, unstable, vulnerable to light and oxygen, and it too fades with time, forming an orangey-grey crust upon the masterpieces of old. This, to me, is an excellent illustration of the duplicity of yellow.

Because yellow, to the unquestioning mind, is the colour of sunshine. And sandy beaches, honey, lemons, daffodils, gold coins, happy things. And yet it is also the colour of pus and stinging wasps and poisonous frogs and sulphur and hot mustard and decaying teeth and old bones and leaves preparing to die.

Over time, yellow has become the colour of Judas Iscariot. You can see him wearing yellow togas in paintings of the Post-Classical era. Jews during the Middle Ages and in Nazi-occupied Europe were forced to wear yellow star badges on their clothing.

Yellowcake, or concentrated uranium oxide, is used in the preparation of fuel for nuclear reactors and in uranium enrichment: an essential ingredient in the manufacture of nuclear weapons. The Oppenheimer diamond is a huge yellow crystal, one of the largest uncut diamonds in the world. Ironically it is not called Oppenheimer because of the man who invented the atomic bomb, but for a

---

[6] We feel it is worth drawing attention to Hope's obvious underlying intelligence at this point. Her academic performance as a child was reportedly poor, but this undoubtedly had more to do with her dyslexia than her intellect.

prominent businessman who owned mines[7] and dealt in diamonds and gold (which is as close to yellow as you can get in the mineral world, really).

In Chinese mythology, yellow is a force for good. Google tells me the Yellow Dragon- an incarnation of the Yellow Emperor- is a legendary hero and deity, a cosmic ruler, patron of the arts. Part of a cosmological scheme in which the colour represents good, powerful things, like the earth.

The point being: yellow is a complicated hue. Deceitful, capricious, unreliable. It is the colour of power and corruption and death and decay, a warning colour denoting poison or a hazard. If someone is 'yellow-bellied', they are a coward. But it also symbolises hope and glory and optimism. Warmth, and succour. Our ancestors made yellow from clay, and daubed it on the walls of caves thousands of years ago. Other shades were later made from cow piss and arsenic. As a species, we cannot keep away from yellow, even when it hurts us to make it.

Tomorrow, Thomas and I are moving into a house that was once painted yellow. It looks like this:

---

[7] *Hope is referring here to Sir Ernest Oppenheimer, who founded the Anglo American Corporation of South Africa. He was a controversial figure. The yellow diamond dedicated to him is now in the Smithsonian.*

Scanned sketch from Hope Gloucester's scrapbook/diary. Dated March 15, 2020.

I haven't told him about losing the baby. I don't think I will. He wouldn't react well to the news.

> With note: Realistic
> Skin tone — Indian Yellow
> Titanium White — Reds / Yellow / Blue
> Cadmium Red / Napthol
> Ochre
> Raw Umber / Burnt Sienna
> Ultramarine

Scanned note from Hope Gloucester's scrapbook/diary, undated. It details the color mix she used when attempting to recreate skin tones with oil paints.

13.

Audio Transcript
File name: Once_Yellow_House_Transcription_04
Audio length: 00:04:36
Date transcribed: 12/22/2022

Kate: So you *are* starting with the house.

Hope: In a roundabout way, yes, but everything needs context, doesn't it? Context is useful. Without it, it's difficult to explain how strange it was.

Kate: How strange what was?

Hope: That we ended up at the Once Yellow House.

Kate: Your first impressions of the place were not great?

Hope: You could say that, yes. I remember when I first saw it. Hunkered down, squat and cowering, like it was, I don't know… waiting for someone to kick it in the ribs. Like a shivering stray dog or cat. Bird shit all over it. Front door hanging wrong on its hinges, lopsided, like it was leering at me, you know? Mounds of other people's rubbish…I mean, trash, just lying around. It was obvious the property had become this unofficial edge-of-neighborhood dumping ground. Not to mention a drug den, while it was empty. There were needles and shit everywhere. I counted not one, but three discarded couches, a chest freezer, uh…oh, and there were car parts all over the place. Over here we call it 'fly-tipping'. I don't know what you call it there, but I do know it's expensive to clean up other people's trash.

Kate: It doesn't sound like an appealing prospect. The house, I mean. And the trash.

Hope: Safe to say, I'm glad it no longer exists, but then I don't need to remind you, do I?

Kate: Remind me of what?

Hope: Don't play dumb, not with me. You heard the whispered gospel. Saw the site. Saw what remains. The burned earth and tree stumps. I bet you went back there, didn't you? Like a good little pilgrim. I bet you stood in the ruins and told yourself you could still feel his energy. The Great God Thomas. *[Snort]* Fuck's sake. A Retinue of acolytes, all in yellow. Not even he could have imagined that for himself, not in his wildest dreams.

Kate: You really hated the house, didn't you?

Hope: Yes. Right from the word 'go'. And I can tell you definitively that the world is a better place since the Once Yellow House was demolished.

Kate: Are there…Do you think there are other houses like it?

Hope: *[Scoffs]* Of course there are. All over the world, probably. Places where reality is thinner within the walls. Places that exude chaos. Take this house, for example.

Kate: What's…what's wrong with this house?

Hope: It has a name, you know. *Taigh Faire.* I don't know what it means, it's Scots Gaelic for something. As to what's wrong with it…we'll get to that. All in good time.

Kate: Do you think…is it possible to you that there are other beings like Thomas?

Hope: I sincerely hope not. What can we do about it if there are? His gospel was falsely spread, but words have power, don't they? It always makes me laugh when people say 'spread the good word'. Like a virus, spreading death and misery. *[Laughs]* 'And in the beginning was the Word, and the Word was…'

Kate: Don't. Don't do that. No dogma, please. Not even in jest.

Hope: You have a point. Shall we keep talking about the Once Yellow House?

Kate: Yes.

Hope: My apologies. I shall continue. But first…

[Sound of more whiskey being poured]

Kate: Yellow is the only color I seem to wear now, you know. Old habits die hard, don't they?

Hope: They do. Cheers!

[Prolonged slurping sounds]

Kate: So the Once Yellow House was a coincidence. Not a deliberate choice?

Hope: There are no coincidences in this life, you know that.

Kate: I'm sorry, I didn't mean-

Hope: I'm not upset. I'll tell you if I am. And no, it was not deliberate, to answer your question. At least, not on my part. Thomas found the house. Or maybe it found him. I didn't make the connection with the name of the place until after we moved in. Even though Van Gogh had long been a hero of mine.

Kate: I can see his influence in some of your paintings. And sketches. *[Pages shuffling]* Like this one. It's very good.

Hope: Stop buttering me up. *[Dismissive sigh]* I lost most of my real art in the...final days? I can't keep calling it what everyone else calls it. End times? I don't know. I think I get too hung up on words. But that's why I painted, you see. Words never behaved for me, much. Although the stuff I churned out was hardly inspired. I sincerely wish I could say my own work was even 'inspired by', rather than 'derivative of' Van Gogh. Still. I know what you're about to say.

Kate: You do?

Hope: You're about to say: at least I'm still alive to be able to paint, which is more than can be said about the others.

Kate: *[Throat clearing]* It says here...cadmium comes from Scotland?

Hope: There's a quarry not far from here where they found lots of it.

Kate: Another coincidence?

Hope: I told you. There are no coincidences in life, only interlocking truths.

Kate: Cadmium yellow.

Hope: Once you start seeing it, you realise it's everywhere.

Kate: Hope, can I ask you something? I know this is going to sound wild, but. Can I ask...

Hope: Spit it out.

Kate: Is there any way...Thomas...is he still alive? His presence? Essence? I'm trying to phrase it right.

[Pause]

Hope: He was never 'self-proclaimed' you know. The media keep using that phrase. He wasn't. I'm not saying he didn't found the Retinue, but...he never asked for any of this notoriety.

Kate: Hope? That's not an answer.

Hope: I know. I'm just gathering myself. *[Pause]* I think it's important to remember that death doesn't apply here, not in the normal sense of the word. What Thomas became, at the end...I don't think death stood a chance. I'm not sure he's alive in the classic sense, but I am pretty sure he is not deceased in the classic sense, either. Does that make you feel any better? It shouldn't. I worry about it all the time. Whether he's watching me now. Somehow. If he has further plans for us.

Kate: I don't really understand what you're saying. He's neither alive, nor dead?

Hope: I'm sure it will all make sense in the end. You'll see.

Kate: Okay.

Hope: Look, I know I'm a lot. I can be intense. I get that. You'll have to be patient with me. It's been a long time since I spoke to anyone, and it's been a lonely existence of late. Or it was, until you arrived. There's no-one else left to talk to, understand. They were all taken away by the Great God Thomas, weren't they? Good old *[Indistinguishable]* Devoured by him. Friends, followers, devotees. My dog, Mimi.

Kate: This is not Mimi?

[Faint whining]

Hope: This is her successor. Mimi, the original sidekick...she ran away. I lost her. I lost everything, just like you. My husband, my sanity. My house, which was once yellow. Gone. You were there. You saw.

Kate: His favorite color was yellow too, wasn't it?

Hope: Thomas? Yes. His favorite color was yellow, too. Which, I suppose, given the context of everything else, makes a lot of sense. Do you think yellow is the color of fate?

Kate: *[Sigh]* I don't really-

Hope: Or perhaps I'm looking at it in the wrong way. Perhaps yellow is the color of love, not fate. Either way, it led me here. And you too, it seems. I have a feeling you'll regret that, in time.

Kate: I hope not. Do you need to take a break?

Hope: Yes. I need to let the dog out.

Kate: Can I use your bathroom?

Hope: Sure. It's at the top of the stairs, on the left.

Kate: Thank you, I'll find it. Pretty hard to get lost in a cottage of this size.

Hope: That's the American in you talking. Up here, this is quite a generously sized house, I'll have you know.

Kate: Oh, sure. I like it. I wasn't being snide. I just mean-

Hope: I know what you meant. Stop being so sensitive. *[Whistles]* Chester! Here, boy! Time to go out!

[Recording cuts out here.]

14.

Audio Transcript
File name: Once_Yellow_House_Transcription_05
Audio length: 00:00:56
Date transcribed: 12/22/2022

[Recording restarts, clearer audio. Kate is whispering. The room tone indicates a change of location.]

Kate: Hope has gone outside with the dog briefly. It's a young collie dog and maybe it isn't house trained properly yet, I don't know. Looks real similar to the one she had at the Once Yellow House, though. I guess that's deliberate.

My first impressions of Hope Gloucester are...ah. *[Sigh]* She seems to have aged a lot since the last time I saw her, far beyond her years, which I suppose I can understand. Her hair is now really grey, although she can't be much older than forty, and there are these pronounced worry lines around her mouth and eyes and between her eyebrows. She is a lot thinner, too, like she doesn't eat well, and is dressed in these raggedy-ass clothes that look like they came from Goodwill, although I'm not sure if they have Goodwill over here. Whatever. She seems happy enough to talk. I'm surprised by that. I thought I would have a fight on my hands. Not that she has given me anything useful yet, but I'll persevere.

The house she lives in now is very run down, but kind of cosy. Draughty though, real cold in places. The kitchen is nice, it has these, ah, windows overlooking the bay and the little island I saw earlier. There doesn't seem to be any heating and I can pretty much see the breath in front of my face when we talk, but Hope either can't feel it, or is doing a good job of hiding how uncomfortable she really is. Or maybe it's the scotch. I thought it would loosen her up, but now I'm worried...I can't tell if any of the things she is recalling are truthful or not. I think she believes what she's telling me, so I'll have to be content with that, for now. I have no way of fact-checking anything out here. I'll just take her word verbatim, and see how it goes, I guess.

I can hear her coming back inside now, I have to stop. *[Toilet flushes]*

[Recording ends.]

15.

Diary Entry, personal Diary of Hope Gloucester
March 16th, 2020

Notes on Love: A Two Handled Suitcase

Thomas and I moved today. The weather was good for us, but the whole experience still felt like the set-up for a poorly executed horror movie. The kind where you start yelling at the screen at the naive idiots buying a fixer-upper thinking it will somehow solve their deep-rooted marital issues. That is us. Hope and Thomas Gloucester. A pair of idiots. Therapy would have been a lot cheaper.

Thomas said 'good riddance' as we cleared the city outskirts, and this made me feel sad. I had been at peace with our life there. I know it was hardly perfect, but nothing ever is. Our old apartment was comfortable and suited our needs, or at least mine, just fine. Or so I thought.

We found the Once Yellow House largely unchanged from our last encounter with it: rotting patiently amongst the discarded couches and rusty train paraphernalia that litters the land all around. We pulled across the disused train tracks opposite the bungalow via a signal crossing and into the long drive, which branches off from the tracks and winds through weed-infested scrubland until it reaches a slight hollow in which our new house hunkers down. As we drew up, Thomas pointed to the roof of the low-slung building, where we saw birds. Hundreds, lining the rooftop. Like they were waiting for us. They flew up into the sky as we turned off the car engine and opened the doors. For a second, I thought I saw patterns in the bird-cloud: a circle, maybe. The image stuck with me after.

The house is dark, which will take some getting used to. Huge fir trees surround the backyard, partially screening the place off from view in one direction, and cutting out most of the natural light. Painting will be tricky, I'll need to get a stand lamp I think. The fir trees will have to go eventually, but it's not an immediate priority. The front yard and drive open directly onto wasteland and the train tracks. The darkness here feels preternatural, somehow. Like an arctic winter where the sun never really fully rises. It makes me tired. I need some Vitamin D supplements, badly.

There is also a lot of junk to clean up, like I said. There's an old train carriage disintegrating right across from our front door. Someone has graffitied the letters *G.E.O.L.U.* inside a triangle framed within a circle on the side. It's an eyesore, to say the least.

Other things I don't like: the back door of the house is opposite the front, which means a tunnel of wind forms if both are open at the same time. Most of the window panes are fractured or pierced with holes. The air moans through them pitifully. Water damage on the ceiling has left gaping maws in the plaster in several of the rooms. There is a stench of damp and mildew everywhere, a mossy, wet smell, wholly unpleasant, completely pervasive, like the bungalow is a stale, unwashed body. On top of that, the distinctive aroma of rats, or mice. It makes me think of chewed wires, squeaks and snuffles in the night.

Thomas doesn't seem to mind any of this. He looked happy the second he set foot in the place. He has been struggling with headaches lately, and lethargy. He's been withdrawn and moody (more than usual), pushing me away every time I tried to ask him what was wrong. As soon as we crossed the threshold here, however, he got his energy back. His eyes are noticeably less red. And he seems to have energy again. Finally. It made me realise how long it's been since I last saw him happy. In an uncharacteristic fit of whimsy, he proposed that we rename the bungalow 'Primrose Hill' although there are no flowers, and no real hill. The name didn't stick for longer than an hour or two, at most. I am glad about that. The 'Once Yellow House' suits me just fine. It is more honest than he has been, and that is all I want, really.

Despite the frustration, despite bone-deep fatigue, mould, the stink of damp and the sound of hundreds of birds sitting on the roof, *shitting* on the roof, scuttling along the tiles with bony little feet, squawking down the chimney pipes, our first night in the new house, so far, has been almost fun, I can't deny that. Despite all the anger that led us here. We ate Chinese takeout on upturned moving crates by candlelight, just as Thomas wanted. Cracked open a few cheap beers. Mimi sniffed out every single inch of the place all over again, sneezing as the dust went up her snout, before deciding on her spot: a corner by the empty fireplace in the living room. We put her bed down for her. She seems to like it. We watched her as she slept like we would watch TV. There was nothing else to do. There is no internet. No signal for data. It's kind of a relief. Thomas has been on his phone so much in the last few months that it's bordering on addiction. He gets twitchy when I ask him to put it away, focus on spending time together. Now, we are forced to actively engage with each other, instead of feigning interest in a movie whilst he scrolls and I sketch. It is, I daresay, almost romantic to have his full attention back.

Or it would be, if I wasn't still mad at him. There is a quote from Marlene Dietrich: 'Once a woman has forgiven her man, she must not reheat his sins for breakfast.' I think that's how it goes. Well, that's nice, but hardly practical. I am finding it difficult to forgive, now I see the scale of the renovation project I've got ahead of me. But, again, Thomas is happy. The Once Yellow House has injected him with a new lease of life.

'We're going to be good here, Hope,' he said, all matter-of-fact, over his noodles. 'I can feel it. We needed a change. We really did.'

It was the way he said it that got to me. As if he really trusts his own hyperbole. I suppose he needs to believe what he needs to believe, despite peeling walls, the damp-ravaged ceiling with one single naked light bulb dangling down from a decaying wire, the smell. The cold. The wallpaper. God, the *wallpaper*. Only in one room, thankfully, but that's enough. It's this vintage gothic velour paper, thick and furry, with an uninspiring repeating scrollwork motif in mossy green stamped all over. The quality of production is really poor. And the strips were not matched properly when hung, so the pattern is interrupted in ways that hurts your brain the longer you look at it. It's a real mood-killer. Not yellow, though, which, as Thomas pointed out, I should be grateful for.

Anyway, I know it is stupid to focus on the paper when so much else is wrong with the house. The biggest problem being, of course, the damp. There are holes in the roof that need fixing urgently before winter. We need a professional opinion on the electricals, which are ancient. There are bare wires coming out of the wall right next to the sink in the kitchen, and all the plug sockets around the bungalow are loose or blackened around the edges where appliances have clearly shorted and burned out. I'm amazed the house hasn't been razed to the ground long before us. Maybe it's too damp to catch fire. Or too stubborn to burn down. I can believe that, living here. There's an atmosphere I have never felt in a house before. Staticky, oppressive, overbearing. As if I am being frowned upon by unseen forces.

Whatever those forces, they seem to exert themselves differently on my husband, who can't stop smiling and bouncing around like a puppy. 'I've got something for you,' he said, again while we were eating. 'A housewarming gift.' I told him we didn't have money for gifts. He said it was only a small thing. He wanted to mark the occasion. He left the room, came back with a bundle under his arms. I immediately felt bad when I saw what it was: a new easel, a set of small blank canvases, a fresh set of oils, medium, white spirit, and some brand-new sable brushes. He bought extra cadmium yellow because he knows I like it so much. He said he didn't want anything that had happened lately to stop me from pursuing my dream. He said we'd find a way to make it work. It was a genius move, all things considered. Heartfelt and vulnerable. It is hard to stay outwardly mad at him, after that. My anger has gone inwards, now, instead. I suspect that's why he did it.

We fucked, after that. Fucking is now a notable event that needs documenting. Thomas said he wanted to christen the place. I didn't want to, but he pouted when I said no, so I let him undress me, knowing we needed the intimacy, knowing it would be good for us, whilst also knowing it would be safe, predictable sex that would end in one way: his satisfaction, but not mine. I would pretend, of course. I always do, else his pride gets hurt. It's not always like that between us, sometimes things do click into place. But tonight was not one of those times. I closed my eyes to begin with, until he told me to open them again. Wished for something more, something fiercer. Like fingers around my throat or my hands tied behind my back or some enthusiastic rimming or even a little light-to-medium spanking, but Thomas doesn't play that way. It isn't a question of desire, or lack thereof. It's hard to explain. He just isn't very intuitive. I have to direct everything. 'Tell me what you like,' he says, but it isn't a request. And I find I don't *want* to tell him. I want him to know me well enough that I don't need to give him directions.

'Let me in, Hope,' he says. 'Let me in.'

But it's difficult.

He came quickly, apologised after. It wasn't perfect, but it was a start. To reconnecting a little.

'You didn't cum, though,' he sulked.

I pulled splinters out of my shoulder blades and told him to stop worrying about it. 'It isn't the be-all and end-all,' I lied.

Now I'm writing in my scrapbook while Thomas sleeps. I don't know why, but it makes me feel more connected to myself. As if I'm already worried about losing myself, here, in this house. In this situation. I feel like something in here with us is hungry for me, in ways I can't quite put my finger on. I know that sounds absurd, but sometimes a mood or an ambience can be influential. Like when you visit an art gallery, or a museum. Or a place where something terrible once happened. Space holds onto energy, I firmly believe that. And the energy here is hungry. For something.

I also found six tins of unopened yellow paint under the front porch, which feels like a sign. Even though I don't believe in signs. Or didn't, until now.

This whole move has gotten me thinking a lot about love, about the various different forms it takes. Requited, unrequited, erotic, romantic, platonic, toxic, self-love, familial love, enduring love, love at first sight. I think we're too preoccupied with love, as a species. We're preoccupied without really understanding what it is, what it truly means for each of us. Aristotle said that love is composed of a 'single soul inhabiting two bodies.' I'm not sure about that. I suppose it implies that love is a game of joint responsibility. Or a two-handled suitcase, an evenly balanced pair of weighing scales. A burden held by two pairs of hands. A shared freight. Perhaps this is the real reason.

Why I stay.

Should love feel like that? A load to bear? I don't have any other frame of reference. There's only ever been Thomas, since I was eighteen. Back then, I imagined love to be a lot less exhausting. Safer. I moved out here to feel safer, or at least I thought that was why. But I don't. Feel safe. I feel on edge.

I should stop now. A good night's sleep will help me feel better, I'm sure.

Scanned sketch of the Once Yellow House, from Hope Gloucester's scrapbook/diary, dated 16th March 2020.

16.

Audio Transcript
File name: Once_Yellow_House_Transcription_06
Audio length: 00:07:56
Date transcribed: 12/22/2022

Kate: So. You stayed for love.
Hope: Of course. What else is there?
Kate: Had you ever tried to leave him, before? You said you met him when you were eighteen. You've been together since? You never left?
Hope: Once. I left once.
Kate: And?
Hope: It didn't go so well.
Kate: I understand.
Hope: I'm not sure you do. Can.
Kate: So, you were stuck. Loving a god.
Hope: I mean…I had a choice.
Kate: I'm sorry. I didn't mean to offend you, or make you feel uncomfortable.
Hope: I'm fine, it's just…You came out of the blue, and now you want all this intimate information…Well, if you must know. Loving him was torture. Fire. It was pain, and confusion. It also brought me moments of intense clarity bordering on ecstasy, if you can believe that. I know you can, because that's why you joined the Retinue, isn't it? You wanted someone to make it all clear for you. I'm sorry if Thomas disappointed you.
Kate: Not disappointed exactly. I had low expectations. Just…I changed in ways I didn't anticipate, is all.
Hope: So did I. Anyway, to further answer your question: it was also boring, in large parts. Especially later on. He said less and less as his transformation progressed. But in his earlier iterations, The Great God Thomas was a fascinating conversationalist. By which I mean, he stopped treating me like a child, and started exploring new ideas and themes with me while I tended to his sores and wounds and gave him his bed baths and hand jobs.
Kate: We're jumping ahead here a little, aren't we?
Hope: Yes, we are. I just…before we go on. I'll try and keep it as chronological as I can but…first…I feel like I need someone to understand.

Kate: Understand what?

Hope: Understand what, exactly, it was like being with him.

Kate: I'm listening.

Hope: It's impossible to describe...to fully convey how... how...frightening he was, sometimes.

Kate: I can't imagine.

Hope: He taught me how a person can learn to live with fear. Especially in the early stages, when he was not yet The Great God Thomas. That would come, although of course I didn't know that. I just thought he was sick. That he had damaged something in his brain in the accident[8]. But he was, actually, what I could reasonably call at that stage of his metamorphosis, a proto-god. A god-in-bloom. An embryonic deity, slowly unfurling like a huge golden sunflower, face to the sky, you know? The seeds would drop when he died, I always thought that, and make more gods. Like dragon's teeth turned into skeleton warriors in Greek mythology.

Kate: I saw that movie. It was a childhood favorite.

Hope: Perhaps you are one of those seeds, some to finish what he started, eh? If that is the case, you'll have to keep me on track before you take me, because my mind wanders, so very much.

Kate: That doesn't make any sense, Hope. Are you feeling okay?

Hope: I know. I know it doesn't. I think there are parts of me that just don't work anymore. Like, I stared directly at the sun for too long.

Kate: Let's get back on track. Talk to me about Thomas. Your routine.

Hope: After the accident, our routine...well, those first mornings back from the hospital, I usually walked into Thomas' bedroom with my eyes firmly closed. Sounds weird, doesn't it, but it made it easier. It used to be our bedroom, but I couldn't bear to sleep near him anymore. This was because I was never entirely sure what, exactly, I was going to find lying in the bed waiting for me. He used to...to change so unpredictably.

Kate: When you say change...describe that to me.

Hope: Kate?

Kate: Yeah? What is it?

---

[8] Ed. note: This conversation references an 'accident' more than once without preamble. For readers who feel as if they have missed something, fear not: Hope documents this event in more detail in several other diary entries. We also found Thomas Gloucester's hospital records corroborating his 'serious neurological injury', which may or may not have been the catalyst for what followed. We will let Hope continue to tell her story, however.

Hope: Can we just stop pretending you're not recording this?

[Pause]

Kate: How...how did you know?
Hope: I can tell by the way you're sitting. Your phone is in your pocket and you're favoring that side of your body. You might as well just come out and ask me.

[Pause]

Kate: I'm sorry, Hope, I... Do you...can I? Record you?
Hope: What do you plan on doing with the audio?
Kate: I was going to send it to a contact I have. Anonymously, of course. A publisher. Back home...what happened...people want answers, Hope. They want the real story.
Hope: You don't for one second think that they'll believe any of this, do you? Better to let it go down in history as one of those great unsolved phenomena, or even better still, wait until it becomes urban legend. Because the real truth...if it was as easy as telling people the real truth, don't you think I would have done it already?
Kate: No, I'm not sure that you would. You went into hiding. You vanished.
Hope: I did what I had to. Why do you care so much anyway? You got out. You survived. Wasn't that enough?
Kate: I can't explain it. I feel like...
Hope: Like you owe it to the Retinue? That's how they get you, isn't it? Cults. Religions. By increments. They make you believe you owe them something, just because they put a roof over your head for a while and feed you. Obligation, right? Well, you don't owe them shit, Kate. All they did was push crazy rhetoric down your throat, dogma that was wrapped around a man who none of them actually knew, not like I did. Before he was a god, Thomas was human, and he was weak, selfish and unremarkable, just like the rest of us.
Kate: You said you loved him.
Hope: I did! I still do. He was only human, and we're all flawed. I was weak too.
Kate: Doesn't sound like a healthy dynamic.
Hope: It wasn't.
Kate: Can I keep recording or not?
Hope: *[Raw laugh]* Oh, do what you want. Like I said, not a single fucking person out there is going to believe it anyway. As long

as you don't go around telling people where I live, you can publish a fucking novel about it, for all I care. Put that thing on the table, though, where I can see it. I hate people hiding stuff from me.

[Muffled sounds as Kate's phone is pulled from her pocket and set upon the table. The quality of audio improves considerably from this point on.]

    Kate: Okay.
    Hope: So what now? What do you want for your big scoop?
    Kate: Can you tell me about the accident? That's when things really changed for you, right?
    Hope: No.
    Kate: No?
    Hope: Not yet. There's more to unpack, first.
    Kate: Like what?
    Hope: Just more. Trust me. Drink?

[More whiskey is poured]

17.

Diary Entry, personal diary of Hope Gloucester
March 17th, 2020

It's a funny thing, being married. Getting along, as people do. We love each other, I think. Before the move, we were not completely happy, but not wholly *unhappy*, either. There were good times. A lot of shit times too, but I was told (by Thomas) that this is normal. It's not like we have a lot of friends to compare ourselves to. I mean, Thomas has plenty of friends, but none that we share. Other couples, that kind of thing.

I can feel us unravelling, slowly. Like someone has a hold of the end of a single strand of wool, and as they pull, row after row of our relationship falls apart, until all that will be left soon is a tangled mess of yarn upon the floor.

He shouts a lot. And puts me down, constantly. He did that before, but now it has intent. Purpose. It's mostly passive aggressive, subtly couched with a dizzying logic, but getting worse by the day. I try not to take it personally. It's hard. I never was very thick skinned.

It is the Once Yellow House that is undoing us, I know this. I am starting to suspect there is something very wrong with this place. Wrong beyond the surface things like damp and mould and leaks and broken window panes. It's more like *reality* is wrong here, somehow. Thinner. I know that makes no sense. It doesn't have to. It's a gathering feeling, like rain clouds forming in a clear sky.

And I have nobody to blame but myself. It is all my fault. We moved to the Once Yellow House because I allowed it. Because I didn't stand up for myself. Because of love. I should have never let myself be manipulated.

Perhaps I should be fairer to Thomas. He says he just wanted a new adventure, he wanted the quality of our lives to improve, he wanted to invest in our future.

It's not as if he hadn't been dropping hints for a while, either. About moving. I can't believe I didn't see it for what it was, at the time. He kept saying things like maybe we needed a 'new challenge' before we got too old and stagnant. He got into this habit of speaking about us like we were a pond full of still, dirty water. I didn't like it. But he kept on. *A new project,* he said. *Somewhere safer. Somewhere we can breathe a bit. Something different, exciting. Crime rates are going up. Living costs. The city isn't safe anymore. Is this the life we really saw for ourselves?*

We need change, he said. He was right, but it wasn't our house we needed to change.

I can't say I wasn't resistant, at first. I did try to exert some influence. I liked our old place well enough, and I could see no real reason to leave- *if it ain't broke, don't fix it,* I told him. But Thomas continued to press. He said he felt stuck. He wasn't ready to admit why. I think he thought we were simply tired of each other. That happens, of course it does. You spend a lot of time with just one other being, and it eats on you, after a while. Well, it eats on me, at least. I like to be by myself, more than he does. Thomas likes company, stimulation, having other people gather around him. He takes his energy from others. He likes to argue, debate, chew things over at length. Impart knowledge. I do too, but only when it serves the conversation properly. Everything above and beyond always feels like wasted time. Time I can be spending on other things, like painting. Quiet things, pursuits that don't make my ears ring afterwards. That's why I don't do social media, but he loves it. Groups, forums, servers, wherever people gather online, that's where you could find him, before moving here. Typing away furiously, thumbs flying. It drove me crazy. The lack of reliable internet has been a blessing in disguise, honestly.

I don't believe in change for the sake of change, as a way of fixing things, but he clearly did. We have never been very alike, come to think of it. Chalk, and cheese, as the saying goes. We make it work, but it isn't easy. Chalk and cheese never is.

Anyway, he built this spreadsheet of houses he said we should look at. He programmed a macro into it that automatically sorted properties into a viewing shortlist, based on a variety of mysterious factors he never shared with me. I think about that now, and how utterly absurd that was: our lives, determined by the sequence of numbers in a series of grey-bordered cells. I realise now, though, that our whole life's span is essentially a numbers game. Nature and maths, inseparably intertwined, because, of course they are. Everything is connected. Fractals. Terrible, beautiful symmetry. Golden ratios. Pi. Fibonacci sequences. All these things turn up in art, too. If you turn a pinecone upside down, and look at the perfect spiral arrangements of the seed scales, you can see it. With paint, it is clearer. If you daub the individual spiral patterns in different shades, you end up with a wheel of colour, and chances are, the number of bract spirals, if you count them, will conform to some natural mathematical principle you would have known fuck-nothing about, until that moment in time.

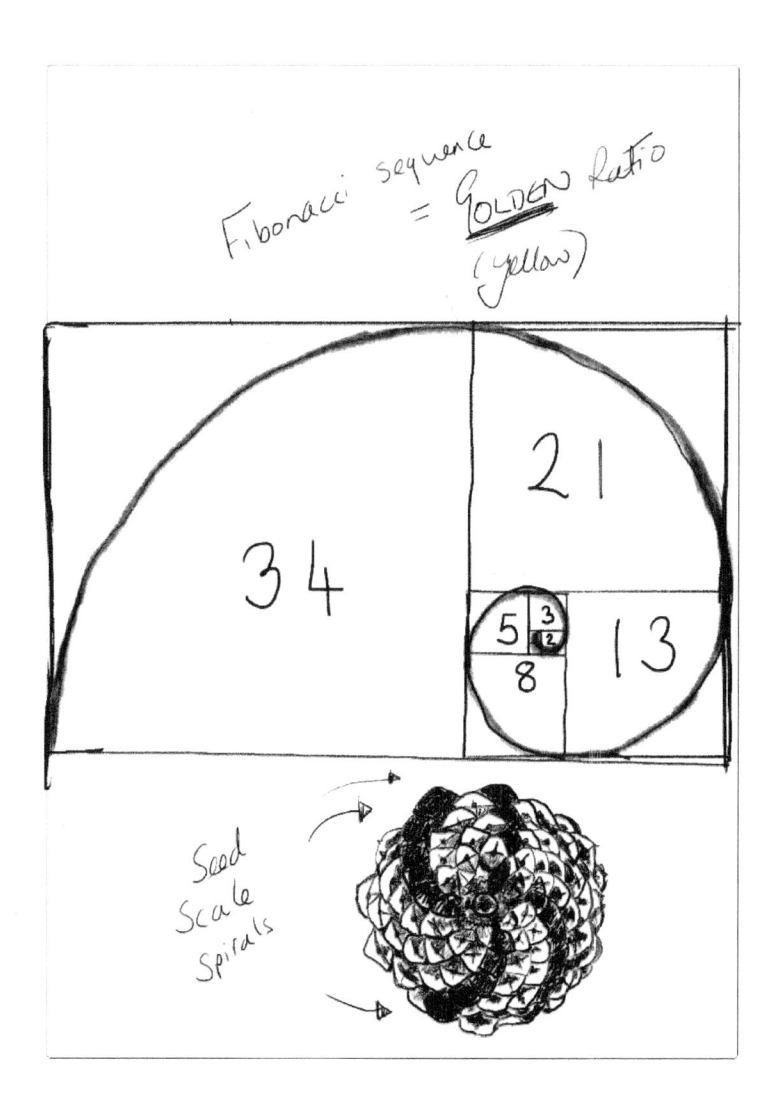

Scanned sketch from Hope Gloucester's scrapbook/diary, dated March 17th, 2020.

I saw a TED talk once, about *Starry Night*, by Van Gogh. He painted it in 1889 while in the asylum at Saint-Paul-de-Mausole. He was sinking into fits of hallucination and paranoia, and for me, it makes sense that he pushed yellow to one side during that phase of his life. *Starry Night* is almost entirely blue. The stars are still yellow, of course. The painting was about capturing not light, but the *motion* of light, according to this expert. Luminance. Turbulence. Apparently, turbulence is one of the 'great unsolved mysteries of physics'. Apparently, Van Gogh's painting of the night sky shows a 'distinct pattern of turbulent fluid structures,' whatever the fuck those are. The idea being, the more psychotic Van Gogh was, and the more he presented that psychosis in his art, the more his paintings displayed clear signs of using definable mathematical principles. As if there was a correlation and alignment between his brain chemistry and the basic laws of the universe.

Art and nature and maths and biology. Chemistry. Physics. Intertwined.

There are no coincidences, only interlocking truths, someone once told me. I can't remember who. Maybe it was me, and I'm smarter than I think I am. He's made me believe I am not the clever one, but I wonder.

Whatever. I am learning that nature likes numbers, and so does fate, and I was nothing if not terribly naive about this until we moved here. And I'm still in shock, in a way. That we did move here.

In the end, it all happened so fast. Once an idea takes root with Thomas, that is that. Thomas said he thought we could save money by doing some of the work on the house ourselves. He says the experience will bring us closer together. I am sceptical. Growing up in England means I understand enough about old houses, renovations and how devastatingly all-consuming building projects can be.

But I let things play out. I think this has surprised Thomas. I read somewhere that surprises are a key ingredient in a successful long-term relationship.

I read a lot of things, and none of them ever turn out to mean much.

Either way, we're here now. Our old apartment has been sold, and I am stuck with the shitheap that is the Once Yellow House. It is a full hour and forty-five minute drive from where we lived in the city, so I cannot easily meet with any acquaintances. A part of me wonders if he has moved us out here deliberately, to cut me off from any external support network I might have, but joke's on him. I have no support network. I have a couple of friends, sure, but only what I would call 'arm's length' friends.

Beyond the isolation, the house is, by anyone's standards, a fucking *wreck*. A rotten, damp-riddled wreck. Even the air in it feels spoiled. A faint shimmer hangs in around the house like a heat-haze. It smells bad. I think there is an underground vent giving off warm air from something, either that or it is gas from rotting leaves and matter. There are flies everywhere too, so that tracks. I keep putting up these sticky fly catcher strips, and have to change them every day. They get crowded with the corpses of hundreds of bluebottles and I hate every second of handling them.

Thomas keeps telling me to 'use my imagination,' and see beyond the gross stuff, to 'look at the potential.' But it's hard. The prospect of spending hours by myself stripping floors and painting ceilings while he wines and dines his clients in a five-star restaurant back in the city because he earns the lion's share of the salary is grossly unappealing, to say the least. But he likes it that way, being the breadwinner.

If I am being honest, this horrible bungalow represents nothing more than a whole chunk of disproportionate labour for me. Although interestingly, Thomas has already ordered internet. The men are coming to lay cables tomorrow, he paid for some weird, expedited service, used his business connections to get it sorted. He cannot go more than an hour or two without social media, I know that is what is driving him. His need for connection with whoever he is chatting to online who is more exciting than I am.

Meanwhile, I have lost all motivation to paint. I have all this new kit, but there seems to be no point. Everything around me is so derelict, and grim. I feel I would only be painting my own hollow ugliness onto the canvas, anyway.

If only I could do it beautifully, like Van Gogh.

I like my ears, though.

18.

Diary Entry, personal diary of Hope Gloucester
March 18th, 2020 (1)

The internet was switched on today. I honestly do not know which god Thomas prayed to in order to get a high-speed connection routed out here, to this derelict old shack surrounded by industrial wasteland, but whatever sacrifice he made worked. It's so incongruous to me that we don't have functioning heating or gas or a complete roof over our heads but he can email people and reply to shitty memes on group chat. But there you have it. Thomas remains happy. Purposeful. I chose not to point out that if he spends all his time with his face stuck to his phone we'll never get the renovations done. Something warned me he wouldn't appreciate this particular nugget of truth. To his credit, sorting the internet was an item on our long to-do list, so I don't feel like I can complain too much. His priorities are his priorities.

Meanwhile I had a good, strong word with myself after reading back over my last diary entry. I didn't like how I sounded at all. I don't recognise that pathetic individual. So I decided to get a grip. Take control. I'm trying to be more positive.

I've started by trying, really hard to actively look at things with more optimistic eyes. In a life drawing class I once went to, I remember we were told not to draw the person sitting naked before us, but instead draw the negative spaces around them- like the shape of the space between their legs, or the spokes of the back of the chair they were sitting on. I think this is what might be meant by 'seeing the bigger picture'- lines, angles, other spaces all converging around a central figure. I'm trying to do this, cognitively. Not see the damage to the house, but see the potential around the damage.

It's not easy but I can see, begrudgingly, that underneath all the mould and damp and peeling paint and rotting plaster there are elements of the Once Yellow House that could be considered quite charming, with poetic licence, like the sales brochure that sold it to us: "A characterful one-bedroomed folk style Victorian bungalow on the outskirts of the Sunshire Chateau estate in Lestershire. A fixer-upper built in 1900, enormous potential and unique aesthetic. Many surviving original features."

That last part is accurate: history and quirkiness in abundance. Many of the original features *do* remain, like the sash windows, plaster mouldings, and cast-iron pipes. Even the original railroad semaphore signal device, still wired up to a small control panel near the front door of the place. This leads me to think the bungalow must have been modified for the nearby Sunshire Estate's own personal rail signaller, which makes sense if you know anything about the history of the Lester family. The Lesters inhabited the Sunshire Chateau which lies about a mile North from here, and owned much of the land around. By all accounts, the estate still does. I did a little research. Turns out there was a private train line that serviced the house with coal and lumber and anything else they needed, direct. Whoever lived here at the time must have overseen all of that. I wonder if he wore a uniform, at all. Some special livery, perhaps, with the Lester personal crest on it. How the other half live.

I'm not envious. The Lesters were a nasty bunch, according to historic society lore. Ghoulishly rich and grasping. *More money than sense*, as the saying goes, although I have no personal experience of that dilemma. The chateau has been closed for years, the windows long-shuttered, but the legacy of scandal and intrigue lives on. They do the occasional tour if you are lucky enough to get a ticket. They sell out fast. Tourists love gossip. Thomas tried to get us on the tour yesterday. He said we should get to know our neighbours better, for they are the closest thing we have to neighbours, I guess. But no joy.

Anyway, to keep things POSITIVE (capital letters because I keep forgetting), the layout of the Once Yellow House is also something I suppose I could find a bit of comfort in, if I tried hard. The bungalow has this simple, uniform floor plan. Living room on the right, kitchen on the left. Bedroom on the left behind the kitchen, bathroom on the other side. Hallway in the middle. Symmetry. Geometry in action. It reminds me of the work of Mondrian[9]. Squares and shapes and lines, everywhere. You can't escape it, once you realise what's happening. Once you realise the grand design of it all.

---

[9] Ed. note: Dutch painter Pieter Mondrian was a pioneer of geometric abstract art, and he dealt mostly in squares and rectangles. He was also a member of the Theosophical Society, which, a little like Thomas Gloucester's Retinue, drew on a wide range of influences and beliefs from the occult to Buddhism, Hinduism and neoplatonism. Interestingly, their 'logo' is an odd symbol that incorporates two equilateral triangles arranged in a star formation, centred in a circle that is depicted as a snake eating its own tail. A lot to unpack there. Mondrian leaned into cubism and symbolism to express himself. His style eventually simplified into one he called Neo-Plasticism, which was limited to painting only in primary colors and grids of lines.

There's no point trying, either. You just have to let the shapes take you where they will.

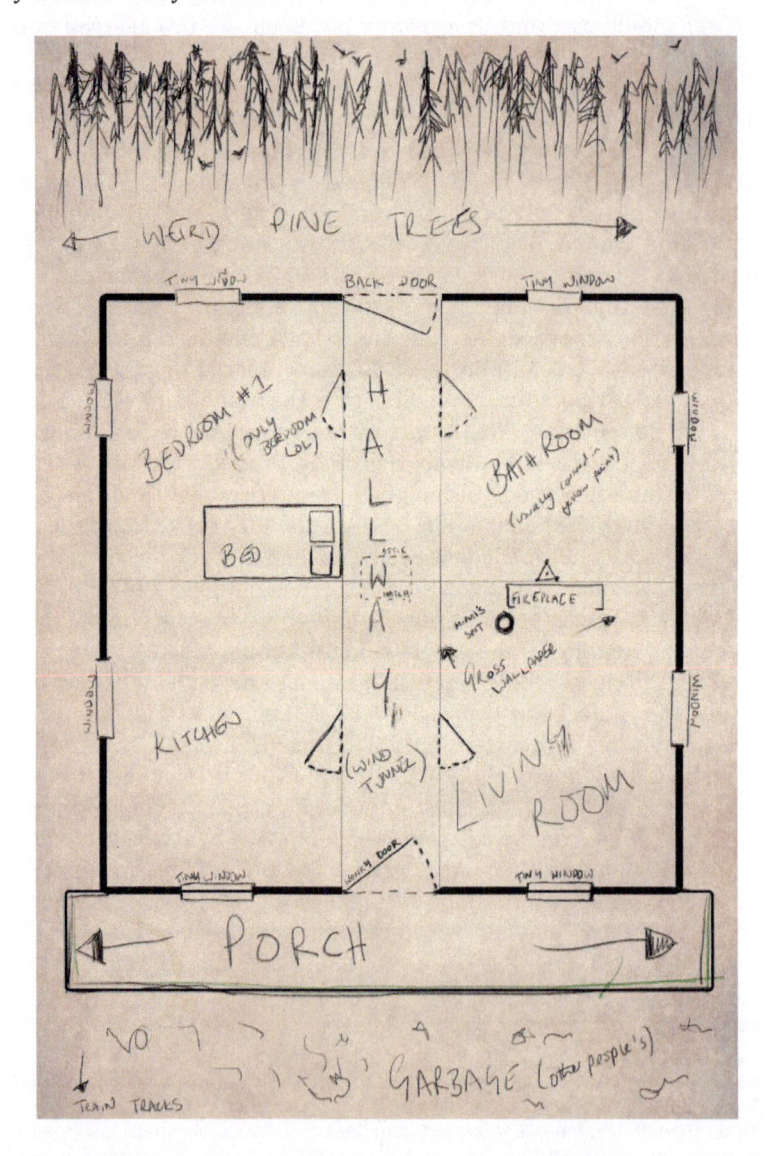

Floorplan, from Hope's sketchbook/diary. Actual floor plans have yet to be located, despite our best efforts with the local record office. Undated.

And it was cheap, I'll allow. Thomas negotiated a good deal, although I don't think the sellers were in much of a position to argue with him. I took down the *FORECLOSURE, FOR SALE* sign out front today. It makes me a bit sad to think of the financial predicament the previous owners were in. You can tell they'd given up on everything, even the most basic maintenance. There are spiders and beetles and roaches everywhere, in addition to the flies. I've used up three cans of bug spray already. I've also put traps down for any vermin hiding under the floorboards, which are, incidentally, peppered with woodworm holes. I'm also pretty sure there are bats and birds in the attic, nesting. More birds constantly line the rooftop, way more than when we first arrived. Like their numbers are growing. I can hear them wittering as I move about. I might get a bird scarer, although they don't seem frightened of Mimi when she barks at them, so that could be a waste of money.

There I go again. Complaining. I have to stop! Writing in here isn't working. I'm going to take Mimi for a walk. Get out of my head for a bit. I would paint but: no point.

But just one thing before I go. I have to allow myself to believe that maybe my funk is justified. *Nothing* about this house is manageable, or easy. And Thomas knew that when he bought it. He's not blind. Or perhaps he was. Perhaps he had the glare of yellow in his mind. Perhaps his eyes were bigger than his yellow-belly. Or perhaps he is just trying to keep me occupied while he's off doing whatever he does during his day.

He's back in the city, for a late meeting. I asked him to take a few days off so we could tackle some of the most pressing chores, and he said he'd try his best.

In the meantime I've got Mimi. And the birds, and the insects and the wallpaper and the holes.

And internet.

What more could a girl possibly want?

19.

Diary Entry, personal diary of Hope Gloucester March 18th, 2020 (2)

I'm back. I went along the train tracks a ways. The walk didn't help much, but at least I got fresh air. And perspective. Mimi enjoyed herself. Dogs have quite simple needs, sometimes. Things to pee on. Smells. Treats. Back scratches. I wish Thomas was that easy to please.

I think one of the main reasons I'm struggling is because I haven't quite dealt with the *way* in which Thomas bought this house. Inflicted it on me. The manner in which he did it was so underhanded, and I am still angry about it. I didn't realise that until a short while ago, but I am.

I keep thinking back to the first time we viewed the place, as an example. I was still recovering from the thing. The loss. I wasn't really in the mood, and when I was–the place–I remember vividly how revolted I was by everything, and how weird and insistent Thomas was, despite my discomfort. Manic, almost feverish. As if he couldn't see anything but his own warped reality. Tapping into his phone as he raced around the place, taking pictures. For what purpose? Who would care? Perhaps that was what he wanted, to generate likes from all my future hard work.

His phone feels like a rival, like the enemy. It has made me into a cynic, and I hate it.

I remember him trying to romanticise me out of my obvious disgust. 'Can you see a nice cosy couple sitting in front of that fireplace in winter?' No, I couldn't, but I kept that to myself. He was enjoying a completely different experience to me as we surveyed the bungalow. His cheeks were flushed despite how cold the place was. We were in the living room, the centrepiece of which is a large chimney breast wall with a generous cast-iron fireplace recessed into it. The design of the fireplace is unusual: blocky in an art-deco style, with tiny details stamped into the ceramic tiling: a series of geometric shapes, triangles, circles, squares, and vertices (no coincidences). In the middle of the brick hearth, barely visible through years of accumulated dust and soot: a triangle centred within a circle. Each point of the triangle is tipped with small dots that shine dimly as if made of glass or ceramic. I crouched down and rubbed a thumb across the soot; underneath, a mustardy-ochre gloss was hiding. The motif reminded me of the work of Malevich[10]. I felt a tingle in my fingertips as I wiped soot onto my leg. I remember the sensation still, clear as day. I drew a shit sketch of the fireplace later, I need to remember to tape it in here before it gets lost.

Image taken from Hope Gloucester's scrapbook/diary. The text in the fireplace grate reads 'Removable grate/hidey hole'. Undated.

---

[10] *Hope's favorite piece by Kazimir Malevich may well have been 'Yellow Plane in Dissolution', an arresting composition from 1917 depicting a bright yellow shape or colored plane slowly disappearing into the background, or, as some critics have interpreted, 'moving through space'.*

There is energy in this bungalow, I maintain. In the walls, the very construction of it.

I remember trying to make Thomas see what I saw. How ugly and derelict and unwelcoming the place was. He was having none of it.

'Snug, huh? With a little imagination, I mean.' He rubbed his hands together and then held them out to imaginary flames, sighing in false contentment. He is not theatrical, not normally. But in that moment he was being hectic, emotionally manipulative.

My alarm bells sounded but he has trained me to ignore them.

I did one final circuit of the bungalow in a desperate search for any redeeming features, because I wanted to make him happy, really I did. I heard the key to a long marriage is the ability to put yourself in someone else's shoes, see things from their perspective, so I gave it my best shot. My feet creaked and squeaked as I moved. Mimi followed me, her claws *tack-tack-tacking* on the wood. She stopped and sniffed at regular intervals as we explored. I watched her to see if there was anything particularly fragrant or juicy I needed to worry about, like a dead rat under the floorboards. I noted large gaps between the bare planks. Perfect for insects and slugs and vermin to squeeze through, not just the damp and cold.

'This hesitance is very unlike you, Hope,' Thomas admonished, raising his voice needlessly the further away from him I moved. His smile as he stuck his head around the doorframe after me was just a bit too fixed. I noticed fresh lines around his eyes. More grey hairs, too. He checked his phone anxiously for new notifications, pocketing it and then pulling it out again seconds later. I remember thinking *maybe he's on drugs,* then dismissing this as nonsense.

'This is very unlike *you*,' I countered, scratching my elbows until they bled. 'There must be a dozen places on that spreadsheet that are a better fit for us. Why are you suddenly so taken with this place?'

He shrugged and shook his head evasively, and he had this odd, cloudy look on his face.

'Just a...gut feeling, I guess,' he said, and that really got to me. Thomas didn't have gut feelings. He had spreadsheets.

Then he changed tack. 'Did you see the yard out back? So much space!' He darted off, another distraction technique. It cemented my slow-dawning suspicions. There was something he was not telling me.

I followed him to the yard as the door screen slapped shut behind us, sealing off the through-draft. Thomas stood with his back to me, staring up at the fir trees, which have these curiously long, slender, pale trunks, the bark almost white in colour. They sometimes seem like they are tall enough to pierce the sky above. It makes me dizzy when I look at them. Or maybe it's all the mould I've breathed in.

Hundreds, no, *thousands* of little birds huddled on the branches of the firs, quiet and still when we looked at them, even though I'd heard constant chatter and noise from them while we were inside the house. Mimi doesn't like them. She barked at the trees and the birds did this weird shuddering thing en masse, rippling their feathers, before settling down again.

'Are you going to tell me what's going on?' I asked Thomas, when he still didn't say anything. Silence from him is never good.

And then it hit me. I realised what was going on, and steeled myself for what I knew he was about to say.

And sure enough: he'd already bought it, he said.

He thought it would 'be a nice surprise.'

He had this broken capillary in his right eye when he finally admitted it. It hadn't been there an hour earlier. It made him all bloodshot on one side. I would have been more worried about it, had he not blindsided me.

When I started to get angry, he snapped: 'It's my money anyway,' turning the tables as if *he* was angry with *me.* He'd been angry with me all along, apparently. And it *was* his money. He is a businessman, I am an artist. Depressingly cliched, but there you are. I pay into the mortgage and bills when I can afford it, which is not often. Creative careers are either famine or feast, but he's always been supportive and understanding of that. He earns enough to keep the ship sailing just fine on his own, he says. 'Paint!' He also says. 'You're good at it. You should follow your dream.'

Does he mean that? I'm beginning to think not. Why else be so angry, so resentful as to buy a whole house without consulting me first?

Or perhaps he does like the fact that I paint, but not because it represents me following my dreams. Perhaps he likes the fact that it means I have to rely on him, financially. Perhaps it's not about the art at all, or his belief in me. I mean, we both know I'm not going to win any prizes any time soon. My stuff is frighteningly mediocre, at best.

It *is* his money, and he can do what he likes with it, but still. We're supposed to be a team.

The birds in the trees took that moment to launch themselves into the sky in a sudden burst of activity that drove Mimi into a barking frenzy. When I think back to that moment now, I remember the mass of feathers, beaks and wings that swirled over our heads like paint in water felt a bit like the noise in my head, a noise that never really goes away. I hear it now. Wings, beating against the wormholes in my brain. Constant chattering. Feathers, a loud and insistent drift.

Ours now, they say.

Thomas filmed the whole performance solemnly on his phone, posing and narrating as if making a documentary, then got frustrated when he couldn't find a strong enough signal to upload it to wherever he was trying to post. He didn't relax about it until we were back in the city and the video finally posted- then he smiled and looked pleased with himself.

And after that, we owned a bungalow.

I need to do something about this house before it drives me mad.

20.

Audio Transcript
File name: Once_Yellow_House_Transcription_07
Audio length: 00:10:35
Date transcribed: 12/22/2022

Kate: You look sad.
Hope: I'm always sad. I miss him. Or I miss who he used to be. He used to be kind, gentle. Into me.
Kate: Was he though? Did he?

[Pause]

Hope: What do you mean?
Kate: I'm just saying…some relationships can be, like…subtly and quietly abusive. Doesn't have to be overt. Ignoring you…ignoring your feelings, making massive life decisions behind your back…it's a form of coercion, which could also be called abuse. By some.

[Pause]

Hope: He was a good person.
Kate: If you say so.
Hope: You didn't know him like I did.

[Pause]

Kate: Who was Malevich?
Hope: What?
Kate: You said the fireplace reminded you of Malevich.
Hope: He was a Russian painter who…he loved geometry and abstraction. And the color yellow, of course. He used to paint triangles. Suprematism, that's what he called it. The art of shapes. The fundamentals of geometry. The artists have always known, you see. They've always known the truth of it all. Perhaps we see things differently for a reason. Read any art history book. It'll tell you. Malevich used the triangle as a vessel, a means to communicate something fundamental to the world at large.
Kate: What do you mean?

Hope: A triangle has three sides, doesn't it? There are also three primary colors of pigment. Yellow being one. Without it, you can't make the other shades and tones we have become so accustomed to. Green, orange, brown, skin tones. Interestingly, it is not a primary color of *light*. That honour belongs to red, green and blue. The two color theories are different systems altogether, one additive, one subtractive, meaning that we process light in two ways—as it comes to us directly from a light source, and as it is reflected to us from an object...

Kate: Hope?

Hope: Fuck, I'm sorry. *[Exasperated laugh]* I'm sorry. I wandered off again.

Kate: No, no. I see. I am interested. It sounds like math, again.

Hope: Divine mathematics, right.

Kate: I don't think it's happenstance that the Once Yellow House sat so close to another house with, um, reported supernatural properties, do you?

Hope: You mean the Sunshire Chateau?

Kate. Everyone told me it was haunted, when I first arrived. I drove past it on my way in from Chicago. I got lost and my GPS sent me in this weird direction, right past the estate. I could only see the tops of the roof though. I thought about trying to get a ticket for the tour once, like you, but then things...I ended up not leaving the camp much. You know how it was. We weren't really encouraged to go outside unless it was on a supply run. When we did, people would avoid us like the plague, I remember that. The yellow tunics put everyone off.

Hope: I'm not surprised, are you? You all had this look about you. Wide-eyed, intense. The Retinue scared a lot of people, I'm sure. You would have scared me, had I any bandwidth for fear left. I didn't, because of Thomas. He took it all. *[Snorts]* Maybe I should have sold tickets for a tour of the Once Yellow House. Made some money out of all the misery that followed. People would have paid.

Kate: People did pay, Hope. Just in different ways.

Hope: Oh stop lecturing me. Suffering doesn't fill a woman's belly, does it? Do you know what I ate for breakfast today?

Kate: *[Sigh]* Tell me.

Hope: Mold-toast. I scraped the blue fuzz off first, best I could. I couldn't really taste it after I covered it in margarine, but the point is...I should have sold tickets.

Kate: I can't feel sorry for you. Not at this point. Not after what everyone else went through.

Hope: Ah, competitive suffering, is that it? I suppose I have nobody to blame but myself for how I have ended up, is that right? Except that you're forgetting. I stayed. I could have left at any point. But I stayed. To care for him! *[Banging noise as Hope slaps her hand on a solid surface]*

Kate: *[Clearing throat]* You did. I'm sorry. This is hard for me.

[Pouring sound of more whiskey]

Hope: This is why I go off on tangents. It makes the medicine easier to swallow. Breaks up the intensity. Extreme tangentiality is a sign of mental instability, I read somewhere. Other people think it's a sign of enhanced brain capability. Something to do with...something like...oh, what is the term... *Fronto-parietal network.* Funny how I can remember that, but not where I left my front door keys on any given day of the week, isn't it? My brain is full of worms, I'm sure it is. Thomas made holes in it and the worms got in and made a home in my warm, sore little head.

Kate: If it helps, I think I know how you feel.

Hope: Did you get the tattoo, like all the others did?

Kate: I did. See?

Hope: Huh. Look at that. There it is. An equilateral triangle, four dots, the last in the middle, surrounded by a circle. There's something so...pure about the arrangement, don't you think?

Kate: I never really thought about it too much. I just got it done because that was what new members of the Retinue did. They told us it made us part of the family.

Hope: I know. I know they did. They told you a lot of things, didn't they?

Kate: You don't have a tattoo.

Hope: I didn't need one. I was the wife of the Great God Thomas.

Kate: *[Sigh]* Let's stay with the house. Were there any other redeeming features?

Hope: One. Lots of room around the property. It came with a sizable plot of land, which I imagine was the appeal for Thomas. The perfect amount of space for a creepy cult tent village to pitch up in.

Kate: We didn't just live in tents. We built shelters too. Some pretty decent structures. And we helped you fix up the house.

Hope: You did. Feels like a shame, in a way. So much wasted labour, given what happened.

Kate: There's power in building things, though, I think. It felt powerful, to me.

[Pause]

Kate: I think what we build is more important than how much effort we put into it. Does that make sense?
Hope: You mean, it's not about the climb. It's what you do at the top.
Kate: Like, do you know how hard it is to find someone who wants to build things with you? Make things? A life, a new home? Babies, a family? Memories?
Hope: You're right. So few people are brave enough to build things.
Kate: Thomas wanted to build things with you. He wanted the Once Yellow House. He wanted the Retinue.
Hope: I don't think he knew what he wanted, actually. The house had gotten to him by then, sure, but I lost him long before we moved in. That was why he was always on his phone. That's how it spoke to him, you see. I'm sure of it. He found a picture or a thread or something about it, and it got to him. It got his hooks into him, started communicating with him somehow. The point is, he was looking. They say a lot of cults are born online, like that lizard-lady cult.
Kate: Mm-hm. Hope?
Hope: Oh, here it comes.
Kate: I know you've already explained this but…Why stay? Really. Why stay with him when he was so…so…*[Makes indistinct noise]* Even before his transformation. Things were clearly not right between you.
Hope: I asked myself that many times. When the fear was so powerfully all-consuming I thought I might go fucking *blind* with it. Why stay? I told myself I wasn't afraid, you know, that I was numb instead, but I was afraid. I was scared all the time.
Kate: So why? Why risk your life, risk your sanity, risk any chance of happiness or peace of mind?
Hope: Because underneath it all, he was just a man.
Kate: So?
Hope: He was *my* man, and I knew he was good. Deep down. I wouldn't have married him if I didn't know that. He was a good guy. Noone else understood him like me. Sometimes you just know. He couldn't help what had happened to him anymore than I could. The

Once Yellow House poisoned him. I believe that. I know that is what happened.

Kate: I mean...perhaps his personality was predisposed to-

Hope: It was the house! Because of the accident, you see. You have to understand that.

Kate: You've mentioned the accident a few times, but I need details, Hope.

Hope: I'm getting to it, alright? I'm getting to it. But first I need a bathroom break. Is that allowed?

Kate: Of course. You seem agitated.

Hope: I'm fine.

[Recording is paused]

[Recording resumes, this time Kate speaks in a low whisper[11]]

Kate: Despite what she says, she's getting agitated, I can tell. I can't decide if she is completely insane, or just deeply traumatised, or both. It's hard not to question her reliability. Hope Gloucester is not what anyone would call stable. She has all these nervous tics and twitches, she picks at the skin of her elbows, both of which are now bleeding, but she doesn't seem to have noticed that. It's like...like she's in a trance when she starts talking. It's so fucking weird. Everything about her is really fucking weird. And yet none of it is any weirder than the stuff I saw at the Once Yellow House when I was part of the Retinue. Maybe that's the problem. My expectations. Maybe by coming here, I thought I would be able to confirm that the things I saw were...hallucinations, maybe. Like I was getting my nightmares mixed up with my real memories, perhaps because of trauma...a coping mechanism...

But the more I talk to Hope, the more I feel like I was blind when I was there, despite the things I was exposed to. Like there was a bigger design for it all than I ever comprehended. She had a front row seat, yet she's in such a huge state of denial. Even about her marriage. He was clearly abusive to her, but she doesn't see it that way. She sees it all as her fault.

And we haven't even really scratched the surface, not yet.

I think I'm going to be here a while.

[Recording ends]

---

[11] Ed. note: presumably so as not to be overheard.

21.

Diary Entry, personal diary of Hope Gloucester
March 19th, 2020 (1)

This morning I woke up determined to stop moping and change things around here for the better. I sent Thomas (who decided to stay at home today, which I was grateful for) out with a shopping list. He was annoyed by this. Whenever I ask him to help, he gets annoyed. He calls it 'tasking,' not 'help'.

'Why are you trying to get rid of me, anyway?' He asked. 'You told me you wanted to spend more time together!'

I told him I needed tools and supplies if we were going to make a start on the house. He grumbled, but acquiesced. Of course he took his phone with him when he finally left.

After he'd gone I stood for a while drinking in the quiet. I closed my eyes, tried to familiarise myself with the new, alien soundscape of the bungalow. It is different from our apartment in so many ways. It breathes differently, this house, creaks and ticks with strange rhythms. Things are louder because we haven't unpacked enough to deaden the acoustics. I could hear birds on the roof, as always. A drip, in the bathroom. Mimi, snoring. A faint whistling, as a draft made its way in through a sash window that had stuck open in the bedroom. Rather than unstick the frame, the previous owners decided to hell with it, left it wedged open, and gave the window a new coat of paint, sealing it ajar. It means I'll have to chip the old gloss away before I can fix the sash, but in this house, that is the least of my worries.

I unboxed our turntable, unsleeved a record and experienced that quiet sense of joy I always do on hearing the hiss of vinyl sliding past cardboard. I love that sound. I set Clams Casino playing, the track that samples Imogen Heap. I made myself a coffee on our camping stove while morning sun spilled in through the tiny square windows of the bungalow. They sometimes feel more like the portholes of a ship than they do the windows of a house, and light is rare.

I remember thinking, *See? This is not so bad*, as I sipped my coffee and tried to figure out the best place to start. But it didn't last. That feeling. The place was just fucking with me, I think. Gathering its strength before it revealed its true intent.

I knew I should be up in the attic checking out the leaky roof, but I couldn't bring myself to go up there first thing in the morning. I was tired, I'd slept poorly, and wasn't ready to face the enormity of damage I might find in the roof rafters. So I put it off, knowing if I perhaps stripped wallpaper instead, I would at least be making some sort of progress while gearing up for the more important tasks.

I decided the fireplace wall in the living room was the most logical starting point from which to tackle the disgusting paper. I wanted to free the fireplace from its ugly stranglehold, because the hearth was the only intact, not-shitty thing in the whole building, and a quick fix as far as aesthetics went. The more I looked at it, the more I liked it: the blocky shapes, the geometric patterns stamped into the tile design. I have developed this habit of tracing my fingertips around the shapes in the hearth, letting my skin drag along the sooty outline of the triangle, finger-walking the dots at each tip, drawing around the circle inside the triangle. Sometimes I can feel my hands tingle faintly when I do this, just a slight buzzing sensation.

I started by scoring the wall around the fireplace with a craft knife, criss-crossing the fuzzy green paper pattern with savage abandon. The wanton destruction felt quite cathartic, once I got into a rhythm. I channelled a lot of my latent anger and frustration into those knife strokes. Then I soaked everything with a sponge dipped in boiling water mixed with dish soap. The water sank into the thirsty paper, which I attacked with a stripping knife. It slowly began to come away from the wall in thin, serrated strips.

I kept peeling. It felt good. Underneath the wallpaper, I was pleased to learn the plaster was smooth. A bit tacky in places, but no cracks. Not the original bare brick, either, which I was immensely thankful for. I began to feel even better about things when I saw that. About the Once Yellow House. The bones were good, it turned out. There were patches of mould and damp, but not enough to worry me. Airing the room out properly will help. Windows open, a dehumidifier. I'll need to wipe the walls down every day with an anti-fungal solution, but that's easy and cheap enough.

I can't avoid the attic any more, though. Not now I've made progress here. The wind is picking up outside. Rain is forecast for later in the day. As pleasant as it was making headway with the superficial joy inherent with stripping away the ugly paper, I have to get topside, check for leaks, mitigate any further damp problems and damage before it all gets too serious to fix without massive expense.

If it isn't already. At the very least, put a few buckets out to catch the rain.

    I was going to wait for Thomas to come back, but I don't know when that will be, and I'm worried I'll lose motivation. I won't wait. I'm going up there now.

    I will write more after.

22.

Audio Transcript
File name: Once_Yellow_House_Transcription_08
Audio length: 00:02:09
Date transcribed: 12/22/2022

Kate: Thank God.

Hope: What?

Kate: Don't take this the wrong way, but I didn't drive all this way to listen to a blow-by-blow account of you stripping wallpaper. I just want to hear about the accident. We all know everything started there. I just...I really want to get to the point.

Hope: I am an artist, young lady. I am just painting a picture. Setting the scene.

Kate: I don't need that much detail. Really. I get it. You were good at decorating and stuff. You hated the house. Things felt...off. Thomas didn't pull his weight. But none of that is as important as what happened *to* him. It's all just...so...trivial.

Hope: You want my memories, you get the trivial along with the momentous, alright? If you have a problem with that, you know where the door is. Don't let it hit you on the behind on your way out.

Kate: I wish I could just go in there and scoop out what I need.

Hope: My mind, you mean? *[Chuckle]* Good luck finding your way around in there.

Kate: Tell me about the attic, Hope. Please. I am begging you. Stop avoiding it, and just tell me.

Hope: *[Sigh]* Fine. Fine. You've got a point.

23.

Diary Entry, personal diary of Hope Gloucester
March 19th, 2020 (2)

I had an accident. I'm in bed now, so I can't write much. I am too sore.
    And angry with myself.
    The house attacked me. I know it did. It attacked me when my guard was down. I should have known better. I feel like that is becoming a motto for my life.

24.

Diary Entry, personal diary of Hope Gloucester
March 19th, 2020 (3)

I slept a bit. I feel a little better. I have to write down what happened, before it gets lost.

The attic is accessible via a small square hatch set into the ceiling of the hallway, dead in the centre of the bungalow. A push-to-open type, with a small hoop sticking out of the drop-down trap door. I was too short to reach without a stick, so I found a chair and balanced atop it. Mimi watched me, tail wagging as I climbed up onto the chair and reached high over my head.

As soon as my fingers connected with the small latch-hoop the dog barked. Just once. This little warning *yip!* As if she knew something I didn't.

The latch clicked as I pulled, and then popped.

The trapdoor suddenly came open faster than I could react, savagely swinging downwards in a lethal arc. It smacked me on the forehead and knocked me clean off the chair.

I had a second to realise, as I tumbled backwards and hit the floor, that a heavy wooden folding ladder was attached to the trapdoor. This ladder unhinged like a cobra lashing out, the solid wooden rungs speeding towards my face. I screamed, rolled to one side before it could knock me clean out. It missed me by an inch. I even felt the wind as it whooshed past me, heavy, deadly.

Then the ladder came to rest innocently in its unfolded state, as if nothing at all had happened. As if it hadn't just tried to kill me. The house. Butter wouldn't melt.

I lay on my back, winded, chest heaving, staring up into the yawning black hole of the trapdoor. I could see scattered bullet holes of light in the black beyond. Holes between the roof tiles, letting in the sunny day.

Sitting up, my head now pounding, I actually shook my fist at the trapdoor like an old man from a cartoon.

'Fuck you,' I muttered, like it would make any difference.

Mimi rushed to check on me, trying to lick the cut that now ran between my eyebrows. I brushed her off, not wanting the wound to get infected. It was not bleeding, but it was thinking about it. I think my skin was in shock, like I was. I scratched Mimi's ears while my heart rate went back to something approaching normal, then I went to the dirty bathroom to check the damage in the mirror over the sink. A large welt had made a statement on my face. I think it is going to leave a scar.

 I deliberately forced myself to stay calm and try to look on the bright side as I cleaned up with an antiseptic wipe. It could have been worse, a lot worse, I know. I'd rolled out of the way in time, I was lucky not to be lying on the floor, unconscious, with a large dent in my skull. Or worse, dead.

 I patched up my face and went back to examine the scene of the crime. I could hear the wind outside and Thomas was still not back. I probably should have waited, at least sat down for a while until I knew I was okay, but I wasn't thinking straight, and I didn't want to seem dependent, like I couldn't handle it myself. Thomas is never great when I'm sick or I injure myself anyway. He gets frustrated, like I'm an appliance that's malfunctioned at the worst time. I knew he'd be disappointed if I'd wasted the time he'd given me, so I steeled myself to go up into the loft, despite everything. A stupid decision, but I knew that, and went anyway.

 It was clear the trapdoor mechanism would need replacing when I examined it properly. On closer inspection, the inner spring catch was rusted and worn away to the point of failure. I've added this to the list of jobs we need to take care of. The thought of the attic door popping open on a whim without warning at any time is terrifying. What if it comes down on one of us again, right when we are walking beneath it?

 I got a flashlight and climbed into the roof space, feeling a little dizzy.

 And that's where everything went to shit.

 The space under the rafters of the Once Yellow House was surprisingly generous when I hauled myself up there. A trussed wooden framework criss-crossed overhead, making it difficult to move around without having to duck and dive through beams and planks, but there was room beyond those. Only half of the joists were covered with loft panels, the rest lying exposed, meaning one end of the attic was cramped with old boxes and bundles of insulation, while the other end was empty, littered with bird droppings and these mouldy old twists of newspaper. The space stank, obviously. There were dried remains of bird nests in the rafters. A few dead baby carcasses on the insulation below, desiccated, these little mummy-birds. A small gable at the far end had a tiny window in it that only let in a small amount of yellowish-green light, for the glass on both sides is green with mould. It made me feel even more like I was underwater, that window. The bungalow often makes me feel like that. Like I'm alone at sea, drowning.

I spent some time meticulously checking the roof holes and cracks and slivers of daylight. To my relief, I found only three or four tiles had slipped badly, which is miraculous given the state of the rest of the bungalow. I knew the house was squat and low enough that I could probably get up there with a ladder the day after and try to refix the loose tiles myself. There was a small stack of dusty spare tiles at the far end of the attic space, so I knew I could, with the right nails, replace the loose ones. In the meantime, I placed plastic sheeting and buckets and a washing-up bowl beneath the unwanted apertures and stuffed plastic bags and rags into the gaps, hoping that would hold things back just until the forecasted rain passed.

Then I knelt on the flimsy floor and thought about whether I could turn this space into a little artist's studio. The lighting was terrible, but it was everywhere else in the house too. And if I laid the rest of the loft panels down, there would be double the floor space. I could paint the boards a pale colour, and install decorating lamps. The clip-on type. Maybe even eventually install some skylights.

And then, as I sat there imagining this all in my head, I began to feel strange.

Hot.

Flustered and flushed.

Horny.

Aware of myself, all of myself. Every single part.

Like you do when you suddenly smell something that turns you on, like a nice aftershave or a particular brand of soap someone uses, something that reminds you of bodies and intimacy, of being close enough to another person to smell those things in the first place.

I licked my lips. Inexplicably, out of nowhere, I was thinking about sex. The kind of sex I like, I mean. Like but am not brave enough to ask for. Fucking, not making love. Hard and fast and ruthless, without shyness or hesitation or any other complicating factors. *Split me in two like a dry tree, nail me to the ceiling.*

I felt myself getting more and more worked up, uncontrollably frustrated. I couldn't believe how tense, how het up I was. Then I realised what was going on. I was finally alone, in a private spot. My body was relaxing, at last. And it told me what I had been ignoring since I lost the baby: that I just needed relief. I needed to experience something pleasurable about my body again. Before the Once Yellow House, before the loss, I had been horny nearly *all* the time, but had to hide it well. It was a frustrating state to exist in, being constantly turned on, a state that seemed to serve no purpose at this stage in my life. Being obsessed with sex felt like a tremendous waste of energy. Except perhaps when it came to relieving stress.

And I had been stressed, I realised. Very, *very* stressed. My head hurt, and my husband had bought a house without asking me first. And I'd lost our baby, and had kept it a secret, because I didn't feel safe enough to tell him.

I ran a hand across my chest, thinking about the attic door, walloping my head.

I thought about Thomas, who had lied about the house, uprooted our entire lives on a whim. About him texting and gazing into his phone at all hours. Was there someone else? Several someone else's?

I thought about all the work ahead of me. All the cleaning and fixing and hammering and peeling and painting and sanding.

I found myself frantically fumbling at my clothing, loosening my tracksuit pants, slipping my hand between my legs urgently. It was an odd place for a quick self-soothe, I know this, and I could hear myself in the back of my own mind saying *What the fuck are you doing?* But I didn't seem to be able to control myself. I closed my eyes, noticing a faint disturbance in the air of the attic before I did so, and I dimly thought *Maybe it's mould, or pollen, or gas*, or…but it was like the thought, half-baked and hardly registered, then sank without a trace. I worked my fingers rhythmically. It felt uncomfortable, grimy and dusty and a bit disgusting and wholly of the moment, which was, as it turned out, exactly what my body needed. I replayed a few favourite fantasies, urgently scrolling through the selection of scenarios in my mind, and settled on an old comforting classic: stuck in an elevator with a stranger, man or woman, young or old, I didn't mind, just so long as they went down on me while I pushed back against the elevator walls for support, legs spread wide, skirt hitched up around my waist, and I always came thrice in that fantasy, so I worked on it furiously, feeling as if I owed it to myself, one, two, three.

And that's when the thin loft panelling I was kneeling on caved in. Just as I was about to orgasm for the last time. I felt myself drop, screamed. I felt my legs jam into the spaces between the joists, becoming stuck. One joist in particular, sharp and splintered, rammed painfully into my inner thighs, scraping all the tender parts of me. In that moment I think I finally, truly understood what it was to feel vulnerable. I felt my left foot punch through what must have been ceiling plaster, because that foot went suddenly cold, and it was clear there was nothing beneath it to support the weight of my leg.

Pain and shame and panic rolled over me in thick, hot waves. I screamed out for help, remembered I was alone, and tried to extricate myself. One foot dangled out of a hole in the ceiling into whichever room was below. It must have looked absurd. I could hear Mimi barking furiously somewhere beneath. My other foot was trapped under me, and quickly started to go numb. My thighs screamed as the deep scrapes began to burn. No matter how hard I tried, I couldn't get a good enough purchase to heave myself out of the gaps between the joists. I was stuck, and stuck really fast.

I have to admit: despite everything, despite the pain, and the fear, I was still aroused.

That is not how Thomas found me, an hour later, when he finally came back: the arousal had died down. Instead he found me wedged, bruised, nauseous, exhausted and incandescent with rage, at myself, at the situation, at the house and most of all, at him.

25.

Audio Transcript
File name: Once_Yellow_House_Transcription_09
Audio length: 00:16:39
Date transcribed: 12/22/2022

Kate: Wow. That's…that's not quite the story I was expecting. *[Uncomfortable laugh]*

Hope: I wasn't expecting it either, trust me. The house was testing the waters, don't you see? It attacked me, but I was never the original target. It wanted Thomas, but thought it would fuck with me, first.

Kate: I wish I knew what that meant.

Hope: I think I've had enough whiskey for now. I'll put the kettle on. Over here, nobody tells a story without a cup of tea. I can still afford tea, although I can't offer you much else.

Kate: I have money, Hope. I can…

Hope: No, I don't want your money. Not a penny of it. Your pity will do just fine, thank you very much.

[Movement and noise in the kitchen as Hope boils water and makes tea. Water is poured. Cups placed on the table. Sipping noises ensue]

Kate: This is good tea.

Hope: The trick is to use a teapot. I was horrified when I first moved to the States and saw people microwaving mugs of tea. You can't make tea in the microwave. It's sacrilege.

Kate: I don't really drink it. Or coffee.

Hope: There's something comforting about the heat of it, I think.

[Long pause and more sipping sounds]

Kate: So, you went up into the attic, after you were hit by the ladder, you…indulged in some self-care, shall we call it, and you fell through the ceiling.

Hope: Correct. Don't laugh.

Kate: I would never laugh.

Hope: I mean, it *was*, objectively, quite funny. Or it would have been, if I hadn't hurt myself so badly.

Kate: I said I wouldn't laugh, and I meant it. Pain is never funny. Anyway, after all of that, you were angry with Thomas.

Hope: You're damn right I was. Furious. The kind of anger you reserve for the people you love most. A romantic kind of anger, in a way? Like when you know you can trust someone, you can just let it all out.

Kate: I'm not sure that's healthy, Hope. Anger isn't romantic. It shouldn't be. And you couldn't trust him, could you? You kept a lot from him. I think it's a little wild how you've rewritten the narrative about Thomas, just because of what he went through. I really do.

Hope: I mean, sure he'd shaken my trust a little over the years, but-

Kate: He bought a house and relocated your entire life without consulting you first. Oh. And he started a cult online behind your back.

Hope: And what makes you an expert on relationships, huh? I don't see a wedding ring.

Kate: Hey, don't look at me. I personally don't...I don't find romance to be...fulfilling. I prefer my own company. *[Awkward laugh]* Love always felt like a pain in the ass to me.

Hope: It can be. It can also be the most rewarding experience a person can go through, but it comes at a cost. And it means people get angry with each other, sometimes. Perhaps most when they can't articulate what they really want.

Kate: And what did you want?

Hope: I don't know. I don't mean to be cagey. I just feel...I felt awkward about it, at the time. Still do.

Kate: Awkward about what? There's something you're not telling me. I can sense it.

Hope: I'm sorry. I don't mean to...It's just...sometimes I can't tell if things are real memories, or if something in my brain is just firing off randomly. It was absurd, climbing up there for a masturbatory adventure, right? It didn't just happen on a whim. You deserve the truth of it.

Kate: I don't follow.

Hope: The truth is I went up there for that one specific purpose. Not to check the roof. I didn't realise it at the time, but I felt *called* up there, somehow. Or maybe the house was just trying to get me to loosen the trapdoor catch. Ugh. I don't know. This all seems so insignificant by comparison to what came next. The *real* accident. The transformation. The Retinue. The massacre.

Kate: But this was in March? Yeah. You moved to the Once Yellow House in March of 2020. The Retinue didn't arrive until at least the end of September, if not October. So we have a lot of ground left to cover.

Hope: Were you one of the first to arrive? You have that look about you. Keen as mustard. I bet you were.

Kate: I was not. I dragged my heels more than a little. I'm not surprised you don't remember me, though. I had a red tent, if it helps. Everywhere had run out of yellow tents by the time I arrived.

Hope: I remember. I remember because it stood out in that sea of yellow like a red poppy in a field of wheat. Huh, imagine, all that time, it was you, camping outside my front door. And we never said hello, not once?

Kate: I did, once or twice. You always ignored me. I didn't take it personally. You had a lot going on.

Hope: Are you comfortable sitting there? There's a draft that comes through under that door something terrible this time of year. I wouldn't want you to catch a chill, not if you're going to stay for the whole story.

Kate: I'm comfortable, thanks.

Hope: I think I'm going to light the fire. I don't use the grate in here much, but it's pretty efficient when I do. I'm cold.

Kate: Me too. How do you cope with it?

Hope: I don't have a choice. Being warm is expensive these days. I have very little left to me. Wood is free though. I collect it from the shore of the lake, driftwood. It burns quite well once it's dried.

[Chair scraping sounds followed by clattering sounds, an iron grate scraping, paper being scrunched, a match being lit. Eventually, the sound of wood crackling as it burns.]

Kate: 'Despair comes in many forms.'
Hope: What?
Kate: It's in your diary. Here. You talk about despair, and all the forms it takes.

Hope: I remember. 'A sunflower, dying. An ear, hacked off and offered as a gift. A bruise on a cheek,' is that it?

Kate: Well remembered. It's a shame you can't remember other things as clearly.

Hope: Are you angry with me? For what happened?

[Long pause]

Kate: Yes. Yes, Hope, I think I am. You're the only other survivor I've met, and you were...well, you were his wife. You were closest to him. You could have stopped him.
Hope: I tried. I did try. I need you to believe that.
Kate: Even if you tried, you failed.

[Pause]

Hope: Can we take another break?
Kate: No, I don't think so, Hope. I think you should tell me more. So I can understand it better.
Hope: I'm taking a break.

[Long pause of 07:45 mins. Indistinct noises as Hope leaves the room for a while before returning.] [12]

Kate: Better?
Hope: A little. Do you care?
Kate: Not really.
Hope: I suppose that's fair.
Kate: Nothing about any of this feels fair.
Hope: How did you escape? On that final day. I keep forgetting to ask.
Kate: I ran. I ran really fucking fast. I don't know. I guess I just slipped through the net.
Hope: Or...or you were under his protection.

[Long pause]

Kate: You got something you want to ask me, Hope?
Hope: *[sudden burst of laughter that stretches out for several minutes]* Well, well, well. Shit. Little Miss I-don't-have-time-for-relationships, eh? Romance is unfulfilling. And all the while she was fucking my husband behind my back.

[Long pause]

---

[12] Ed. note: Clearly the interviewee found this line of questioning particularly difficult.

Kate: Is that what you've concluded? Because I survived, I must have been screwing your husband?

Hope: I bet you snuck into the house while I was sleeping, right? I used to wonder if anyone did that. I have a feeling they put things in my tea so I'd sleep heavier and not hear it. I don't think you were the only one, by the way.

Kate: If it helps, I never slept with him when he was…you know.

Hope: When he was his real self? The original Thomas? That's comforting.

Kate: There were so many versions of him, Hope, just like you said. I just…I wanted to see what it was like. We were all encouraged to do it, you know. By the Seniors. Especially the young ones, and the virgins. Like me.

Hope: Wait. Wait. Are you telling me…my husband took your virginity?

Kate: I'm sorry. Yes. That is what I'm saying.

[Long pause]

Hope: Well. And what was it like? Fucking a god. Giving your cherry away to a god. To *my* god.

Kate: The entity I got close to… *[Awkward laugh]* If you must know, he had four dicks. They moved around like the tentacles of a sea anemone. Spongy, questing. They had these little leaky openings at the end that looked at me like eyes. I didn't know whether to laugh or cry. I had no experience at all of sex, up until then. And I haven't since.

Hope: Wow. Wow. I…*[Sigh]* I cannot quite believe we are having this conversation. But, I can see how that would be hard to come back from. If you'll forgive the choice of words.

Kate: *[Shuffling sounds]* I have nightmares about it. It was so…so…alien.

Hope: I am beginning to reassess my opinion of you.

Kate: I don't really care what your opinion of me is.

Hope: You're in my house, remember. Looking for answers only I can give.

Kate: Well that's just it, isn't it? You haven't given me anything useful, yet. Just a depressing amount of backstory. And your musings on the color yellow.

Hope: As I said. The front door is over there, Kate. Feel free to use it at any time. On your way out, though, why not check out the symbol carved into the lintel above the door?

Kate: Symbol?

Hope: Another non-coincidence, yes. A familiar symbol, carved into the stone. I'll never escape him, you see. Ever. Neither will you. I would feel sorry for you, but you literally fucked my husband while I slept in the room next door. Don't deny me my cynicism.

Kate: I didn't fuck your husband, Hope. I fucked a *celestial version* of your husband.

Hope: Did he make you cum?

Kate: Several times, since you ask. In several ways. *[Pause]* I think. I don't actually know. I'm not sure I know how it's supposed to feel.

Hope: You know when you know, kiddo. Did you imagine yourself in love? *[Pause]* Wait, wait. *[Laugh]* You're *still* in love with him, aren't you?

[Long pause]

Kate: No. No I am not.
Hope: Turn that fucking thing off. Right now.
Kate: Hope, listen, I-
Hope: Right *now!*

[Recording cuts off abruptly.]

26.

Diary Entry, personal diary of Hope Gloucester
Date: ???[13]

Thomas keeps asking me if I still love him. He asks me this at least once on any given day, whenever his mouth is human enough to form speech. His eyes are these vast, pained holes in his face as he says the words.

'Do you love me, Hope?'
'Of course,' I reply. And sometimes I mean it.
Sometimes I don't.
It all depends on which version of him I wake up to.
Whatever he is, I am my own deconstruction.
But I still have my art. And Mimi. That's something, at least.

---

[13] Ed. note: the date of this entry was smudged and impossible to determine. It is worth noting this entry was crammed into a tiny corner of a page in a manner that looks as if Hope wrote it there only because she had run out of room in the rest of the diary, and was perhaps unable to purchase herself another. We reiterate that we have, as with all other entries, presented this entry in the same order it was presented in the source material—not chronologically.

27.

Diary Entry, personal diary of Hope Gloucester
Date: March 19th, 2020 (3)

Thomas keeps telling me to rest, but I can't. I'm in too much pain. My legs are burning, and it's so uncomfortable I don't know what to do with myself. I'm not able to rest in any position. I keep wondering how much dust and mould and old paint and splintered wood is now festering in my skin. Probably asbestos, too. In for a penny, in for a pound, with this place.

Thomas scolded me immediately for what happened.

'I should have been the one to go up there,' he said, angrily cleaning the cuts and gashes on my knees and thighs while I held a cool flannel to my forehead. Mimi would not stop barking, so we both had to make a fuss of her until she calmed down.

I told him it was fine, but secretly I do blame him, because I wasn't the one to buy the stupid fucking rotten house, was I? This is all on him. He knows it. I know it. He made a dumb, rash decision that I am paying for.

It took a long while to pick out the splinters and tufts of loft insulation that had stuck to the gore on my legs. I also have a large egg-shaped lump on my head, which aches.

Thomas said we should probably go to a hospital, but I told him I was too tired. I just wanted to nap, but I can't. It's miserable. I am miserable.

He took Mimi for a walk while I lay down, to give me some more peace. I noticed his phone in his hand as he left. He can't be separated from it for any length of time, not even to take the dog out. I hate it more than I hate this horrible yellow bungalow.

Alone in the house, I started to feel weird, as if the walls were bending inwards, leaning on me. Unable to get any relief lying down anyway, I got out of bed and went to assess the damage my foot had done when it had gone through the ceiling of what turned out to be the living room.

I hobbled like an old crone back to the spot where I had dangled. When I saw the aftermath, I nearly cried. The living room is now trashed, which feels deeply unfair. It was the one place I was making progress in. Now the space is completely ruined, and I'm back to square one. One step behind square one. Square minus-one.

Even before I got in the room properly I could see the piles of debris, insulation, bird shit, nests, bird carcasses and plaster dumped across the whole length of the space.

But that is not the worst of it.

The worst of it is the clean, blank wall I liberated from the wallpaper and mould.

Because on that wall, which was **<u>clean and bare</u>** except for a few stubborn fragments of paper when I'd last seen it, I swear, right before climbing into the attic, something is now growing. Festering. Propagating. Has spored? Was written? All of these things.

It looks like mould. Thousands of small yellow and black mould spots, standing proud and distinct. Like blood slowly welling up from the fresh wound on my forehead. It flourishes not in randomised patches, but intentionally. In shapes, distinct geometrical shapes: triangles, equilateral. Blobs at the end of each point. A blob in the middle. Over and over again, filling up the wall. Like wallpaper of a different kind.

It freaked me the fuck out.

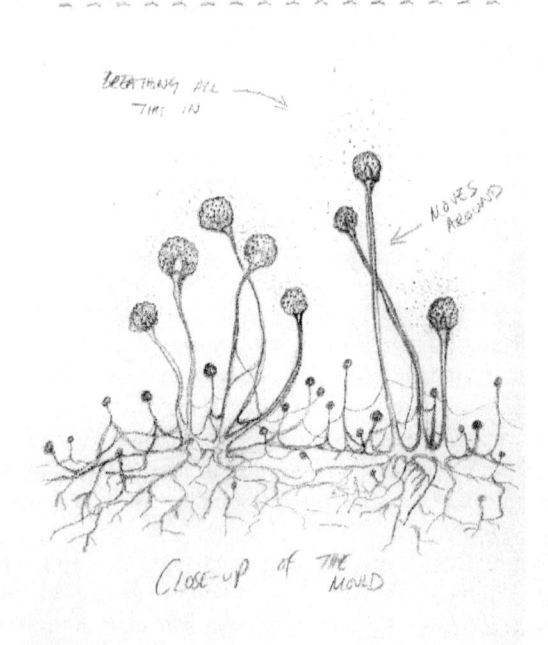

I backed out of the room. Then, like a madwoman, I did a little arbitrary circuit, limping around the tiny house, ending up back in the living room, lurching through the door quickly like a cartoon detective, intent on catching the house unawares, like it was a burglar or something, like I could take the fucking mould by surprise, make it scared somehow, disappear. Or prove to myself I was imagining it.

But the mould was still on the wall.

I know mould doesn't grow that quickly.

I pushed my face up close to it, which sounds really stupid now, but I had to see it properly. I had to understand. I covered my mouth and nose with my sleeve so as not to breathe in anything bad, and, after a good few minutes of staring with the flashlight of my cell phone turned up as bright as it would go, I saw something on the wall that I hadn't when the paper had first come off, perhaps because the light hadn't been good enough. It was the remnants of a tacky, sticky residue on the plaster beneath the mould, like a sheen. The sheen was laid out in distinct ways, as if someone had daubed something there a long time ago, right before the paper was laid, using something sugary, or gluey. Wallpaper paste, perhaps. It would make sense. Something organic could have attached itself to that glue, way back then, something that simply blackened with exposure to light, or as the air got to it, all these years later. It wasn't visible under the paper until oxygen started to affect it, maybe.

Like yellow paint, oxidising. Dormant mould, biding its time beneath shitty, ugly wallpaper. I cannot think of a better metaphor for the predatory, sneaky energy that dominates this house.

I kept staring. It was like the stuff hypnotised me. I still felt weird, my pulse slowing, the blood going *womp-womp-womp* in my ears, my groin and legs throbbing in time. And I can't be sure, but I thought I saw the black spots pulse a little too, expand and contract. Almost as if breathing. Or responding to my heartbeat. I know that sounds impossible, but that's how it felt. As if I were syncing with the bungalow. We were moving in time with each other. Like music.

I think the attic ladder must have hit my head really, really hard. Or maybe I've breathed too much of the black and yellow shit into my lungs and now it is sending me off. I read about toxic mould, about the effect it can have on your general health and wellbeing.

Either way, I won't rest until I have gotten rid of it all.

How exactly is another matter.

I tried washing the offending wall down with boiling water and soap, several times, throwing bowl after bowl of black murky liquid out the window in my attempt to scour things clean. I know I'm making the room damper, and I don't care. I just want something to be clean, tidy, nice, and liveable.

When Thomas came back with Mimi, the patterns had grown through again. Whatever has infested the plaster has taken root deep within the mix of it. We will have to get the walls treated and replastered completely, I told him.

'No,' Thomas replied. 'We couldn't see any of that stuff when the wallpaper was covering it, could we? So we just buy more wallpaper. Thicker stuff. Something bright and modern. Seal it in. Smother it. You said it wasn't there until the air had gotten to it, right? Like it had been dormant. So let's put it back to sleep. Trap it underneath. It'll be fine.'

I knew from his tone that he was lying to me about something, but I don't know what.

'But what do they mean? The patterns,' I kept asking him.

Thomas rubbed my back, soothingly, but it made me want to scream. I felt like clawing my own skin off.

'They don't have to mean anything, babe,' he said, gently. 'It's just shitty mould in an old house, that's all.'

He sounded so confident, but I know better.

Later, when he didn't realise I was awake, I caught him rubbing his face along the mouldy wall like a cat rolling in catnip. He was making this weird groaning noise, almost like purring, only more desperate, and as he turned his body slightly, I saw he had a hard on.

I must have said something, made a noise of some sort, because he spun around, caught me peeping. His face was so twisted and ugly with anger that it scared me. I backed away without breaking eye-contact, and he just stood there, fists balled, breathing all heavy, his dick levering down reluctantly, and I felt sick to my stomach. He has never looked at me that way before. I mean he has, or versions of that expression, but never with as much force, vehemence. It was like coming face to face with a completely different predatory species, not my husband.

I don't know what is happening to us, but I think I want out. I want to move. This place is bad for us, worse than bad. This place is transforming us into people I don't recognise.

Where we can go though, I don't know. Thomas sold our lovely old apartment. I don't think we have enough money for a motel, not for as long as it would take us to sell up and buy again.

I think I'm going to try and go into town by the end of the week and get a steady job. Waitressing, working in a store, anything, just so long as it pays. Money gives me options. Thomas won't like that, he says he has plenty of money, he has a good income, but something tells me I need to build a reserve. Of my own.

I keep seeing triangles and circles. My head throbs.

28.

Audio Transcript
File name: Once_Yellow_House_Transcription_10
Audio length: 00:03:09
Date transcribed: 12/22/2022

Kate: Have you calmed down?
Hope: It would help if you apologised.
Kate: For what? Being brainwashed? Being inaugurated into a cult at the age of twenty-one? For wanting more? For wanting to help and protect people?
Hope: I'm not sure swivelling around on a four-penised man counts as divine connection.
Kate: I was…fed to him, you know. Like a sacrifice. I told you. It wasn't just me, either.
Hope: I would like to change the subject now.
Kate: Fine.

[Pause]

Kate: So the mold was growing in geometric patterns. *[Sigh]* And it made you both horny.
Hope: Yes. Now that I think of it, it must have been the mold. Maybe it had some aphrodisiac quality, some pheromone in it or something. That doesn't account for the way it grew, though. Like I said, it's the same pattern you'll find over the door of this house. It's elsewhere around here, too. It means something significant, something widespread. Not just a Once Yellow House Thing. *[Pause]* You have an odd look on your face.
Kate: Hope. I've been here a while now. All I've heard about is mold. Triangles. Wallpaper. Sex. Masturbation. Are you ever going to get to the fucking point?
Hope: I beg your pardon?
Kate: Tell me about his accident, Hope! I am begging you. You've put it off for long enough.
Hope: I *am* telling you. Shut up and let me work through it, would you?
Kate: I'm trying, it's just…I've been awake for nearly twenty-seven hours straight, now! I need you to be succinct!

Hope: You're welcome to take a nap upstairs and we can start over once-
Kate: *Tell me what happened to Thomas now!*

[Loud bang on the tabletop]

Hope: Well. That was unnecessary.
Kate: I want to know what happened to Thomas! What *happened* to him?! What happened to all those people?!
Hope: Are you crying?
Kate: Just tell me. Please.
Hope: I told you already! The house got him, okay? Is that what you want to hear? The house, or whatever was waiting for us there, got him. It got him good. You have to stop shouting at me. Get a grip, Kate. You're still alive, that's what you would tell me. Get a grip.
Kate: Fine. *[Panting]* I'm fine. I'm listening. I'm sorry.

[Long pause]

Hope: You sure?
Kate: Yes. I'm sorry, I told you. I didn't mean to shout.

[Pause]

Hope: It's okay.
Kate: What happened, after the mold? After you fell through the ceiling. Tell me. I'll be patient, I promise.
Hope: Fine. *[Pause]* Things after that went...downhill, rapidly.

29.

Diary Entry, personal diary of Hope Gloucester
March 21st, 2020

We argue a lot. My health is getting worse by the hour. The mould and dust is in me, coating my insides. I feel sick all the time. I cough and wheeze, my eyes itch constantly. My hair has started to come out in thin handfuls in the shower. They say stress can do that. Make you bald on top. I can't believe how miserable a person can get in the matter of a few days. We moved in on March 16th. It is now the 21st, but I feel as if I have aged years and years in only five days.

I want to leave, sell the house, cut our losses, and get out. I told Thomas I wanted a break from this situation, from him too, if needs be. I told him I was forgetting who I was, in the Once Yellow House. It is eating my identity. I need to take a rest, I keep saying, from the mess, the chaos, the dirt and grime, the stress, the discomfort, just for one night, just for perspective, to reset.

He won't hear of it.

Probably because Thomas is thriving more than ever. The longer we stay here, the more robust he seems to get. Healthier. His hair is thick and glossy and his skin is bright, and his eyes are clear. It is like the Once Yellow House took all of my strength and syphoned it off into him.

I've shouted at him a lot today. He largely ignores me, until he doesn't. Then, he shouts back. His temper, when aroused, is worse than I've ever seen it. And it's different. Before, if he got angry, it was in a quiet way, sometimes broody, but always the type of anger that had a lid on it. Because Thomas was always the patient one. The kind of person who controlled himself, who came across outwardly as the reasonable one, took the time to add perspective and nuance to a situation. I found that a little patronising, I'll be honest. Patronising but manageable. But now…I am left with this volatile, unpredictable person who is either completely closed off, or blows up like a volcano. He swings between frenzied bouts of enthusiasm to wild drops in mood and energy.

Wondering what I am going to encounter at any given hour in the day is shredding my nerves.

30.

Diary Entry, personal diary of Hope Gloucester March 22nd, 2020 (1)

I tried to leave the bungalow to walk Mimi. Thomas got strange about it. Physical. He forcibly blocked the front door so I couldn't leave the bungalow. I kept trying to squeeze past him, getting more and more agitated. Eventually he gently grabbed the back of my neck to steer me around, back to bed, like I was a dog, like we grab Mimi by the collar sometimes.

After that I stopped trying to leave.

All the warmth and fun has gone out of our lives completely. It has also gone out of me. It feels like a synchronous race to misery that I think I might win, for like I said: he thrives here, even as I feel hollow.

He has started painting the house using the yellow tins I found under the porch when we first moved in. He does not know how to paint, or decorate, or do any DIY at all, and he is making a terrible sloppy job of it, but doesn't seem to care. He won't listen to reason. The house was Once Yellow, he keeps saying, and now he wants it to be 'Truly Yellow' again. The paint gets all over his clothes because he does not use the right brushes, or a dust sheet, or anything, and he treads in puddles of it and has started tracking the stuff in and out of the house with his paint-covered boots, and there are yellow footprints all over the floors, and yellow splodges on the walls where sometimes he brushes past, and in between those yellow splodges, the black mould still sprouts in patches, spreading freely throughout the bungalow now, this slow and steady encroachment of blight, and yes, it still grows in patterns and shapes: sometimes distinct concentric circles, sometimes lines and curves and circles and configurations that interact and play with each other like patterns and crop circles pressed into cornfields. Only it isn't a cornfield, it's my house, where I sleep (hardly) and eat (barely) and breathe (with difficulty), and I have given up trying to wash the stuff away. No amount of soap or fungicide is going to get rid of it, I've accepted that now.

I can't stop thinking of the time I saw a crop circle that the abstract artist Herd[14] made into a Van Gogh painting (because there are no coincidences, only interlocking works of art) that you could only see if you were in an aeroplane, flying overhead. Herd's Van Gogh interpretation was stunningly beautiful, I remember, a rendition of *'Olive Trees'* made from corn and grass and soil in a field in Minneapolis. I always thought Van Gogh would have liked it, and now I wonder: what would he have made of the Once Yellow House? And I can't shake that idea, and when I look at the mould patches I see the swirling patterns Van Gogh used to depict clouds in his paintings, only now it's weird yellow-black mould, not paint-clouds, and I think everything in my head is getting scrambled up altogether like so much whisked egg. Yes, that's it. Someone has put an electric whisk inside my skull and *whizz*, all my ideas and thought processes and recollections and ideas are now just muddled egg slurry.

I recall thinking this as I pressed a butter knife to my ear earlier this evening. I was trying to cook pasta, anything more complex is beyond me at the moment. You don't need a butter knife to cook pasta. I don't know why I was holding a knife. But I was, and I nicked my ear lobe, which sort of woke me up.

Then Thomas came in and took the knife off me, only he wasn't angry like I thought he would be, but smiling.

I know I need to leave the Once Yellow House, with or without Thomas, before it gobbles me up whole. *How* is the scary thing. How does one leave? How.

I miss art.

---

[14] Ed.note: Stan Herd is an expressionist painter-turned earthworks and crop artist operating mostly in Kansas. His 'living sculptures' utilize nature and the land around him. One wonders what he too would have made of the geometric mold patterns in the Once Yellow House.

31.

Diary Entry, personal diary of Hope Gloucester
March 22nd, 2020 (2)

He won't let me leave.

He wants me here with him, he says.

While the house disintegrates around us. While everything is subsumed by mould.

There is something really wrong with my husband, I can see that now. I'm so worried about him. I don't know what to do. The only thing I can think is that I need to leave, and then I can get some help for us.

He painted over the windows entirely today, slapping thick yellow emulsion right onto the glass, painting the sash windows shut, so everything is a lurid, yet somehow dark, French-mustardy yellow inside the bungalow. I feel like I'm living in a beehive with honey dripping down the walls. It all feels so sickly and sticky and like a horrible, horrible dream.

The mould growth everywhere has begun to look like this strange sort of forest, with sporangia (I had to google the right word before Thomas smashed my phone screen, it's still useable at a pinch, but you have to squint really hard to make out what's on display) that keep growing outwards and elongating, so it sometimes looks like a bed of kelp, moving horizontally. You can run your hands along the walls and it feels like fur tipped with beads of sap. Your fingers come away coated, but I can't tell if it is powder or residue or pollen or a fluid secretion. It's both wet and dry at the same time, resistant whilst still fluid, and it's all under my fingernails and no matter how hard I scrub, soap won't get it off.

I keep planning my escape, but Thomas is not making it easy for me. He told his office about my accident, said he was taking leave to care for me. He watches me when he isn't on his own phone, and he has this off-kilter accent to his voice that was never there before. A bit like he is talking to a child when he talks to me, a child he doesn't like very much.

Eventually, though, he has to leave the house, for some reason. To buy food and supplies.

When he does, I'll be ready. I'm going to run. I'll run with Mimi, take some time for myself, heal a bit, and when I'm stronger, we'll try and work things out. I'll try and lay down some firmer boundaries for how I want to be treated, and we'll have to come to an agreement about the Once Yellow House.

But for now, I just need to run.

32.

Diary Entry, personal diary of Hope Gloucester
March 22ⁿᵈ, 2020 (3)

He is leaving the house. We have run out of toilet paper and he said he needs more paint. The tins under the porch were not enough. He wants to paint the roof too, and the porch. I will pack surreptitiously and go as soon as he leaves. I am taking Mimi with me. I hope he'll forgive me, but it isn't safe for her here, either.

33.

Audio Transcript
File name: Once_Yellow_House_Transcription_11
Audio length: 00:04:08
Date transcribed: 12/22/2022

Kate: You didn't leave.

[Long pause of twenty-three seconds]

Hope: Obviously.
Kate: You tried, though.
Hope: I tried. It wasn't for lack of trying.
Kate: What happened?
Hope: He went out for supplies. Even he had to eat, I guess, and Mimi's food was low and we had no toilet paper. I took the opportunity while he was gone to pack a small suitcase. I called a taxi, not an easy feat with my phone screen as fucked up as it was. I found ways around it, I used voice search to find a company, ordered a cab and hoped it would get to the Once Yellow House before Thomas got back.
Kate: You sound as if you were really scared of him, by then.
Hope: Angry, scared, more than a little heartbroken. He wasn't the same man I loved, you see. Something about living in that place...it deconstructed him. You see why I am telling you all this, now? Because it wasn't just the blow to the head that changed him. There was something blossoming in there long before that. Something latent, maybe, like you said. Something that had been hiding in him, lying dormant. The house brought it all to the surface.
Kate: The taxi didn't arrive in time?
Hope: It did not.
Kate: I'm sorry, Hope.

[Pause]

Hope: Thomas came back, found me waiting with my suitcase all packed, Mimi ready to go, too. Her leash was on, and I had her travel crate ready.
Kate: You had a fight. Is that how it happened? You had a fight, and he got injured?

Hope: No. I mean, sure, we had a fight, then, but that wasn't it.

Kate: I'm listening.

Hope: Like I said, he came back suspiciously early, like maybe he had been calling my bluff and only pretended to leave to see what I would do, except he had brought supplies, some paint, I could see a bag of groceries, so I don't know. Maybe I just got unlucky. And his face was all hurt and lost, you know? It was hard to look at. I started to cry. I told him it was the house, or me.

Kate: He chose the house.

Hope: He chose the house. Said he would choose it a dozen times over. Then he threw a tin of paint at my head.

Kate: He what?

Hope: It only just missed me, too. Made a huge hole in the wall behind. Paint showered everything. Covered the walls, the floor, Mimi, me.

Kate: I'm so sorry.

Hope: It wasn't him, you have to understand. It was whatever force, energy, I don't know what to fucking call it—cosmic residue *[Laughs]* was inside of him. The taxi pulled up outside then, perfect timing, and he went out, told it to turn around. Said there had been a mistake. Stupid taxi driver didn't question him, not even for a second. Men stick together, I guess.

Kate: What did you do then?

Hope: I ran into the bathroom with Mimi, and locked the door. I didn't know what else to do, so I hid from him until he calmed down. I thought about climbing out the bathroom window and running away on foot, but I didn't think I would fit through. Besides, I couldn't run very fast. My legs were still a mess, I was struggling to breathe by then, my lungs were congested with all the house shit, and the wounds on my thighs hurt a lot. So I decided to pretend like everything was fine, and wait him out. Until he left again. No matter how long that took. I'd make sure this time that he would be gone for a long while. Then I'd try to escape again.

Kate: Couldn't you call anyone? Family? Friends?

Hope: I should have, long before then. But everything seemed to happen so fast, I don't think I could fully believe the way things were going. Maybe I was worried nobody else would believe me either. My family liked him, you see, and the few friends I had I didn't know well enough to ask for help. Anyway after that, my phone stopped working properly. It fell out of my pocket into the paint and I could never get it to turn on again for very long. The house phone wasn't connected, of course.

Kate: What happened next?

Hope: *[Sigh]* Thomas was mopping the spilled paint up when I came out. He was doing it in a weird way, with a bedsheet, swirling it around and across things in these large, sweeping streaks. I think by then he thought of himself as an artist too, you know? The house put that idea into his head. Every surface of it was a canvas, and it was like watching a kid explore textures and colors. He sloshed all this paint around as innocently as if nothing was happening at all, and looked at me as if he'd calmed down a little, but I knew that meant he'd be feeling melancholy inside instead, which, I was learning, was far worse. Because his melancholy made him angry in turn, and it was all this horrible cycle of up and down, self-pity followed by frustrated rage followed by crying and so on. So toxic. Like the fucking mold on the walls. Anyway, when I approached, I saw him standing right where he shouldn't: underneath the attic trapdoor. And then I had a thought, you see. If I could keep him there long enough, maybe. In that exact spot. Bang the walls a little. Make some vibrations. Work the catch loose. Perhaps the house would do me a favor, for a change. Take control of the situation.

Kate: You thought...you wanted the ladder to come down?

Hope: It was this, like, vain hope. Desperate. That someone would solve the problem for me. Fate. Circumstance. The house. It was only a thought. Just a fleeting thing. But I had it. Then I saw the broom, leaning against one wall nearby. The handle was just long enough to reach the ceiling.

Kate: What was Thomas doing?

Hope: Oh, he just stood there, you know? And everything was yellow. He looked me up and down. Mimi was behind me, cowering. She hated all of this, I could tell. Thomas' mouth was all tight at the corners, like he was a puppeteer with a ventriloquist puppet. He called me a coward for trying to leave. He was struggling with himself, like he was about to cry. He said we could have gone to therapy. That I was ruining everything.

[Long pause, broken by shuddering breaths]

Hope: I remember feeling completely broken. After everything he had put me through with the house and all of it, I still felt sorry for him, you see. Love really is a two-fucking-handled suitcase. I was carrying the load of his behavior with both hands, even though he'd imprisoned me in that nightmare house, you understand? It was all fucked. And I could see his phone glowing through his jacket pocket.

He'd left the screen unlocked and I could see all these blurry blocks of color lighting it up, hundreds of messages, I realised, pinging in second by second, and I knew he was talking to someone, multiple people, maybe, about us, or the house, and I couldn't stand it any longer. I had to do something. I had to get close to the broom without seeming suspicious. So I went over to Thomas, ripped the paint-sodden sheet out of his hands, threw it to one side, and got down on my knees.

Kate: Okay.

Hope: He needed reassurance, you see, and because I was scared, and I didn't have any weapons left in my arsenal, I needed to give him what he so clearly wanted. Reassurance, even though I started to gag as soon as I took him out, you know. As soon as I put him in my mouth.

[Uncomfortable throat-clearing noise][15]

Kate: What...ah, what happened then?

Hope: He tried to push me away, but I kept going, trying to make the best of a terrible situation, so he pushed me harder, rough. I kept trying to administer what I thought he'd see as comfort, because I wanted to distract him, and I guess I also wanted us to experience something normal and intimate together, perhaps because I was trying to find out if anything of him was left inside at all, and I figured a man resides in his dick if he resides anywhere, but he got angrier still. He shoved me hard off him, with both hands, furious. I went sprawling backwards across the hall floor. Past the broom. Mimi went crazy, barking and snarling at him.

Kate: Go on.

Hope: I landed heavily. The house shook, but it shook with a vibration that was like...I can't describe it. Like a belly rumble. It had nothing to do with the impact of my body hitting the floor. I didn't weigh a lot back then, even less now. I knew, then. I knew that things were shifting. As I felt the floorboards beneath me, I knew what was going to happen. It was like a switch being flicked, this small moment of violence. I suddenly heard the familiar and unmistakable *click* of the attic door coming open without warning. I knew Thomas had stepped forward to push me, and that would put him directly beneath the trapdoor, and in the path of the ladder. I knew I couldn't

---

[15] Ed.note: unclear if this noise is made by Kate, or Hope.

prevent what was about to happen. The Once Yellow House had finally taken matters into its own hands, just like I'd hoped.

Kate: Maybe it was more on your side than you realised.

Hope: Maybe. I don't really want to think about that.

Kate: What then?

Hope: There was this, like, metallic *ping!* And the trapdoor clicked outwards. The folding ladder extended itself and swung down in this swift, deadly arc, and I heard it connect with the back of Thomas' head. At high speed. That's a sound I'll never forget. I could hear bone crunching. It was horrible. I felt the impact of him landing on the floor next to me, then. And again, it was like the whole bungalow shook with it. Like giant's footsteps, shaking everything for miles around. In a daze, I remember I touched my face, pulled my hand away. I was covered in bright red blood. *His* blood. I found a small, pink chunk of his flesh, sitting on my left cheek.

And the Once Yellow House fell very, very silent, as if it had just realised what it had done.

Kate: And then what?

Hope: I screamed, that's what. I screamed.

[Recording ends]

34.

Diary Entry, personal diary of Hope Gloucester March 22nd, 2020 (4)

Everything is my fault
Everything is my fault
Everything is my fault
Everything is my fault
Everything is my fault
Everything is my fault
Everything is my fault
Everything is my fault
Everything is my fault
Everything is my fault

35.

Diary Entry, personal diary of Hope Gloucester
September 22nd, 2020 (1)

Thomas is going to be discharged from hospital today. I am preparing to move him back to the Once Yellow House. The doctors have all told me in no uncertain terms that I will need help taking care of him. He still has significant swelling on the brain and a whole range of issues resulting: mobility, coordination, mood, speech, regulation, toilet issues, not to mention the threat of infection. He will need round the clock care and attention for a long time. *You won't be able to do it alone,* they said. But I insisted. I can cope. We are haemorrhaging money keeping him in the hospital, money we don't have now he can't work. I cannot believe how much it has cost us, having Thomas under professional medical care for nearly six months. It will take me the rest of my life to pay back the debt we owe, even though he had insurance. Our healthcare system back in the UK isn't perfect, but it's free, at least. Most things. Maybe we can move there when he is a bit further along the road to recovery.

For now, home care is the only option. The worst has passed. It's been a long journey, but I think he is ready. The doctors are impressed with how Thomas has recovered, considering the severity of the traumatic brain injury he received. He still struggles with migraines and seizures, moodiness, speech and other things, but on the whole, physically, his recovery has been better than we all expected.

His mental state is another thing altogether. So is mine, for that matter.

Mostly, Thomas has been pining for the house. Not pining. Longing. The more time he spends away from it, the more diminished he becomes. When he first came out of his concussion coma and regained consciousness, he sank into a deep, deep depression that got worse by the day and continues to do so. I'm constantly worried he'll try and do something stupid, even bedridden as he is. The only thing that brings him any degree of joy to him now is talking about the Once Yellow House.

Oh, and his phone, which he clutches like a sweaty-palmed lover.

I'm still angry about the phone. After his accident, I went through it, determined to see who he was messaging all the time. What he was doing on there. When I saw, I immediately wished I hadn't.

It took me a bit of digging but I eventually found a page he'd created on Facebook. The title of the page was 'The Great God Thomas,' and the profile picture had been changed recently to one of my husband covered head to toe with yellow paint, the same stuff he'd used on the house. The page had over 2,000 followers and was full of absolute insanity. Posts about multiple realities and dimensions, about cosmic beings, about interconnectivity, about energy and colour theory and divinity and fate and something called sacred geometry. And yes, the equilateral triangle with the four dots featured heavily. Like it was their logo, or something. None of these things in themselves were particularly worrisome or transgressive (although the repeated use of the word 'sacrifice' made me feel grimy), but the way he had woven it all together by borrowing snippets of existing belief systems bothered me enormously. It felt manic, frantic. I saw quotes from the bible, I saw Buddhist principles, I saw Nostradamus mentioned several times right alongside Zoroastrianism and middle-eastern ideologies and yoga routines and meditation guides and that wasn't even half of it, and all of them were mashed up into this weird narrative that spanned time and space and the principles of physics and science in general. It was horrifying. It made me realise how much he had masked his true self from me, how much effort it must have taken to disguise his real state of mind. The group had been set up by him years ago, you see. The Thomas I married had been agnostic, a churchgoer in his youth, but he'd eschewed all that long before he met me. He'd never professed an attraction to any particular beliefs beyond what we all knew to be the basic tenets of wrong and right. He was clearly lying. Or maybe not. He hasn't, after all, prescribed to any one type of belief system. He's prescribed to all of them, at once.

Worse, he tried to couch what he was spouting on his page as a set of philosophies and practices that would somehow help and liberate people, regardless of intersectionality. He said he was offering enlightenment and freedom and a chance to transcend 'earthly bonds'. The key to spiritual longevity, he said, lay in proper preparation. In making sure a soul was ready to cross over when the time came.

Basically, Thomas had started an apocalyptic doomsday cult behind my back.

His followers call themselves the Retinue, and they talked ceaselessly about things like Revelations and End Days and used all manner of indecipherable jargon to egg each other on. The more I scrolled, the more I felt like I had a front row seat to an amateur digital orgy. These people were all getting off on each other's lies and fanaticism, had convinced themselves they had found other 'like-minded' thinkers, and it all reeked of barely-concealed masturbatory glee lubricated by buzzwords like 'truthseeker' and 'higher state of consciousness' and 'salvation.' It made me sick to see how keen they were to lose themselves to each other like that. How keen they were to be led. People want to be escorted through life, don't they? They want to be led and they want to believe.

The worst thing about this cult wasn't the deception or what Thomas posted or 'taught'. That wasn't the most deranged element. Thomas was always smart, and the way he laid things out actually came across as reasonable when you first read his posts, which was frightening in itself- how logical and sensible and knowledgeable it made Thomas sound.

The worst part was the way people responded to his logic and 'teachings'. It was the comments from members of the Retinue. They made me sweat. The whole page smelled rabid to me. Digital sickness, plain as day.

I deleted The Great God Thomas' page promptly using his phone. I went through all his direct messages from fans and adoring Retinue members and deleted those too. They were largely philosophical in nature, just a man and his dedicated followers going back and forth on questions of faith, but a few message threads worried me. Specifically the ones implying I was holding him back from fulfilling his true potential as a deity. Thomas always implied he had a 'plan' that would make everything right, but I could tell there were more than a few heavily invested female Retinue members who were actively trying to displace me as his wife, and as his link to a 'normal' world and way of living. I deleted the message threads too. Then I smashed his phone and threw it away. I threw my own away with it: it was useless, paint-logged. I felt the absence of both devices like a massive weight off my shoulders.

And that was that, I thought, until he woke up from his coma. A week later, somehow, he had a new phone. He would not tell me where he got it from. I angrily questioned the nursing staff and all his doctors but nobody knew. I confiscated that device too, went back in, saw his Great God Thomas page had been revived and that there was also now a Youtube channel full of his ramblings- audio only, he must have been whispering into his phone at night when I left. Each video was set to a backdrop of yellow and some pulsing royalty-free music he managed to find. I didn't listen to any of it, I didn't want to be poisoned like the others. I deleted the channel and the page again, and checked for any new messages, but there weren't any. He must have started deleting them as they came in.

That phone went in the trash too.

A week later he had a new one.

I gave up, then. I realised he wasn't going to stop. He had started something and he was committed to it. I could not hold back the tide.

I will write more soon, I have a meeting with the consultant now. There's more I have to say, though. While I still can. I won't get much time once Thomas is out. May as well get it all down now, it's the only form of self-expression I have.

I remember when I used to paint.

36.

Diary Entry, personal diary of Hope Gloucester
September 22nd, 2020 (2)

I'm so tired. The meeting with the consultant went well, but there was so much information to absorb. I'm pretty sure I've forgotten most of it. Medical people use a lot of long words and my attention span and short-term memory was never very good.

Anyway, the time approaches. The ambulance is being prepared. We're going back to the Once Yellow House. It is what Thomas wants. The house has him. Maybe it will always have him. It has burrowed into him like a botfly. I have tried to argue. Tried to get him to see sense. I told him we could sell the bungalow and move, it would be easier while he was in hospital, but he went on strike when I suggested it. He stopped eating for four days until I agreed to take him back there. Four whole days. Ripped all his tubes out, refused his meds too. He is so stubborn. It got to the point where refusing him became worse for his health than just giving in. It's like being away from the bungalow causes him physical pain. More than he is already in, from the accident.

I have a feeling that putting him back in the Once Yellow House will help him mentally, if not physically as well. Which is something, I suppose. Some small comfort.

When he is better, I can leave him.

I don't feel like I can abandon him like this. No matter what he did to me in the past. I am better than that.

Besides, there is no-one else to take care of him. His parents are both dead. Mine live thousands of miles away, and there would be no room for them in the bungalow if they came to visit. And I certainly don't want them to see how we live, even if there *was* room.

I suppose I could always reach out to his adoring online fans for help but…I'd rather swallow nails than let them into our lives in any real, concrete way. I won't let them win, no matter how much it impacts my day to day. If I have to be a nurse for him, so be it.

There is still a small amount of money left over from the sale of our old apartment back in the city, which I've put towards outstanding medical bills and the hugely expensive cocktail of supplies and medications Thomas needs. I have filled up the car, too, and prepared the house thoroughly for his arrival. The hospital is helping us move him and deliver a special bed and any other equipment we need. I can only hope they don't see the house and report us to the authorities for neglect or as a public health hazard. I've tried to make the place as liveable as possible while Thomas has been convalescing. When not at the hospital, I've been scraping paint off of windows, scrubbing walls, sanding floors, filling holes, hacking down weeds, cutting back trees, clearing up trash. Doing my best. And surprisingly, the bungalow has settled down a bit. I don't feel the weight of that hungry presence as much as I used to when we first moved in. I had a man come in to fix the broken ceiling in the living room. He did an okay job, not amazing, but he was cheap. I am slowly winning the battle with the mould, too. I have found that bleaching the walls works better than the fungicide and soap, as does a wire-bristled scrubbing brush. I do this twice a day, morning and night, right after I wake up and right before I go to sleep, like a ritual. Other people have skincare routines, I scrub walls with neat bleach. Such is life. It's incredibly good exercise, if nothing else. My arms are getting toned and taut.

I'm trying not to give into the bleakness that is clawing away at my insides. I am trying to be hopeful.

It is hard.

37.

Diary Entry, personal diary of Hope Gloucester
September 23rd, 2020

So he has moved back in.

On a purely practical level, ignoring the recurring mould and damp and everything else, the Once Yellow House is better for Thomas because everything is laid out on a single floor. That makes it easier to navigate when it comes to wheelchairs and special beds and drip stands and all the other paraphernalia he needs.

And so I have a new career now. Nurse. I look after Thomas on a full-time basis. I supposed I do owe it to him. The doctors told me not to feel guilty about things that were completely beyond my control, but I can't stop. I owe it to him. I wished that accident upon him. The least I can do is try and make up for it by looking after him now. *For better or worse, in sickness and in health.* That's love. That's marriage. I think. I don't know.

The neurologist warned me, shortly before discharge, that his accident would have a 'lasting impact on his personality'. An injury of that magnitude, he said, had major consequences for a person's behavioural inhibitions. I was warned: I might find him quick to anger, prone to drastic mood swings, and unpredictable. He might even lash out, physically. I tried to keep a straight face when he told me all this, but all I could think of was *honey, we already crossed that bridge.*

The neurologist was all concerned and serious as he gave me the lowdown. 'You are going to need some support,' he said, for the hundredth time. I told him I would cope. Forewarned is forearmed, I said. And Thomas has been peaceable and placid for a while, ever since we agreed to move back into the Once Yellow House. His mood swings and angry outbursts have calmed. He just lays in his bed now, patiently staring out of the bedroom window. And he has been like that since we first returned home. Kind of inert. I don't trust it, not entirely. It almost feels like something in him is incubating. But I'll take whatever peace I can get.

38.

Diary Entry, personal diary of Hope Gloucester
September 24th, 2020

I spoke too soon.

Thomas woke up today and told me his name was Sue-Ellen, and that he was five years old.

His voice was the perfect imitation of a five-year-old American girl's voice. His mannerisms, too. He had a deep south accent and a lisp. He twirled imaginary braids around his fingers and smiled at me shyly. It was so convincing I went cold. For a second, I almost thought it *was* a little girl waiting for me rather than a fully grown man.

Then I saw that his two front teeth were missing. They had been right there in his mouth yesterday.

And still, this is not the strangest thing.

The strangest thing is that he sat up in bed, which he has not been able to do since his accident, not without a lot of help, and swung his legs over the side of the bed, which was raised up a bit as it makes it easier for me to change the sheets and get to his pillows, and he sat there, bright eyed and bushy tailed, for all the world like a small kid sitting on a bench in a play park, humming a tune to himself.

'See with the soul,' the little girl said, then. 'To participate in the cosmic we have to recognise the impact of nature, and see with the soul! Did you know that, Hope?'[16]

'Do you need anything?' I stammered, stunned and unsure of what else to do. Some strange instinct told me to go along with things, rather than fight them.

'I like ice cream,' she replied, and then Thomas fainted, plunged headfirst out of his high bed and smacked face-down onto the floor.

I got him back into bed with a lot of effort. I had to use a fireman's lift in the end. Despite how much weight and muscle mass he has lost, it was almost too much for me, but I got there in the end.

---

[16] Ed.Note: Something about this quote struck a chord with us, so we did some digging and found the original quote, a variation of the sentence above, from a Dutch Painter called Charley Toorop. She was part of an artist's collective called The Signal, and her work was typified by bold color contrast and thick outlining. She often mused on the nature of reality versus unreality, and which was which.

With a lot of effort. I'm pretty sure my back will be screaming at me tomorrow.

When I eventually managed to heave him back onto the mattress and tuck him in, tightly, I noticed his two front teeth were back in place. His lip was cut badly from the fall.

I patched him up, cleaned him up, and left the room, shaken to my core.

Then I saw how aggressively the mould has started to come back. It's like Thomas is fertiliser, or something.

I hate my life.

39.

Diary Entry, personal diary of Hope Gloucester
September 25th, 2020

I have this theory about Thomas. It's a simple one.

I call it the cuckoo bird theory. They call cuckoos a brood parasite, even though they look like innocent birds. They lay their eggs in other bird's nests, so the invaded birds have to act like foster parents to an alien chick. Sometimes the cuckoo offspring, when hatching, push all the other eggs out of the nest. That is what this feels like, with Thomas. Like whatever laid an egg in him pushed all the old parts of him out. Usurped his old self. What remains is something I don't know. And it seems to change, all the time.

At first I thought maybe it was a dissociative disorder, a multiple personality thing, maybe brought on by his injuries, but now I am not so sure. Besides, it isn't just his personality that changes.

It is his physical self, too.

When I went to him today, he had an enormous beard, and was a foot shorter than he should have been. He told me his name was Frederick. I asked him where he was from, but Frederick disappeared almost as soon as I started to talk to him, as if he were shy. Thomas was back on the bed, looking at me with this intense expression.

'Do you like the person you are, Hope?' He asked.

I stared at Thomas. 'I don't understand,' I said, carefully.

'I'm asking you if you are happy with who you are.'

I thought about it. What answer did he want to hear? I had to hedge my bets.

'Yes, Thomas. I *do* like who I am,' I said, eventually.

'Really?'

'Yes, really.'

'Huh.'

I tried to placate him. 'I think I've changed a lot, some for the worse, some for the better. I've come to terms with myself, at the very least.'

He was silent.

'You weren't expecting that?' I tried to keep my tone as neutral as I could, but it was difficult.

'You wanted to have sex with other people, didn't you?' He asked then, casually.

Speechless, I felt my face go red.

'What?'

'You wanted to fuck people who aren't me. You still do.'

My cheeks flamed. 'I'm sorry. I don't...I'm not sure this is a helpful conversation.'

'I only wanted you. I only thought about you. I only fantasised about you.'

'What do you want me to say, Thomas?' I felt deeply uneasy.

'I want you to say 'Thomas, I love you.'

I swallowed. 'Thomas, I love you.'

My husband didn't answer right away. Instead, he looked at me with wandering, red-rimmed eyes. I could see a faint dusting of yellow on his skin: mould spores. They made him look jaundiced, like his skin was dyed. I flinched, realising I hadn't had time to bleach the walls today.

His right hand, I saw then, was active, and working under the duvet.

'Thomas,' I said, staring at the hand. 'What's going on?'

'I'm horny, honey,' the man in the bed replied, and this time he had an accent I couldn't place. His head changed shape, right there in front of my eyes, elongating, and his teeth went brown, nicotine stained. His eyes dimmed to a low grey colour. Long fingernails grew on his visible hand, which made a move towards me, a grasping, hungry motion. I slapped it away.

'Wanna fuck?' he said, then.

'No,' I replied. 'What's your name?'

'Dick,' he replied, giggling, and he suddenly pulled back the covers to reveal himself, naked and erect and a full two to three inches larger than he had been yesterday. And not just in one place.

He had four penises.

I screamed and quickly flipped the covers back over his various erections. The sheets undulated regardless, and I had the overwhelming urge to throw up all over him, burn everything down with this abomination inside, and then run.

'Come on honey, you know you want it,' the man rasped.

'How about we get to know each other a little, first?' I smiled weakly at the stranger who lay looking at me with a foul grin on his face.

It didn't always used to be like this.

I turned to leave, unsure whether putting my back to him was a good idea or not, and a different voice followed me out of the room.

'I'm so sorry,' it said, and I turned to find that Frederick was back. His eyes were filled with tears. 'I'm so sorry for what he is putting you through, Hope.'

I didn't know what to say. I felt dizzy, and everything spun around me.

'It's okay,' I whispered. 'I don't think he can help it.'

I decided to leave with my dignity intact and take the first of many of my daily scalding hot showers. Not least because I knew the bathroom was the only room of the house with a functioning lock on it.

I would have to rectify that if I was going to continue to be his nurse, I realised.

And, not for the first time, I began to question first, my own sanity, and second, my own safety.

In the shower, which was so hot it nearly peeled off my skin, I got to thinking. And I came up with the cuckoo theory.

Whatever has invaded Thomas, whatever got into him and lay dormant, was woken up by the Once Yellow House. I'm sure of it. Probably when the attic door smacked that huge hole in the back of his head. It opened him up like *he* was the trapdoor, and something terrifying in him is now hatching out. Something parasitic in nature. Something cosmic. Grand in scope and ambition. I think this house is a conduit. There is an infectious energy all around, in the walls, in the mould, in the ground, in the birds too, the ones that live on the roof and in the trees. Mimi seems immune, somehow, but the rest of us are changing, Thomas more than me.

I could call for help but who would I call?

Who would believe me?

This is my burden to bear.

Besides, I said I wouldn't leave him.

40.

Diary Entry, personal diary of Hope Gloucester
September 26th, 2020

Regret is one of those things, isn't it? One of those things that you don't recognise in others until you recognise it in yourself. It's the tired lines around the edges of your mouth, the small, bunched frown between your eyebrows. It's a faraway look on the rare occasion you catch sight of your strangled reflection in the mirror, because who has time to look at themselves these days, who has time to leap from the constantly escalating stairway of tasks, the cooking, the cleaning, the fixing, the sanding, the painting, the laundry, the medical bills, to indulge in a spot of introspection, or a skincare routine. Who has time?

It didn't always used to be like this.

Spending time with my husband was never something I had to actively and consciously prepare for. He had always just been Thomas.

Now, it feels like spinning a roulette wheel.

Which I suppose, when I think about it, is what love is like, in a way. We spin the wheel to see where the needle lands. Red or black, this number or that. Happy life, or ingrained servitude to a constantly shifting cosmic abomination.

I don't believe in fate, but I have started to believe in probability. Love is all about probability. *It's a losing game*, someone once sang, and I didn't know much about that, but I do know that it didn't always used to be like this.

But I still love him, despite everything. At least I think I do, otherwise why am I still here?

Everything is fucked.

41.

Audio Transcript
File name: Once_Yellow_House_Transcription_12
Audio length: 00:02:03
Date transcribed: 12/23/2022

    Kate: Stop.
    Hope: What?
    Kate: Let's just stop for a little bit.
    Hope: Alright. *[Clears throat]* Would you like another cup of tea?
    Kate: I'm fine.
    Hope: Well, you might be fine, but I'm not. I need something… *[rummaging sounds as Hope moves about, exploring cupboards]*. Damn. I'm out of tea bags. And milk. And everything else too *[Sigh]*.
    Kate: You know what? There is a small village down the road. I passed it on the way in.
    Hope: Laide. Yes.
    Kate: I saw a small store in the gas station? I assume they sell food.
    Hope: They do. Bread, milk, cheese, that sort of thing.
    Kate: How about I go for supplies? Don't give me any of that nonsense about money and owing anything. I'm going. I need some fresh air.
    Hope: Are you alright?
    Kate: I won't be long. I think maybe…jetlag. Fresh air will help.
    Hope: Suit yourself. I'll be here when you get back. And Kate?
    Kate: Yeah?
    Hope: See if they have any bundles of kindling or bags of firewood. The fire's running low.
    Kate: Of course. Anything you want. I'll be back soon, okay?

    [Recording ends]

42.

Audio Transcript
File name: Once_Yellow_House_Transcription_13
Audio length: 00:02:03
Date transcribed: 12/23/2022

[Sound of car changing gear and clutch grinding]

    Kate: Well, it's way icier now than it was when I first drove here. I think it might snow again, judging by the color of the sky. I don't care. I won't be long, I just...ugh, I just needed to get out of there for a little while. Hope is an intense person. It's odd, because she talks like Thomas was the weird one, the intense one, and sure, he was. He was magnetic. You don't gather people around you like that unless you have charisma, you know? That's why he was able to form the Retinue.

    But the way she paints herself as the passive one in their relationship...it kinda drives me mad. Because she's a lot, as a person. You'll hear that and come to the same conclusion, I know you will. Like, she has this huge force of personality, but I'm not sure she realises it. I know she was abused, like, it's obvious he was always very controlling. But the things she is telling me...you'll hear it all when you go through the audio. It's a lot. It sounds unbelievable. It requires a suspension of disbelief I'm not sure I'm capable of. Me, who saw some of it. It still sounds crazy, all of it. The house, the mold, his accident, the way she said he changed afterwards. I'm sure some of it is rooted in truth. Like, I know people that followed that Facebook page. I saw the things that Thomas posted there, so that much of her story I can verify. And I'm sure his hospital records can be checked too[17]. And. *[Laughs]* I *do* remember the guy with four dicks. Well, I kind of remember. I just assumed I was hallucinating at the time. It was part of being drugged, because they used to make you drink this herbal tea shit before they sent us to him. I think they used to scrape the mold off the walls of the Once Yellow House to brew it, so it was probably some natural psychedelic, whatever. It made you shit black for days, that tea.

    But the rest of it? I don't know. She talks like *she* is drugged. Don't get me wrong, I've seen shit I do not understand. But I'm still

---

[17] Ed.note: checked and confirmed.

having a hard time putting this all into some semblance of a truthful first-hand account of what happened. And yeah, if I'm honest...this is all making me really angry. The stuff she's saying. Hundreds of people died and she's talking like he used to talk. Kind of...fanatical. Like she is still part of the Retinue, even though she never was. She hated us all, but now, ugh, now she sounds kind of brainwashed. She's smart, but she sounds like...like Mom used to sound. Like she swallowed the red pill. *[Sigh]*

I'll let her get to the end of the story and see how I feel then, I guess. I came out here looking for answers, but I have this feeling I'm going to leave Scotland with more questions, not clarity. I mean that's my fault, that's on me. I chose this, I chose to dig it all up, so I have to be okay with what I find.

But, fuck. My head is spinning! I can feel the Retinue tattoo *burning* on my skin. What is this triggering in me? I'm not sure it's healthy. It's like digging up all my trauma again, rolling around in it, instead of helping me to heal.

The worst thing, despite all my reservations...is that I find myself liking Hope. Even though she's a lot. I feel like, I don't know... if none of this had happened to either of us, I think we could have been friends, in real life. She's funny and smart, and weird, and intense and neurotic, and really fucking closed off...but I like her. Despite all that.

Perhaps that's why Thomas chose us both the way he did. Perhaps gods have a type, too.

[Recording ends]

43.

Diary Entry, personal diary of Hope Gloucester
October 21st, 2020

The only way to keep track of all the different entities that now live inside my husband is to paint them. I need physical proof of what's going on. I don't have a phone to take pictures with, and I can never find his.

I am able to paint. I've already used up the canvasses he gave me so I've taken to painting portraits on little squares of cardboard instead. I keep them up in the attic, and yes, I am aware of the irony of that.

It's hard standing up for long periods of time at the moment. Exercise in general is difficult, but I make myself move around. My legs still hurt periodically from where I fell through the attic floor. It was months ago, but the scars won't heal properly, and break open every now and then. And then I found mould sprouting from my left thigh wound this morning. It was gross and fascinating in equal part, this discovery. I got a magnifying glass and tried to get a really close look at what was going on, and then promptly wished I hadn't. The growth in my raw scar tissue looked like a cross-between cress seedlings, and the mouldy fuzz you get on bread when it goes bad. All these delicate little stamen things coming out of my actual flesh, reaching for the light. I used the white spirit I clean my paint brushes with to flush the laceration out. The seedlings dissolved instantly. It hurt a lot, but I figured it was the most industrial thing shy of bleach that I could pour on myself. It seemed to do the trick, but I have a feeling the stuff will grow back, just like it does on the walls, and I know I'll end up losing the battle, and giving in, and letting it spread across my body. Bigger battles to fight, and all that.

My brain seems to be my biggest adversary right now. I can't find any light within myself, or any strength, any hope. I've given up, accepted this weird slide into wherever I've headed. I barely eat, because there seems to be no point. I barely sleep, because I just see a shifting wall of faces and forms whenever I close my eyes.

I am unbearably sad at losing Thomas, the real Thomas, without saying goodbye to the old version of him properly. Even if he did lie to me. There was good there, once. Way back when. I wish I had known how much things were about to change. I wish I had done so much differently.

Wishes are wasted energy, though, energy I don't have.

Frederick is the only entity that seems to come back, so far. He comes back quite a lot. All other manifestations carousel into Thomas once, and once only. I have gotten into a habit of listening for Frederick's voice, then spoiling him when he makes an appearance. He likes toast with jam on it, and weak tea, made British style. He told me I needed to start preparing myself. He told me that what is happening to us is only going to start escalating, now the transformations have begun. I don't know what he means, but I trust him. He feels like the only friend I have in the world now. I think he is, or used to be, a mathematician, or academic of some sort. He speaks like one.

I asked him if he thought I was safe living here. He looked at me sadly as he started to cycle into something furry and blue and said 'I think we're beyond that, now, don't you?'

I don't know what to make of that.

44.

Diary Entry, personal diary of Hope Gloucester
October 22ⁿᵈ, 2020

To add to my problems, there is now a fucking cult on my stoop.

Currently, there are eight little fabric carbuncles, bright yellow in colour (of course), parked out in the scrubby strip of wasteland out front.

It feels like every time I start to work up enough courage to think about leaving, the Once Yellow House sends me something to make me stay.

Well, now it has sent me the Retinue.

I suppose I should have seen it coming. Thomas aggressively guards his phone when he is himself, and when he is not, I don't have the courage to go near him to confiscate it. It makes sense that he is using all that time lying down to spout god-stuff. I feel like maybe his fanaticism feeds his transformations, or possibly it is the other way around, that his rotations feed his rhetoric.

Whatever he has been saying out there into the void of the online church has proven effective, because now, they have started to come. Like pilgrims on a trail. Only the trail leads to the Once Yellow House. Frederick was right to warn me: this is an escalation, if ever I saw one. Taking something from the digital realm to the real world is an escalation of intent and a sinister shift in momentum, for us. I guess he got bored, lying in bed all day, with only me for company.

Well, now he has lots of new friends to talk to.

Does this mean I live in a temple now?

More of a compound. There are the tents, and a temporary fence that went up overnight. On my land. Without anyone asking me. It ends just beyond the railway tracks. I would be angry about it if I wasn't so tired.

I use the word 'cult', but I have a feeling the members of the Retinue wouldn't like to hear me say this out loud. They prefer to call themselves 'followers' or 'believers,' assumedly because this is more marketable to future potential members of the group than the actual word 'cult,' which sounds aggressive and frightening. And yet, aggressive is a good descriptor for these people. Aggressive, paranoid, maybe. There is something in their eyes that frightens me.

Something fervent and hopeful and blank, like a person smiling even though they can only see the fuzzy outlines of something, and that something is Thomas.

They think he is the Great God Thomas, you see.

They wear these yellow tunics, and they hold firm to their belief that he is here to usher in the 'End Days', whatever those are. I can't make head nor tail of what that actually means, it's all buried in amongst the tangled roots of their jumbled ideology, but all I need to know is that this supposed event revolves around Thomas, *my* Thomas, their saviour. Or guide. Omnipotent, omnipresent.

And perhaps he is. I barely know what he is anymore.

I live in a world of infinite possibilities.

Thomas continues to cycle personalities and entities on a daily, sometimes twice-daily basis. The frequency of change increases without warning. He reminds me of an overloaded electrical circuit, becoming more unstable as power is forced through inadequate circuitry.

And it's hard to explain, but I think that circuitry is sending out signals, somehow, to the world, the universe, the wider cosmos- I don't know. The signal is proving very effective, because the first tent appeared outside the Once Yellow House yesterday evening, and since then several more have come, and they keep on coming, as if a floodgate has been opened.

Mimi spotted them first. She'd been trying to tell me about the new arrivals since I'd woken an hour earlier from an exhausted pseudo-nap, but I was slow to react and respond, slow to understand. I find it hard to react to things quickly. Thankfully, Mimi didn't give up. She growled and whined and yipped at my ankles until eventually, she gently gripped the fabric of my jeans at my ankle between her teeth and tried to drag me over to the living room window, which overlooks the tracks opposite the house.

I grumbled but went where she pulled, peering through the mildewy glass- I've not had time to wipe the walls and windows much this week. The mould has taken advantage of this laziness. It's been appearing and disappearing in different places all week, depending on the Once Yellow House's mood. Or on Thomas' mood. Or perhaps the growth patterns are related to neither of these things. Perhaps it's down to climate and humidity and air-pressure. It feels like it is fucking with me, though. Sometimes, in the evenings when I am alone and Thomas is sleeping, I stare at the walls in the living room and I fancy I can see faces in the black and yellow splotchy patterning. The faces are trying to communicate something to me, but I am too far gone to listen. I try and air out the house as much as I can, propping open the sash windows each day, wedging open the front and back doors to let the wind howl through, because I know breathing all that spore shit into my lungs is not good for me, or for Thomas, or the dog, but it doesn't make much difference. I felt dizzy all the time, and out of breath. Mimi sneezes and scratches at her face to the point where I am considering housing her in a kennel outside.

At least nobody I know has to see us live like this. I would be so ashamed if they could see me.

I don't give a shit what the Retinue thinks.

Anyway, I saw the tents, eventually. I watched them for a while, trying to assess the lie of the land before I did anything else. I saw two women most frequently, setting up gas camping stoves, issuing instructions. I noticed that on the side of each tent, symbols are daubed in black and red paint. *The* symbol. Triangle in a circle. Dots at each point. Once you see it, you see it everywhere.

It is still strange to me that Thomas has a symbol to go with his shiny new God-name. And his shiny new Retinue.

Names, symbols, and an attic stuffed with portraits.

I hope they do not try to talk to me. Unless they are here to help me wipe his arse when he shits black again, which he so often does. What use is a Retinue unless it is to wait hand and foot upon the thing they worship?

I have a feeling they'd stop worshipping him pretty fast once they see him turn into a shrieking Sea Biscuit.

What does he want with them all?

Time will tell.

45.

Diary Entry, personal diary of Hope Gloucester
October 23rd, 2020

I bit the bullet today. I took my coffee and the dog out the front door this morning and went over to talk to the two women I spotted before. I thought I'd give them a little while, see if they got bored, or if they would pack up and leave of their own volition, but they didn't.

The women were friendly enough as I eventually approached. Of course they know all about me. I don't like that much but there is not a lot I can do about it. The sensation of being spoken about behind my back is uncomfortable, but not the worst thing about my present situation. Still, I find myself craving friendship, of any sort. Maybe that's why I went over to them. Perhaps I was hoping to find comfort, even in this, the most unlikely of circumstances.

I wish I could talk to Frederick again. Frederick could be a friend. He makes me calm. He seems to have things figured out. He predicted this. He would probably know what to say to the erupting cult camp in my front yard.

I didn't, so I approached, and then hovered, not saying anything at all.

One of the women is very tall, and *very* good looking. She is called Lisa and is physically very intimidating. She radiates confidence and tilts her head back to look down her nose as she talks, although this is more about her natural height advantage than any superiority complex, I think. She does have one of those, too, I can see it plain as the nose on her face, but it feels understandable given the circumstances. Why else would she be camping in front of my house, if she wasn't completely and utterly convinced of her own correctness in doing so? Thomas has filled her head with her own significance, which was clever of him. *Target the ego, and the rest will follow,* I thought, as I looked at her.

The other woman is shorter, and very blonde, with an old-fashioned permed hairdo that reminds me of my mother's hairstyle when I was a child. She is called Theresa and is more reserved than her tall friend, but has the same look in her eyes. A determined gleam. These are women on a mission.

Which is nice for them, but I'm too tired for bullshit. I have laundry to hang, dressings to change. Pills to count. Bedpans to empty. Entities to paint.

Maybe I can ask them to lend a hand, I thought, sizing them up. *May as well earn their place here in this provincial hell like I have.*

'Hey,' I eventually said out loud, 'You know this is private land, right?'

'We were invited,' the tall woman replied. 'By him.'

'By who now?' Of course I knew who, but we were sparring. I had to establish dominance by not backing down.

'By him.' Lisa pointed at the Once Yellow House.

My mouth twitched.

'By who now?' I repeated myself. I wanted her to say it out loud. To hear how ridiculous it sounded.

'The Great God Thomas,' she intoned, without an ounce of irony or self-consciousness. And it didn't sound ridiculous in her mouth, that's the really irritating thing. It sounded impressive. Portentous. Dare I say *spiritual.*

I rubbed the hand not holding my coffee over my eyes.

'Jesus fucking Christ on a bike,' I muttered.

'That's not very respectful,' Theresa admonished, eyes glittering like hard jewels in a brooch. 'He is not to be-'

'His name is Thomas, and only Thomas, nothing else, and he was my husband before he was your shiny new god toy.'

Lisa licked her lips. 'He may have been Thomas once. But now, he has risen. And he will continue to rise as we help him fulfil his teachings and his destiny.'

I blew out my cheeks. I would not find any friends here.

'Point is,' I snapped, scratching the top of Mimi's head. 'You can't pitch up here. This is my house.'

'As I said. We were invited.' Lisa's whole demeanour shifted into one of false understanding, of barbed sympathy. I wished she would stop. I hated her smile. It meant she had become a one-way transmission. She could only communicate outwards. There would be no receiving of anything other than what The Great God Thomas had told them. What do they call that, an echo chamber? The same message bouncing off the walls, coming back at you from a thousand different directions. My own words were falling on deaf ears.

What happens when the chamber is dampened by mould? I thought, but I knew my brain wandering off was not going to help me much at that moment.

I gave it one last shot.

'Well, he is not the only one living here. I live here too, and *I* didn't invite you.'

The smaller woman was not smiling. 'You have power of attorney?' She asked, in a matter-of-fact tone.

I blinked. 'What kind of question is that? It's none of your fucking business.'

Theresa shrugged. 'Thought not. My understanding is that as the property and the land around it is jointly owned by both you and Him, an invitation from only one party is a valid enough premise upon which we can camp.'

'You a lawyer or something?'

Theresa examined her nails. 'I was a legal secretary. Before He called me here.'

'About that.' I shifted my weight from foot to foot. 'He called you here? Why?'

Lisa sidestepped the question with remarkable dexterity. 'You will be treated with respect by us,' she said, 'Because you sit on His right hand, and serve Him, but it's important you know that we answer to Him and Him only. Only He can tell us to go away, or ask anything of us.' She emphasised the 'h' of each 'He' and 'Him' so hard it made me wince.

'Is that right?' At my feet, Mimi was growling now, a low, continuous grumble of discontent.

There was a moment or two of silence, where we all said nothing with our mouths but covered a lot of ground with our eyes. Like a Mexican standoff in Yellow frontier land.

Then, I sighed.

Because, ultimately, it was simply another situation where I knew I could not change anything, so what was the point in fighting it?

My shoulders sagged.

'What are your intentions?' I asked, wearily. 'No blood sacrifices, I trust? Orgies? I don't have the energy for any ritualistic shenanigans.'

Both women stiffened, offended. 'We hold meetings,' Lisa replied, eventually. 'We hear His words, and we live by His teachings.'

'Teachings. You keep mentioning those. What can he possibly have to say that is so life-affirming? He's just a guy, a guy from Ohio, who had a very normal upbringing and has gone on to have a very normal life. What is it about him that you find so...instructive?'

I was genuinely interested, not trying to insult them, but this may have gotten lost in translation. They bristled.

I blundered on, feeling my face heat up.

'I mean, seriously, what are two obviously very smart women like yourselves doing getting wrapped up in all this? How does one man override a person's ability for critical thinking so completely? I don't get it.'

Lisa skewered me with her eyes. 'Then you have not been listening to Him properly,' she said.

I began to get a sense that none of them knew what they were letting themselves in for, not really. Thomas may have fooled them with his intellect, but he wouldn't be able to teach them much beyond his phone ramblings. He was too busy morphing from one freakish form to the next. What lessons there were to be found in the constant, agonising flux of a man who used to be human and is rapidly turning into something, or a succession of things that are not, I didn't know.

They would not be put off, though.

'We want to grow vegetables,' Theresa muttered, glaring daggers at me.

At that, I burst out laughing. 'Vegetables?' I looked down at the earth on which we stood: thick with scrubby weeds, stones, garbage, the soil scratchy and pale. Thin white roots thickly matted under the topsoil. 'This time of year?' It was late October, and cold, too cold to grow anything much at all. They would have their work cut out for them.

Theresa straightened up, trying to grow an inch or two, and failing.

'Beans,' she said, then. She pulled some out of her pocket. They were yellow wax beans. Of course they were.

'Beans[18],' she repeated, like she had forgotten what other words sounded like.

---

[18] Ed.note: Another infamous cult, the ascetic religious group known as the Pythagoreans, were vegetarian because of Pythagoras' belief in the transmigration of souls—reincarnation, even into other animal species. According to some sources, Pythagoras himself refused to eat beans because he fervently believed humans and beans originated from the same source. He 'tested' this by planting beans in mud and then noting how the germinating sprouts looked like a human foetus. More interestingly: the Pythagorean theorem is a mathematical calculation that applies to the lengths of the sides of right-angled triangles. Pythagoreans later went on to practise 'numerical mysticism'. Pythagoras himself thought maths (not art) was the path to enlightenment. His claim 'Ten is the very nature of number' is interesting because ten is a 'triangular' number: meaning a number depicted by objects that can be arranged in equilateral triangles. Diving into this further, some sources state that the largest triangular number is 666, but we do not have the time/mathematical expertise to verify this.

Mimi wagged her tail and yipped, lending me her support.

The women would not be swayed. My scorn was fuel for their conviction, I realised, so I calmed myself.

'You might want to consider moving out from under this tree, then,' I said, trying to be helpful. 'Unless you want to wake up covered in bird shit every morning. Your choice, though.'

Lisa nodded. 'We appreciate the warning.'

I fired a final shot across the bow then, knowing I could not do anything else. 'And if you want to help him, *really* help him,' I said, 'Then we could use a hand around the house. It's falling to bits around His ears.'

Lisa blinked. 'Alright,' she said, begrudgingly impressed by my moxy. 'Tell us what you need.'

I thought it best to divulge a little more truth, instead.

'He's very sick, you know,' I informed her, weariness coming over me in rolling waves. 'I don't know what he's told you but…He is in a bad way. Sometimes…it's too much for one person to handle.'

The women looked at me with inscrutable faces.

I left it at that and walked away, back to the Once Yellow House, where I double locked the front door firmly behind me. Then, I headed straight out the back to the small square yard sheltered by the tall, weirdly white trees, and I stood there looking at all the millions of birds in the branches, trying to get a handle on what my life had become, and failing.

You could always kill him, an inner voice said, the words stabbing my heart as I stood there, and it was a sweet, tempting prospect, but not a realistic one.

I breathed in the fresh air, which was far colder than it should have been for the time of year. It carried a sharp scent tinged with cooler things to come. Clouds moved fast in the sky overhead. Wind chimes sadly sang on the back porch. There was a sense of see-sawing turmoil, turmoil that peaked and then faded, leaving me feeling peaceful for a fleeting moment only. A sense of calm that then dissolved, exposing me to the turmoil once again.

Turbulence, I thought. *One of the great unsolved mysteries of physics.*

I started to laugh, then to cry. I felt like a tiny flower petal on the fringes of a gathering storm. I tried desperately to anchor myself to that single fleeting moment of quiet, so I could remember what it felt like, so I could return to the calm in another moment when I needed to. It didn't work. Instead, I felt my own loneliness like the weight of a galaxy upon my shoulders, and yet somehow I also wished it could always be this way, just me, the breeze, the trees gently moving all around, Mimi pottering about nearby, unobtrusive but there if I needed her. Birds chirruping bossily, feathers impatient, shifting from foot to foot as they too waited for winter.

Except that when I looked at them, *really* looked at them, I saw they had arranged themselves on the branches of the trees in a strange pattern, one bird facing towards me, the next bird with its back turned, front, back, front, back, like beads on a string, it was all so artificial and contrived and odd, because birds weren't able to organise themselves like that, I knew.[19]

And the weirdness of this sight drove home to me that any small respite I ever experienced, no matter how wonderful, was temporary. Did that make it more intoxicating? Possibly. It felt like a stolen moment. Something that didn't really belong to me, something borrowed.

Something blue.

Something old, and something new.

You could always kill him.

Put him out of his misery.

I would be lying to myself if I said the abhorrent thought was not growing more tempting by the day.

---

[19] Ed.note; readers may be interested in the book *Sensitive Chaos* by Theodor Schwenk, first published in 1962. Schwenk believed in 'unifying forces' that underlay all living things, and how those forces affected the water movement in rivers and streams, the way bones and bodies are formed, the formation of mountains, weather systems and, most relevant to this story: the flight movements and behaviors of flocks of birds.

46.

Audio Transcript
File name: Once_Yellow_House_Transcription_14
Audio length: 00:01:53
Date transcribed: 12/23/2022

Kate: And that's where I came in.

Hope: And that's where you came in. Do you need me to go on? I feel like you know a lot more about what followed than I do.

Kate: I only know what I was allowed to know. Life in the encampment, as you called it, was not fun. Nor was it free. Not by any stretch of the imagination. It was camping in the cold, with very few possessions, not a lot to eat, and no real structure to the day, not to begin with. It was just a…a congregation of people, milling about. Making a big mess. Trampling mud around. Until the ground froze hard, anyway.

Hope: So why did you come?

Kate: I don't…I'm not comfortable answering that, yet. I didn't exactly leave a life of glamour behind me. I left a shitty trailer. Life with the Retinue wasn't much of a downgrade, to be honest. Eventually, the powers that be started getting their shit together. There was a daily schedule. Everybody got a task, which kept us both warm and out of trouble, too tired to think much. I didn't mind the work, to be honest. Except when it came to latrine duty. I hated latrine duty.

Hope: All this while, I was inside, working myself to a nub to keep Thomas alive and healthy, and you were outside, digging toilet trenches and ploughing the earth. I'm starting to think this is a woman's lot in life, you know. To just work, for other people.

Kate: There's work, and there's the business of living. The two are intertwined, I think. Even insects work, Hope. Ants. Bees. The Retinue camp felt a lot like a beehive, come to think of it. Less honey, more mud and shit, but there was a kind of…natural engineering that just occurred as a by-product of all those bodies coming together in common purpose. Living together, by choice. Everyone had a role. Without that, the whole thing would have collapsed a lot sooner than it did, I'm sure. I'm not saying it was efficient, but…there was *something* there. Something…a force. Keeping us all together. Keeping us going. Some energy. Quorum momentum, or…

Hope: Your vocabulary is a lot more developed than mine.

Kate: Growing up in a trailer doesn't mean I'm stupid. Poor kids can read too, you know.

Hope: I know. I know that all too well. I just never got on as well with words, like I said.

Kate: Anyway, this is where our stories converge, I guess. I'd like to hear more. Your side of it. If you want to.

Hope: Is it making you feel better? Hearing all this.

Kate: It's making me feel...something. I haven't figured out what, yet.

Hope: Well, I guess that makes two of us.

[Laughter. Recording cuts out]

47.

Diary Entry, personal diary of Hope Gloucester
October 25th, 2020

Today was quieter. Thomas lay in a semi-comatose state for most of it, thin eyelids closed, mouth slack, chest rising and falling slowly. I didn't like the way he was breathing. I decided leaving him alone for long periods wasn't wise, so I got a chair and put it in his room and brought in a small square of board and my easel, and painted him as he lay there, tubes and all. The tubes made me remember stories he had told me of his birth, which was premature, and how he had only weighed a few pounds when he was delivered, and how he had to be incubated (intubated?) for months before his parents could take him home. I thought about those tiny tubes, then, and how circular our lives can be.

Mimi curled up on the floor next to me, a rare concession for her, usually the bedroom puts her hackles up. I can't say I blame her. Mine were up too, but Thomas was out of it for most of the time we were in there.

I put Rachmaninoff on the record player while I painted. *Rhapsody on a Theme of Paganini.* The needle didn't run smoothly, it kept snagging over clumps of mould and fuzz clinging to the grooves, but it was good enough. Thomas always told me I was basic for loving this piece of music as much as I do, so it was nice to listen to it uninterrupted. I heard somewhere that Rachmaninoff thought sounds had colour, and he had once told a protege to 'play in gold.' I realised the canvas in front of me was smothered in cadmium yellow, primrose and gold, and the brushstrokes in the oils corresponded to the music as it swelled around me. It felt like how I always imagined magic might feel if I believed in that sort of thing. Pure energy flowing. This got me thinking about another composer, Scriabin[20]. He had synesthesia and thought the world would be saved by the music he wrote[21]. The colour yellow, for him, was

---

[20] Ed.note: Research tells us Rachmaninoff never liked Scriabin much.

[21] Scriabin is a curious figure to mention here, most notably because he was known for the use of something called a 'mystic chord', around which his music was loosely arranged both harmonically and melodically. The mystic chord is also known as the 'Prometheus Chord', and is a six note synthetic cluster chord which,

represented by the pitch "D". When you start to look into it, it's a bit like falling down a long, twisty rabbit hole[22]. How everything comes together. Art, music, religion, spirituality. Maths. Nature. Physics, and geometry. Our senses are malleable, is what I think I am trying to say. Perhaps reality is also malleable, by the same logic. Because we perceive what we experience via our senses. So if they become interchangeable, if our senses merge and warp and reflect and redirect and interact with each other in unpredictable ways, our reality is going to do the same, by that logic.

Or perhaps I simply have spent too much time in the Once Yellow House. The place feels like a dampened prism for the senses. Like that Pink Floyd cover. It takes one sensory faculty, one colour, and refracts it into a multitude of others, only the fuzzy, pillowy walls absorb a great deal of the intensity, leaving only a residue of sight, of sound, of taste, like a nightmare residue, like the sour taste and fur on your tongue when you wake from a long sleep.

But none of that makes sense, does it?

I never was the smart one. I should leave the existential musings to Thomas. Clearly that is his forte.

These kinds of days, the quiet ones where he sleeps and doesn't cycle, make me both sad and relieved at the same time. I hate to see Thomas like this, I hate to see this deflated, diminished version of him, but I also know it means I don't have to steel myself for problematic encounters. For horror. When he sleeps, he stays Thomas. Like his body knows it needs to rest, sometimes. It means I can relax a little.

I am so tired. So very, very tired.

I finished the painting and watched a vein in his neck throb gently for a while. I could hear the low chatter of conversation outside the house. More of the Retinue have arrived, more tents, more people. They don't make a lot of fuss or noise, considering,

---

apparently (please note, we are not musical experts) when rooted in C, consists of C, F♯, B♭, E, A, and D (again, to our uncultured ears, this chord sounds highly dissonant). Scriabin was intensely interested in theosophy and mysticism. He also called the special chord a 'chord of the pleroma'. Pleroma is a Greek word that refers to the totality of divine power, and it is used frequently throughout the texts of the New Testament. We find the recurring themes and symbols in Hope's world view fascinating, and they give us some real insight into the complicated, interconnected way in which she viewed the events going on around her.

[22] Other composers, musicians and notable people who saw sound as color or other sensations—Liszt, Sibelius, Rimsky-Korsakov, Aphex Twin, Tesla, Billy Joel.

preferring to go about their business as unobtrusively as the wind in the branches of the trees in the yard, but it still serves as a reminder of my own unique loneliness. Alone in a crowded space, always.

The vein pulsed and I had a sudden memory of kissing Thomas' neck when I was younger, of standing on tiptoe to push my face into his, of exploring his mouth with my tongue. He always loved it when I did that, had always craved physical reassurance, but over time I had felt less and less like giving it to him. Neither of us really understood why, but gradually, I closed myself off, became a sealed-up type of person.

It's ironic to me that now, Thomas is the one who has withdrawn access to his true self.

While I stood there, I felt, not for the first time, an overwhelming desire to speak to Frederick again. And it occurred to me that I'd only ever been able to *react* to Thomas' changes, not *influence* them.

Maybe, I thought, *if he is sleeping, I can...dial into what's beyond him, somehow.*

'Frederick?' I said, out loud, softly. 'Are you in there?'

I've never tried to speak to any of the entities directly before. I've been in receive mode, frantically trying to understand what's happening most of the time, but never proactively engaged. Largely, I suppose, because I haven't needed any of the things that live inside (or outside of) him, before now.

'Frederick?'

Thomas' eyelids fluttered. Mimi, who was curled up asleep nearby, roused, pricked her ears and thumped her tail anxiously on the floor.

'I know, I know,' I said to her miserably. 'But I need someone to talk to. I really do.' I heard my voice crack as I said it. Sometimes, it isn't until I hear myself say something out loud that I know the truth of it.

Mimi kept an eye on me and one ear cocked.

'Frederick?' I tried again. 'Are you there? I don't know how this works, but are you...I need...'

Thomas opened his eyes. They were blue. Frederick blue. With flecks of yellow in the irises.

That was easy, I thought.

'Hello, Hope,' he said, in Frederick's voice.

I nearly wept with relief. 'I'm sorry. I needed a friend. I'm sorry.'

'Don't be.' Frederick sat up, slowly. 'This body is disintegrating, Hope. You should send him back to the hospital.'

'I know, but I just...I'm scared.'

'What of?'

'That they'll see something they shouldn't. Thomas is so unpredictable. What if I take him to a hospital and he hurts someone? At least this way, it's just me. And he hasn't shown any signs of wanting to hurt me. Not yet. Besides, I don't think they-' I gestured to the people camped around the bungalow- 'Will let me take him away.'

He asked for some water. I rushed out of the room to bring it, terrified he would be gone by the time I came back. He was still there, to my relief. I handed him the glass with trembling hands.

'This is taking a toll on you, isn't it?' He asked me. I started to cry.

'I just wish I knew why this was happening,' I sobbed. 'Or how. Or *what*, even. I have no fucking idea what anything is, anymore!'

He held out his arms. I hesitated, then let him fold me up. It was the first time I had gotten close to Thomas for reasons not related to caring for his body in weeks and weeks.

Frederick gave me a hug. He felt warm, and although his body stank, and I could smell a mixture of different people on him, as well as an underlying stink of something pungent like sandalwood, a smoky aroma, I sucked it in greedily. It smelt almost *normal*, you see. Warm. I nearly lost my mind, at that moment. The relief was overwhelming. Pathetic.

Mimi thumped her tail on the floor. She liked Frederick too. I took that as a barometer reading.

'Do you know what I think?' He asked me, then. I pulled away with reluctance. His eyes were sad, and I think they were Thomas' eyes for a second, not Frederick's. I found sad Thomas almost more difficult to deal with than angry Thomas or French Thomas or glowing eyes Thomas. Preferable to seaweed Thomas though, in many ways. And vastly preferable to squealing horse-head Thomas.

'What?'

'Think of a pack of cards,' Frederick said. 'A normal fifty-two card pack. Fifty-two is the key thing, here. Specifically, something called a Fifty-Two Factorial.'

I told him I didn't understand. It sounded like maths shit, again.

'Fifty-two little rectangles of cardboard.' He started shuffling imaginary cards in his hands, expertly chopping the non-existent deck in half with fingers that were a good deal more supple and deft than they ever had been before the accident. *These hands would know how to paint a wall properly,* I remember thinking to myself unexpectedly, and then hating myself for it.

'Wait,' I said, remembering something. I went to a small chest of drawers in the bedroom and rummaged for a minute or two. When I came back to the bed, I was holding a pack of playing cards. I gave them to him.

Frederick beamed at me.

'Fifty-two cards. Perfect.' He started to shuffle them for real.

'Now, how many different ways can I arrange each card in this deck?' He asked, and I thought *how can we possibly be having a normal conversation like this.* But I went along with it. I had asked for him to come, and here he was.

'You mean, the order or sequence?'

'Sure.'

'I don't know. The number...it's too big for me to figure out.'

He smiled. 'Fair. The actual number is something called 52!' He had to spell out the exclamation mark for me at the end, saying it like this: *'Fifty-two-factorial-which-is-also-an-exclamation-mark!'* I'm not sure if I have written it down correctly here[23]. The exclamation mark, I think, is meant to illustrate how big the number is, or can get, really quickly. It's like a growth symbol, I suppose.

Symbols, everywhere. There is no fucking escape from anything, ever.

'Fifty-two factorial is the number of different ways you can arrange the cards in this deck,' he continued. 'No matter how randomly or logically you order them, that is the number of permutations possible.'

'Why is that important?'

'Because the number 52! is huge. *Enormous*. More than most people on earth could ever visualise or fully comprehend.'[24]

'So?'

'The chances that you shuffle this pack of cards, and then that someone else could come along and shuffle it in the exact same way, are absolutely infinitesimally small. That makes this pack of cards quite unique, because it contains potential arrangements that are almost impossible to replicate, by the laws of mathematics.'

---

[23] Ed.note: She has.

[24] Ed. note: for more information on fifty-two factorials, readers may like to visit the following sites:
https://czep.net/weblog/52cards.html
https://www.matthewweathers.com/year2006/shuffling_cards.htm

I didn't see what that had to do with me, or him, or Thomas, or the Once Yellow House, or the growing number of weirdos camping on my doorstep. I said as much.

Frederick put down the cards and took my hands in his, instead. His fingernails, I saw, were starting to fall off, exposing yellowing, sticky, pus-filled beds. Thomas' sickness, seeping through the Frederick veneer.

He didn't seem concerned by it.

'Think about that. An endless possibility of different combinations, of different sequences, a random arrangement.'

'What are you trying to tell me? I'm not that smart. I don't work well with allegories.'

'This is not an allegory, simile, or metaphor. It is a theory, of sorts. A theory explains known facts; and these are the facts: every day the person you know as Thomas wakes up, and there is a new person inside his head. Inside his body. Person, or being. Creature. Thing. Sometimes several in one day. You most likely think this is as a result of his accident and the head injury he sustained, and maybe it is, maybe it isn't. Maybe there was a pre-existing susceptibility that meant this was always going to happen.'

'Susceptibility to what?'

Frederick made a shushing motion with his hand.

'For this theory to remain a viable theory, I must anchor it, as I said, in the known facts. Fact: there are multiple entities existing in this one body. Including my current permutation, the man you know as Frederick. Correct?'

I nodded.

'So, why don't we think of Thomas' brain, or body, for that matter, like a deck of cards. And each card in his brain deck is a different entity, or personality, or character, if that's easier for you to visualise. Every time we shuffle the deck, we get a brand new combination of cards, right?'

I remained silent. I saw where he was going, and it made me dizzy.

'And, as long as we keep shuffling the cards, the chances of coming across any single familiar person or entity or character more than once are, well...unpredictable, aren't they?'

'Fifty-two factorial unpredictable.'

'Precisely.' He smiles, and his teeth are more crooked than I remember, his incisors much higher up in their gums.

'But I was able to summon *you*,' I said, confused. 'Just now. Just by speaking your name.'

Frederick nodded. 'You were. Or maybe it was just the deck of cards, and you got very, very, very lucky.'

'Fifty-two factorial lucky?'

'Just so.'

I sucked in a breath, sadly. 'Does that mean I might never see you again?'

He dipped his chin. 'Maybe. But think about this. Your husband's brain is a revolving door of entities and personalities, a shuffled deck of cards, the variations of which, you haven't even really begun to scratch the surface of, I fear.'

'None of this explains why. How. *What*.'

'I think it does. Thomas is a mathematical exercise in real, physical form. Physical laws can be expressed in mathematical terms, and now, I suppose this is the reverse of that.'

'But what does any of that *mean?!*'

Frederick stared at me, his confidence fading. 'I don't know,' he whispered, and Thomas was underneath him, I could tell, awake once again, and staring out at me. The way his eyes shifted colour, in and out of blue, brown, yellow, green: it was hypnotic. And, although I'll never understand this- arousing. I could feel myself moving closer to them both, them all, and I could feel body heat rising through the bedding.

An overwhelming urge to experience some intimacy overcame me. I put my hands under the covers and felt for him. The man/men in the bed went hard quickly, and then, I don't know why, but just like I had up in the attic all those weeks ago, I felt this wild burst of sexual desperation wash over me, and it culminated in a persistent desire to climb up onto the entity nearby, whether Thomas or otherwise, and feel him inside me one last time. So I did just that.

I rode whoever/whatever it was like a devil, and Frederick's face shifted into other people's faces several times as I brought myself off, and when he came, explosively, it was, of course, yellow, and accompanied by a pained bellow that sounded a lot like a cow or a bull lowing.

We both cried a little after. Then I lay down next to him on the sodden bed, which was drenched. I smelled discharge from yet another wound that had re-opened while we fucked. I felt both ashamed and elated, disgusted and cleansed, full and empty, sore and healed, traumatised and calm, everything, every feeling, all at once.

I liked Frederick, and was happy he had given me a small gateway back to Thomas.

Something struck me then, as I recovered next to him. The Fredrick smell was waning, which meant I would not have much time left to enjoy the moment, or explore it. Explore *him*. Perhaps ever again.

'Where do you think you were before? Before you came into his body?'

Frederick shrugged Thomas' shoulders. 'I don't know. I don't know where I was before. Dead, maybe. Purgatory? I don't think I was a religious man, though.'

The nubs of horns crested out of his forehead, then disappeared again.

'I think you were a kind man, Frederick. Or maybe you still are. Religious or not.'

'I hope so.'

'Frederick? The next card shuffle won't be as nice as you. The possibilities...I'm scared. What's going to happen? I feel like the deck is shuffling faster and faster.'

'Well.' A new card shuffle had already begun, I could tell. His skin was changing colour, slowly.

'You could always kill him,' Frederick's voice said, before it died.

I stood up abruptly, feeling suddenly nauseated. My head spun.

But Frederick was gone. The body on the bed was changing, but I didn't want to hang around to see it. I had things to do.

48.

Audio Transcript
File name: Once_Yellow_House_Transcription_15
Audio length: 00:00:23
Date transcribed: 12/23/2022

Hope: Frederick never came back.

[Here follows a section of damaged audio, approximately seven minutes in length. The recording resumes after.]

Kate: ...Theory allows scientists to make predictions, predictions of what they can observe and learn and experience if a theory is proved true. Like seeing into the future.
Hope: Only I failed. If I had been able to predict what would come next, don't you think I would have tried to do something about it?
Kate: Honestly? I'm not sure. I'm not sure at all, Hope. I don't think you were capable.

[Pause]

Hope: You're probably right. That pack of playing cards was one of the few things other than my diary to survive the fire, by the way. I have it somewhere.
Kate: Of course you do.
Hope: Want to play a game of patience?
Kate: Maybe some other time, Hope.

49.

Diary Entry, personal diary of Hope Gloucester
October 27th, 2020

I let some of them into the house. I didn't have much choice. Lisa and Theresa strong-armed their way inside under the guise of needing to discuss 'matters of faith' with TGGT (I can no longer be bothered to write this ludicrous name out in its entirety).

Within seconds of me standing to one side of the front door, they were down the corridor, as if they knew exactly where to go. I remember calling a warning after them, because you never really know what will be in there waiting for you, but they ignored me.

I followed wearily, watched from a small distance as the women rushed to Thomas' bedside.

Luckily for them, he was human on this occasion. He wasn't Thomas, but he was human. A wild-haired, wide-eyed woman with whiskers and decaying teeth, to be exact. Her skin had a weird sheen to it, but otherwise she didn't seem to present much of a threat. I was mildly disappointed. Why is it me that has to deal with all the batshit wild stuff?

Lisa sat on the bed next to the woman, careful not to disturb any of her tubes or the bed pan I had not emptied yet. The tubes, at this point, are largely for show. The bedpan still gets a lot of action.

'How are you feeling today?' Lisa asked, and I watched as she reached out to stroke the wild-haired woman's wrinkled, age-spotted forehead tenderly. Why was Thomas' altered appearance not strange to her? How much did they know about what was happening to him? Did any of them even know what the real version of him looked like? I thought back to the Facebook group. Thomas' profile picture was of him covered in yellow paint. He had posted no other pictures of his own face, as far as I could remember.

Maybe none of them knew. What he really looked like.

I found that oddly comforting.

The old woman licked dry, cracked lips and whispered something almost inaudible.

Lisa leaned in, putting her ear closer so she could hear better.

'I wouldn't do that if I were you,' I said, and Theresa gave me a funny look, as if properly seeing me for the first time.

Lisa ignored me. 'Tell me again,' she implored, and if she could have climbed on top of the woman then, she would have. I felt a familiar surge of revulsion in the face of her devotion. It was obscene. She had no idea who Thomas actually was. How he would spit into the toilet after he cleaned his teeth every night. How he picked off his toenails and flicked them across a room. How he snored bubbles of snot when he slept. How he ate hotdogs, deep-throating them in an obscene pantomime display. How he put on funny voices and comedy accents, all of which sounded the same, were just high-pitched versions of his real voice. How he stacked the dishwasher. How he put his socks on. How he liked his coffee. None of them knew any of this, and yet here they were, eyes filled with stars. It made me furious.

The woman in the bed tried to speak again, but her words were still too difficult to hear. Lisa scooched closer.

'Again,' she said, and I saw her hands were trembling.

'Kill me,' the old woman said.

Lisa reared back. 'What?'

'I SAID KILL ME!' The old crone started to change in response to her own anger, and Lisa fell backwards off the bed, startled. Theresa backed away, looking from the bed to me to the bed and back again.

I folded my arms and examined my fingernails as Thomas arched his/her back, arms splaying out like a woman about to be crucified, and light poured out of her mouth, as if she were vomiting incandescence instead of puke. It was yellow light, flecked with streaks of pink and green, and it reminded me of the northern lights, of aurora borealis.

When all the light had gone, Thomas remained, but he was deflated, an empty skin. All his insides had gone. What remained looked like someone had stripped off a fleshy suit and left it discarded on the bed. His hands looked like gloves, his legs like stockings. His face was a leather mask. I'd seen a version of this strangeness before, and knew that he would most likely fill out again, but Lisa and Theresa did not know this. They both burst into tears, awed and overcome. I gently ushered them out of the bedroom and back along the corridor. They went meekly, but Lisa turned to me as I yanked open the front door, which was still lopsided on its hinges and would stick at the bottom.

'How can you not believe, when you see what He is? What He can do?' She asked me, her face white and pinched. Her bottom lip wobbled. 'How can you be so empty inside, so devoid of hope that you refuse to entertain the reality in front of you? How can you take the evidence presented so definitively, and…and…*refuse* to believe it?'

I thought about that. She was right, I realised. I don't know why I found it so hard to believe that Thomas was, in fact, what he said he was. Hadn't there been enough proof of otherworldly powers, abilities, tendencies, potential, to persuade not just me, but everyone?

'How do you define a god?' I said, eventually. Theresa had bolted by this point, scurrying off to her tent. I saw her dive inside and zip the door up tight, and I didn't see her come out for a while after that.

Lisa was made of stronger, dare I say more fanatical stuff.

'How do you define a person?' Her lip stopped wobbling. She shrugged, and that really got to me, because she was right. 'We are multitudes. We are nature's paint palette.'

And with that, she left, walking a little unsteadily, and I knew I had a real problem on my hands then, because now she had seen enough to add fuel to the zealot fire.

Which reminded me of something I read once that stuck with me, but I cannot for the life of me remember where I read it. Anyway, this writing said that there is only one life that we all live, and we share it, in 'varying degrees of consciousness', whether we are man, animal, vegetable or mineral. And because of that, the ideal of 'humanity' should not be something to which we all aspire. There are other things, you see. Other aspirations. *How do you define a person. What exactly is humanity. How do you define a god.*

And maybe that's what Thomas figured out. Maybe he had this revelation, religious, spiritual, or otherwise. Maybe he figured out that the real purpose to this life is about more than just being a good man, or a bad man, or a man at all.

I don't really know what I'm saying, but it feels as if all of this is happening because Thomas realised that life is…about more. More than paying the bills, eating, shitting, sleeping, sex. There is more, and he was looking for it, I think. Before we moved here.

I wonder if he has found it yet.

50.

Diary Entry, personal diary of Hope Gloucester
October 30th, 2020

More and more have come, but then I knew they would. Tents like yellow-headed pimples on sore skin, one, two, three, six, twelve. He doesn't need to use his phone any more to call them. He can't anyway. He's not able to stay human long enough to even hold a phone, not now. It doesn't matter. Word spreads, and the word is Thomas. Or Yellow.

Persuasive, regardless.

Now there is a tent village around the Once Yellow House.

To their credit, they have started growing vegetables. Or at least preparing the ground, turning over long strips of earth between their tents. They've put up plastic polytunnels, too. They look like shiny worms from a distance.

This morning I found two of them up on the roof of the Once Yellow House, replacing the broken roof tiles. Something I had been meaning to try and do myself, then never did. I watched them work in silence, feeling annoyed and also experiencing a deep-seated, unshakeable sense of relief that someone else was shouldering the responsibility of the house. Thomas has taken all my time, energy and what little money we had left. It felt nice to let someone else deal with the maintenance shit for a little bit. Making the best out of a bad situation. Next I'll be donning yellow robes and marking my skin with weird geometry, if I'm not careful.

Something about allowing people into the Once Yellow House to visit Thomas has, like I predicted, fanned the flames of the Retinue's adoration. They have decided to show this by fixing up the house in which their god resides. Just like I asked them to. After the roof, came the windows. Sash window frames stripped, sanded, oiled, re-painted (white, not yellow), all in a matter of hours. Broken glass panes replaced. Beading redone. Lopsided shutters fixed. Now, they are sanding the floors. It seems now that they've started, the Retinue can't stop. They are on a mission to make their god as comfortable as possible.

And I am just going to let them.

I am going to let the cult fix up my house.

I figure they owe me.

I went into Thomas later today than I meant to, because of all the renovations. I let the Retinue distract me. It was mid-morning by the time I got to him, but I found to my surprise (and again, relief) that he'd already been cleaned and turned and medicated by someone else. A younger member of the Retinue, a girl with a nice smile. She looked at me strangely as I passed her in the hallway.

'Did he behave for you?' I asked.

She ducked her head and kept on walking. She had a guilty, complicated look on her face.

Thomas was sitting up when I went into the bedroom, his covers rolled down to below his waist. I wondered suddenly what he had been up to, for his hair was mussed and he was covered in sweat.

Then a thin red tendril, like the curling peduncle on a grape vine, poked itself out of a split that had opened up along one of his ribs. It reached for me, and I could see other things beyond it, glittering things roiling behind the slit in the flesh. Thomas is a seething sack of different entities, of potential, and I don't think it will be long before they all take over, erupt. He is a cosmic volcano about to go off.

He was talkative today, perhaps for this reason.

'I think love is the ability to let someone go, don't you?' He said, his face and voice still his own.

'What do you mean?' I asked, feeling blindsided.

'I mean, you could help me. I can't...do it myself.'

'Do what?' For a moment I assumed he was talking about sex. Then: 'Oh.'

His eyes were pain layered upon suffering. His eyelashes, I saw, were wriggling.

He will ask me again.

He can ask me as many times as he likes.

I won't kill him.

I know I've toyed with the idea but...I *can't* kill him.

Thomas collapsed then, into a pool of tiny red squiggly worms, and I left hastily, shutting the door behind me and hastily grabbing a towel from the bathroom, rolling it up and stuffing it in the crack beneath the door to minimise the risk of the worms escaping into the rest of the house.

A scratching sound made its presence known as I retreated to the living room. There are still rats in the walls.

And the mould is so thick it looks like a living forest has carpeted my walls.

I have stopped trying to bleach it all away.

I'll get the Retinue to do it instead.

Perhaps I can get them to solve the other problem too.

I looked out the window. One of the tents outside, someone has painted 'END DAYS ARE COMING.'

I hope so. I really do.

51.

Audio Transcript
File name: Once_Yellow_House_Transcription_16
Audio length: 00:00:15
Date transcribed: 12/23/2022

Hope: I just realised. That was you, wasn't it? Coming out of his room. Caught red handed.

Kate: I hoped you wouldn't remember.

Hope: It just hit me. Why he was sweaty. Why you had that look on your face. Weren't you...weren't you worried about getting pregnant?

Kate: I...it wasn't something I thought about. I told you, I was...I was drugged, I did as I was told.

Hope: But why? Why give yourself over like that?

Kate: I...I...I need a break.

[Recording ends]

52.

Diary Entry, personal diary of Hope Gloucester
November 1st, 2020

The attic is now full of all his little portraits. I realised today that I have not washed in weeks. I caught sight of myself in the bathroom mirror this morning. I'm covered from the top of my head to my ankles in blotches of oil paint and fungus (it has taken over all my broken skin and scars now) and hair and dirt and paint bristles and house debris like some weird, wild, living work of surrealism. An organic sculpture. I don't have any desire to wash any of it off, although I do hope there is no lead in any of my paint. I think modern paints are safer these days, but there were a few old tubes in my kit that my mother gave me, so who knows. I quite like the feel of the paint on my skin, to be honest, and the fear it inspires whenever anyone from camp catches sight of me. I spend a not insubstantial amount of time moving the oils around with my fingers and creating different patterns and textures on my body-canvas. It's endlessly satisfying. I recreated the swirls from *Starry Night* the other day, and felt every part of me vibrate in recognition.

Outside, a large canvas and pole structure has gone up in the centre of the tent village. A meeting place, I think. I heard chanting coming out of it last night. Or it might have been singing. Either way, it kept me awake.

I've been thinking about Thomas' request. I'm confused about why he needs me to do it. Why can't he end his own life? Why does he need *me*? Why not a member of the Retinue? Perhaps he can't control himself that much. Perhaps they won't let him, which I guess makes sense. No Thomas, no Retinue. I don't know. I know I sound callous. There is emotion in me, but you might have to wipe away all these oil paint layers first to find it, and I'm out of white spirit.

It's getting colder, but the Retinue have fixed my broken heating and for once, the bungalow is almost comfortably warm. The bedroom exists outside of this regulation and maintains its own environmental temperature. This morning I found what can only be described as a mass of ice crystals and frost-flowers choking up the doorway to the room I once shared with my husband. I couldn't get past the ice build-up to get to Thomas, and part of me didn't want to. The crystalline formations were beautiful, the first actively beautiful thing I have seen for a very long time. They glowed. I didn't know if the ice was part of Thomas or something he had excreted but I left it as it was.

Later, I noticed water all over the floor, and after I mopped it up, I found something thawing on the bed. It was too grotesque for me to actually get a handle on, visually. The best way I can describe it is like that movie, the one about the Antarctic research station that gets invaded by an alien. It looked like that impossibly mutated thing that Kurt Russel obliterates in a rush of fire. Pink, sticky, molten, pained.

Which makes me think. I could always burn the house down. Burn Thomas, burn whatever lives under his skin, burn the rats, the mould, the strange shit drawn on the walls under the wallpaper, burn the now freshly painted yellow wooden cladding, the shingles, the attic door with its faulty catch (the Retinue haven't fixed that yet), the ladder, the portraits of Thomas I paint to stop myself going insane, the stupid skinny white trees, the land, the tents, the signal equipment, the garbage...

I could burn it all, and start over.

But I will never be able to start over, will I?

I will never be able to forget Thomas, and what happened to him. He has changed everything, forever.

Lisa came to me and asked me if I wanted to join them later when they had a 'meeting'. I declined, politely. She then asked me if I wanted her to run me a bath. I declined that offer politely, too. Their discomfort is not my problem. I like my paint skin.

53.

Audio Transcript
File name: Once_Yellow_House_Transcription_17
Audio length: 00:02:03
Date transcribed: 12/23/2022

    Kate: Do you know some of the common markers of abuse, Hope?
    Hope: Here we go.
    Kate: I'm serious. It's relevant. I did a lot of reading, after I left the Retinue.
    Hope: *[Sigh]* Enlighten me.
    Kate: Signs of abuse. Criticising someone constantly. Destroying a person's confidence. False remorse. Anger, and violence, obviously. Lying. Destroying a person's self-esteem. Name-calling. Gaslighting. Manipulation. Controlling of finances. Treating you like hired help, or a servant. Refusing to talk about emotional issues. Shaming. Ignoring your boundaries. Stonewalling. Triangulation.
    Hope: What's that?
    Kate: The practice of making you think that everyone else is a threat by lying about things they supposedly said. Projection.
    Hope: Astral projection? *[Laughs]*
    Kate: This isn't a joke, Hope. I'm not laughing.
    Hope: What are you trying to achieve? Why are you telling me all this?
    Kate: You lost a baby, didn't you?
    Hope: What?
    Kate: I saw it in your diary.

    [Pause]

    Hope: I don't see how that is relevant.
    Kate: What triggered him wanting to move out to the Once Yellow House, Hope? Did something happen between you both? Some…catalytic event?
    Hope: No. I don't know what you're talking about.
    Kate: He was doing all those things to you before you moved, wasn't he?
    Hope: Shut up.

Kate: He was abusing you before, wasn't he? Long before you moved to the bungalow.

Hope: Shut up! I don't see what difference it makes if he was or if he wasn't! It isn't relevant!

Kate: How did you lose the baby, Hope?

Hope: Time's up. Get out of my house. *[Chair scraping]*

Kate: How did you lose the baby? Did he hurt you?

Hope: Shut up.

Kate: Hit you?

Hope: I said stop it!

Kate: Kick you?

Hope: That's *enough!*

[A loud slap, followed by a sharp intake of breath from Kate. A protracted pause follows, filled with heavy breathing from both participants.]

Hope: I lost the baby because we had an argument. He was…he was being aggressive. I backed away from him, tripped, and fell down a flight of stairs. It was my fault.

Kate: Is that what he told you?

Hope: I never told him I was pregnant. He didn't know. But it was my fault. All of this…all of this is my fault. Everything. All the things that happened to you…to all those people…Kate, I feel sick.

[Retching sounds, followed by clattering and cupboard doors opening and closing.]

Kate: Here, use this.

[Protracted vomiting, spitting and heavy breathing.]

Kate: There we go. Let it all out. Come on, spit it up.

[More vomiting, spitting and heavy breathing.]

Kate: I knew I shouldn't have let you drink so much whiskey.

Hope: I've never told anyone…about the baby. Never out loud.

Kate: I figured.

[Recording ends]

54.

Diary Entry, personal diary of Hope Gloucester
November 3rd, 2020

The new structure in the tent village is a temple. Of course it is.

There is an altar inside, and a triangular hardboard platform in the middle, around which chairs are arranged in a spiralling pattern. Guidelines on the ground marked out with yellow spray paint help with chair placement. It wasn't until later that I figured out what those spiralling lines represented: a perfect Fibonacci sequence spiral.

At the tips of the platform, there are small iron braziers for ceremonial fires. Triangle, dots etc. Lying on the platform's heart is a thick, soft mattress, easily king sized, if not bigger. I asked Lisa what the mattress was for. She made an evasive noise, and then several hours later, as dusk was beginning to fall, she came for Thomas with a dozen members of the Retinue.

They went straight to his room, sweeping me easily to one side as I protested. When I wouldn't quit asking (yelling) what they were doing, what their intentions were, they restrained me. Of course I fought back. Mimi, furious at the intrusion, bit one of them on the ankle. That did the trick. They let me go and this big, bearded guy went for her with a baton he had clipped to his belt (later, I found out that wooden batons have become a thing around camp- big men armed with them everywhere). Terrified, I tried to get between the man and Mimi, but he was determined and so was she. I screamed at her then, screamed at her to run, waving my arms furiously to scare her off, but she refused to go until I yanked the baton from the man's hand and threw it at her. It missed her by an inch (intentional) and the look on her face broke my heart, but I had to do it. She whined and backed off. I kept on yelling and cursing and throwing things, and eventually she yelped and turned tail and ran right out the open front door, and it was the biggest betrayal, I could see it in her eyes, and it made me sick to my stomach.

And now she's gone, and I miss her, but at least she is safe.

Then they took Thomas outside, carrying him reverently above their shoulders on this long stretcher they had built for this specific purpose. At first I was terrified they would damage his human form by moving him, by disconnecting him from all his tubes and wires, but then I figured he is human now for such small periods of time, it couldn't make much difference. His body is fighting this titanic cosmic battle with itself, the very nature of his cells and atoms changing constantly. A little fresh air and a change of scenery would hardly be the worst thing he'd have to endure.

He remained Thomas while the Retinue carried him in a solemn procession out of the Once Yellow House and into the new temple, which obviously has yellow symbols and glyphs painted all over it. I have a feeling they chose this time of day because they knew his entity cycling speed slows down as he prepares for sleep, so he was less likely to melt into a pool of goo on the stretcher or burst into a cloud of a million ants or something equally inconvenient.

I followed miserably. Once they realised I wasn't going to make a fuss, they let me. I think they thought if I saw what they were up to, I'd join in, volunteer to become part of it. I feel almost sad for how delusional they are. Almost.

Thomas was taken past the chairs and up to the platform, where his body was shuffled and rolled onto the mattress with great care. I stood to the back of the temple near the entrance flap and watched as his arms and legs were arranged neatly, and someone slid a yellow silk pillow under his head.

A gong was struck. The temple began to fill up. That's when I truly understood the power my husband had over these people, the depths to which they had immersed themselves in this cult lifestyle. There were so many of them, and there was this hum of anticipation in the air as the Retinue gathered, exuding this energy akin to electricity, staticky and full of potential. They were excited, hopeful, babbling to each other about lessons to be learned and how he was going to save them all and usher in a new age of understanding and wisdom and I just stood there, grinding my teeth and trying to appear as unobtrusive as possible.

When the temple was full, which didn't take long, Lisa appeared, accompanied by Theresa, who looked a bit green about the gills. They were wearing different clothes than normal. Still yellow, these garments were longer than their usual tunics, and floor length, like ceremonial robes or a bishop's cope. Wide in the shoulders with padding and brocade, the robes were smothered in embroidery- the usual geometry. I am getting very tired of that imagery. I sometimes see it when I close my eyes at night to sleep. Triangles, circles, squares, trapezoids, rectangles. Rhombus. Some people count sheep, I count angles and sides and corners.

Lisa and Theresa lit the braziers and held hands over Thomas, who had started to sweat and moan. I had the feeling he was fighting against the change this time. That he was deliberately trying *not* to transform. I was amazed he had held off as long as this, and felt fiercely proud of him for a moment. There was still good in there, a speck of it, spinning in the void.

A hush fell over the temple, an anticipatory lull that brought goosebumps up on my crusted skin.

Then they all closed their eyes and started muttering indistinct prayers, or perhaps it was a mantra- either way I couldn't make out, it all sounded like gobbledygook to me.

I realised they were waiting for him to cycle. I saw instantly that Lisa was the brains behind this idea. She had been plotting, a marketing manager trying to packet a brand. Practical demonstrations were best, she had decided. An effective way of convincing the consumer that their money (or faith) was well placed. This was a spiritual circus. Roll up, roll up, get your tickets for the greatest show on earth, etc. Lisa wanted my husband's transformations to be a public event, insofar as his manifestations now belonged in her ceremonial domain. She wanted a visual spectacle to reinforce the rhetoric. Perhaps people were starting to question that rhetoric, and what they were doing there at all, or the veracity of the Great God Thomas as a deity they should all be slavishly worshipping.

So, she had decided upon a public demonstration.

I couldn't fault her logic. She was smart. I just don't think she expected it to go so far.

The Retinue waited patiently, their lips moving in the ceaseless dedication that had brought them this far, and after a while, their diligence was rewarded.

Thomas started to change. Which was not the normal way of things, not at night, but maybe he sensed his audience wanted a display. Maybe he felt obligated. Or, like showing off. Either was possible, with Thomas. He always liked doing things for people then immediately making them feel guilty about it.

This particular transformation had all the hallmarks of a dramatic one, and my senses lit up like a dozen warning signals. His body went tight and straight, like a plank of wood. His skin rippled. His thin, now wispy hair, rose up from his scalp and stood on end.

The audience opened their eyes, gasping, clapping hands, whispering, leaning forward in anticipation.

I started to edge back so I was half in, half out of the temple doorway. I should have warned people then, but I was so fully immersed in the spectacle that I didn't.

Lisa and Theresa broke their grip, stood back to give Thomas space. His form began to swell and yet also reduce at the same time, compacting itself into a dense, fleshy ball. Bones snapped and refused. Gristle creaked. Blood leaked out of him and splattered across the mattress. The audience on the closest seats got sprayed with a fine red bloodmist, which produced mixed reactions. I saw one woman very deliberately rub the redness into her skin, eyes closed in ecstasy. Several others gasped in terror and confusion and shot up out of their seats immediately, retreating to a safer distance. A small child wailed in fear and confusion, and I was quietly livid on her behalf.

And yet nobody left.

'Hey!' I shouted, then, shaking myself and realising I had to do something. 'You know this is dangerous, right? You should run!'

But they all ignored me. They were caught in a rapture, and I had no hope of breaking it.

A keening hum made its presence known, loud, sharp as a blade. It sliced, that sound, the vibrations scalping the unbelievers and the dedicated alike. I put my hands over my ears, but it still razored my brain. Quite a few members of the audience started to cry, unable to comprehend what they were seeing and hearing. More of them got out of their seats and began milling about, raising their arms up, kneeling, wailing, ululating, huddling together in prayer, holding each other up.

'Hold firm!' Lisa intoned. I could see her chest heaving with fear and excitement, a potent cocktail judging by her eyes, which were wide and fanatical. Theresa's lip wobbled, and I thought she might bolt, but instead she started thrashing the gong that hung nearby with a manic sort of rhythm that whipped the members of the Retinue up into further frenzy. I could see it travel, this madness, or perhaps it was the sound[25], travelling outwards from the centre of the temple, as if carried by the undulating soundwaves of the gong, and it passed through the audience in this rippling wave of ecstasy

---

[25] Ed.note: readers may wish to do their own research around the term 'cymatics'. Cymatics are vibrational modal phenomena best described as 'Visible Sound'. There have been studies on how cymatics can physically affect and influence matter and molecular structure. The first supposed documented instance of cymatics was by Galileo in 1632, who scraped a brass plate with a sharp chisel and observed strange marks appearing on it when he made this particular sound.

and terror that I could *see*. A woman towards the back began to rip her own tunic off, baring her breasts and shredding at them with her nails and squeezing them as tears leaked down her face. Others dropped to their knees and repeatedly banged their heads and fists against the floor until they were bloody. A man off to my left vomited all over the person in front of him, and then promptly soiled himself but didn't seem to notice.

I began to feel terrified for the children present. I could not fathom what being in this sort of situation would do to their brains. I looked to the back row of the spiral, and saw a small toddler sitting on his mother's hip. I ran forward in a strange, lurching burst of speed, and tried to wrestle him from her, thinking *At least I can get one of them to safety.* His mother screeched and clawed at me and the little boy screeched too.

I gave up. The hum made it hard to function, to do anything but stagger around, half-paralysed, as it all played out, and besides. I still had this inherent faith. That underneath all of it, Thomas remained.

And the Thomas I had known was a good person, who would never hurt anyone.

Wasn't he?

The fleshy round mass on the platform doubled in size and sprouted feathers, pristine white in colour. Small nubs of gristly bone erupted from six points in the ball, elongated out into bony phalanxes, and more feathers germinated from these limbs, flight feathers this time, primary and secondary, and I understood suddenly what Thomas was turning into.

I started to laugh. I couldn't help myself. Once I started, I found it impossible to stop.

And sure enough, within moments I was looking at a round object out of which six wings grew, and those wings began to flap, expelling a tremendous wind that knocked most of the Retinue in the front row backwards off their seats, propelling them across the temple.

The ball then lifted itself into the air and hovered, great pinions beating, and it started to shudder and shake with an intense, urgent series of movements that got more and more violent as its wings beat faster and faster and the wind grew stronger. Tiny pink erect stubs emerged from the gaps between each wing, and they looked engorged, pink, wet at the tips.

The wings whipped the air into a feathered, frenzied soup within the tent, and the juddering, jerking movements sped up and became more desperate, and the hum reached a pitch which nearly dissolved my ears clean off the side of my head, and there was a moment of complete stillness as the wings slowed and the shape stopped shuddering and shaking, then suddenly, the airborne abomination erupted and showered the entire temple with an energetic spray of white, sticky fluid that came down like heavy rain.

A few drops of it landed on my arm. I rubbed it between my fingers, and I sniffed at it and yep, I knew that smell. It was *his* smell, an intimate smell of love and passion and vulnerability. I had powerful surges of memory, us naked in bed, me sitting behind him, legs dangling either side of his off the side of the mattress, and I had wrapped him in an embrace, big spoon little spoon, and I was using my hand to bring him off from behind. He used to go stock-still before he came, just in the instant before release, a statue, fully focused, everything held tight in place before the explosion would come, and I would think *I have done something right, then,* and after he would collapse like an airless balloon as I kissed his back and told him how proud I was of him.

And it was at that point, as a bolt of sadness speared my heart, that I thought *you should probably run, Hope,* and so I did, but not before catching the finale of the Great God Thomas evening performance in that last split second before I left: a huge, blue, watery lidded eye that opened in the centre of the feathered ball. And it blinked, and turned itself on Theresa, whereupon she melted from the top down, like hot wax. Simple as that. She screamed briefly, then her face went all soft and ran down her skull and I turned and high-tailed it out of there, sprinting back to the Once Yellow House and screaming at Mimi to follow, before remembering Mimi was no longer with me, and I was thankful then, that I had done what I could to scare her off.

And in hindsight, had I been thinking clearly, this moment could have been my golden opportunity to escape while the entire camp was distracted. I could have hightailed it out of there while they rolled around in supernatural spunk and kept on going, and nobody would have stopped me. But I didn't escape, because my brain had been sabotaged by the warping hum sound, because he had his hooks in me, and still does, and always will, because maybe love isn't a two-handled suitcase, maybe love is more like a net, or a barbed arrow, or a fishhook from which we can never free ourselves, and instead I ran back to the house and into the living room, which was like running into a room carpeted with sentient, breathing weeds, and I used one of my last scraps of cardboard, and I painted Thomas as he had presented himself to us, as a biblically accurate angel, and then I wondered, after I had finished and I was covered in more layers of paint, a suit of oil-crusted armour, I wondered, after the screaming had died down outside, whether my husband had been taking the piss, whether the angel had been a particularly subtle joke, or whether God (the real God) who I have never believed in, had been fucking with us all along.

55.

Audio Transcript
File name: Once_Yellow_House_Transcription_18
Audio length: 00:01:43
Date transcribed: 12/24/2022

Kate: That is the most cogent first-hand account of that evening I've heard yet.

Hope: You weren't there for that meeting? Lucky you.

Kate: I was not. I had been running a low fever. I stayed in my tent. I heard the commotion, though.

Hope: You didn't think to come and look?

Kate: With everyone screaming and carrying on like that? No thanks. I hid in my sleeping bag and waited for it to all blow over. What else could I do? I knew I was better off out of it.

Hope: And there you were, judging me earlier. Huh.

Kate: I never claimed to be perfect, Hope. Just...angry, I guess. It was a waste of a good man. Of good people. All of it. The whole circus. I keep thinking about all the things he could have done, with that power. All the good. The retinue, too. What a waste of energy, and devotion. When you think how many people are struggling in this world...the challenges we face, as a species...as a planet...he could have...I think he could have made a difference. Where it mattered.

Hope: I think you're over-estimating how much control he had over himself.

Kate: But still, maybe there was *some* good inside of him, you said it yourself. Or if not good, at least some rationality. Even bad men can be brought along a better path. It hurts to think about the *potential*. What he could have been. It hurts.

Hope: Oh it hurts you, is that right? *[Bitter laugh]* I remember him before. You don't know the meaning of the word hurt.

Kate: I know. I'm sorry. I'm still mad at everything, I think.

Hope: I'm still mad at you, too.

Kate: I probably deserve that.

Hope: No, I think you might have helped me, maybe. I can't keep it all buried, for the rest of my life. It'll rot my insides.

Kate: I know how you feel.

Hope: Did you go to any of the Meetings? At all?

Kate: Only one. I tried to stay away. They always smelt crazy to me.

Hope: What happened? What did you see?

Kate: He was a No-Show, on that occasion. No transformation. He just slept. I think he snored a little, actually.

Hope: So you missed most of the theatrics.

Kate: I tried my best to. I'm not sure how to explain it, only…I didn't *want* to see him like that. And you were right about Lisa. I never liked her. She was hard, and short-sighted. And greedy. And yeah, she wanted nothing more than to exploit him, for her own gain. You know she started charging entry fees to the camp?

Hope: She did?

Kate: You could only join the Retinue if you paid a membership fee on arrival. Cash in hand. I think it was five hundred dollars minimum. Some people gave three times that. Some people gave up their life savings to join the Retinue. The word spread, I guess, and curiosity is a wild thing. People are just looking for something to believe in. I never knew where that money went. It didn't get spent on food, or the camp, I know that much. It was a circus, in every single sense of the word. Children in rags, the toilets were always overflowing. We went hungry and she told us it was good for us. That it would put us 'more in touch with our divine selves', whatever that meant. I think she stole that from Buddhism, the whole starving yourself thing to reach enlightenment, but we never did. Reach it. We just got thin and cold and sick as winter came in.

Hope: And she seemed to eat just fine, right?

Kate: Right. So much hypocrisy, but by then it didn't matter, you have to understand what it was like out there in the camp. It was like a fever had us all. We were swimming in fog, constantly. She had the spectacle of Thomas to keep people around her, and it worked. It really worked. He was glue.

Hope: I always wondered about that. Why people didn't leave. Why they weren't terrified enough of him to leave.

Kate: Because she wouldn't let us! That's what the batons were for. Subjugation. Intimidation. People came in, but they didn't leave, unless they died. She put together a squad of bodyguards, followers who would get wind of anyone threatening to escape or expose the camp and beat the offending parties into submission before they could.

Hope: She was a gangster, not a religious devotee.

Kate: Whatever. I was scared of her. We all were. Almost more scared of her than we were of your husband, hard as that is to believe.

Hope: That was your mistake then, wasn't it? You should have run while you had the chance.

Kate: So should you. And yet, here we are.

[Sigh]

Hope: Here we are.

[Recording ends]

56.

Sun Bulletin November 3rd, 2020
Letter to the Editor

Dear Editor,

As another long-term resident of the 'once fine and pleasant Village of Lestershire within the Town of Union' (Letter to the Ed, Oct 31st, 2020), I also feel compelled to write about the growing encampment over at the old Mackenzie bungalow (also known affectionately as the Once Yellow House by most in these parts). I am not writing from a position of anger and intolerance, however, but from one of compassion and empathy, and I must express my complete dismay and disappointment at the sheer number of fellow Lestershire residents that have voiced similarly unsympathetic sentiments to those expressed by Mr. Zielewicz in his letter.

I am not usually one for publicly contradicting a presiding sentiment, no matter how ardently I disagree with it, however in this case, I feel I should point out a few uncomfortable truths.

The first, that the Once Yellow House remains an eyesore and a dangerous building. This is simply not the case. Since the arrival of the makeshift encampment, anyone venturing out there can see immediately that the entire property *has* been renovated, to what appears to be the highest standard. The paintwork gleams, the roof tiles are all repaired, all weed growth obliterated, and the land around, despite the addition of tents, temporary toilets and other makeshift structures, is well-cultivated and tended to. I saw no evidence of 'vermin' or rodents, and must confess, it's been many years since I saw that sad old bungalow looking anywhere half as good as it does now. These encampment folks have proven themselves hardworking and diligent, and I was impressed at how quiet and peaceable the place appears to be—hardly the 'immoral, misguided vagrants' Mr. Zielewicz complains of. The addition of temporary fencing around the property and associated land is, admittedly, not the most attractive thing I've ever seen, but hardly indicative of the ghetto or 'eyesore' in the formerly mentioned letter.

Furthermore, it is clear to me that many of those who have joined the encampment and the 'Retinue' who operate there have done so because they felt driven to some higher purpose or noble cause, not because they wished to band together and cause the residents of a small town on the edge of a dying Estate any particular trouble.

I would argue that the 'impact this enormous and rapid influx of strangers has had on the community of Lestershire, and on the wider area of Sunshire Hill' has not 'been profound', not by any degree. Is it jarring to see people who dress differently to us and behave differently to us walking down the street? Only for those of us who are narrow-minded and bigoted, whose worldview does not extend beyond a population of folks who all look and sound and walk the same.

Furthermore, I can find no concrete evidence that indicates crime rates have risen, and have not noticed any increase in littering or any other antisocial inconvenience. The strain on our resources is also apparently minimal: the Retinue seem to be operating in a mostly self-sufficient manner and, by and large, ask for very little when they do come into contact with the residents of Lestershire.

As to the claims of aiding the spread of the virus and contributing to the pressures of a pandemic: the community over at the Once Yellow House seem to be the only people in these parts truly comfortable with the idea of self-isolating and staying away from others unless strictly necessary. By that measure alone, they are doing a lot better than many of my fellow townsfolk in fighting the spread of the disease.

I do agree with my esteemed neighbor on one thing: Lestershire within the greater Town of Union used to be a 'fine town', a fine town indeed. It would continue to be a fine town if we could all remember that a little compassion goes a very long way, especially in these trying times. America was founded on an ideal of religious freedom, and this town was built on the tenets of religious tolerance. Its residents would do well to remember that whenever possible, rather than conform to a Republican stereotype of predictable proportions.

Russell M. Petrosky

57.

Diary Entry, personal diary of Hope Gloucester
November 4th, 2020

You would think last night's display would have put Lisa off, or put an end to things. You would think the Retinue (having lost five people, Theresa included, before Thomas transformed once more into a small hard rock that sat innocently on the platform while the Retinue carried out their dead and cleaned off their living) would have been persuaded to disband.

But it hasn't. Last night's 'meeting' only made them believe more. Thomas is a god, it is proven now, and they will worship him and die for the pleasure. Lisa was absolutely right. The practical demonstration has sealed the deal for anyone on the edge of doubt.

And so I shouldn't be surprised that dozens more arrived today, more than the Retinue can provide tents and tunics for. This place is bursting at the seams, and I know I've missed any opportunity I might have had to stop this madness. I am no longer allowed private access to Thomas. I have to be supervised at all times now. Probably because they fear I will try and kill him.

Because he has become what I hoped to avoid.

He has become death.

So now it is no longer a question of suitcases, or love, or anything but duty. He wants me to do it, I'm sure of it, and now he's shown me how dangerous he is, I should try to honour his wishes. Somehow. I'll have to come up with a plan soon. I can sense tensions running high and a certain escalating stress surrounding Thomas on the rare occasions he is in his own body. Like a god-bomb, about to go off.

Perhaps that is what the yellow tunics mean when they start parroting their spiel about 'End Days' and so on.

The Once Yellow House seems to be gearing up to something, too. The mould is rampant, infesting every surface and corner of the place. It seems frequently agitated, and moves like seaweed as I wander around the house. There is almost something comforting about it. Familiar. I don't get splinters in my feet anymore. Dozens of patches of the stuff have rooted in the paint scabs on my skin. Turns out, oil paint is a rich compost for this particular type of fungus, and it mimics the colour of whichever paint patch it has sprouted from. I look like an odd sort of tropical parrot, walking around barefoot. I maintain that it wants me to make art with it somehow, like my body is a palette. There's not enough yellow on me to be tempted, though. I am still in love with yellow, whatever else there may or may not be.

I wonder if all artists have one preferred colour (I am thinking here of Klein[26], and his obsession with blue), or if I remain the worst type: a painter with a reduced vision, a tunnel vision. I can't help it. Yellow has its hooks in me.

Other things about the house are more energetic. I catch the symbols on the fireplace glowing, sometimes. I wonder if they were put there as protection or for some other purpose, to ward off evil or good. I wonder a lot of things about this house, before we got to it. About who lived here before, and what happened to them.

I constantly hear things moving on the roof, in the attic, in the walls, beneath the floorboards. I used to worry about my paintings in the roofspace, whether or not they were safe up there, but art is transient at best, I've realised. It doesn't much matter what happens to my daubs, the power was in the construction of them, not their longevity after. Like a song on the breeze, unrecorded. Only those within earshot hear it, if at all, but it doesn't mean the song is any less tuneful.

The Retinue dug graves for the five lost acolytes out by the train tracks, buried them with small yellow markers denoting each body. I can see them through the kitchen window. Theresa's grave looks more of a hole than anything else. She had to be mopped up with rags and squeezed into a bucket before they could bury her, so I'm not surprised. Takes a lot of effort to dig, in this cold. No point shovelling more frozen earth than necessity dictates.

Despite this (the deaths) Lisa says they will call a Meeting every night, regardless of the outcome, until his Message is Received. Whatever it may be. (I am the Lord of the Dance, said he.)

All these capital letters are making me as tired and numb as the geometry. I think that's how they get you, these religions. With Sheer

---

[26] French artist Yves Klein was, indeed, obsessed with blue, so much so that he invented and patented an entire new color in his pursuit of the perfect shade. One of Klein's most memorable art performances included an exhibition called 'Blue Epoch', where three naked models coated themselves in blue paint and imprinted themselves on a large canvas. Klein called the models 'living brushes'.

Readers will no longer be surprised to learn that Klein was also interested in magic, the arcane, mysticism, and was influenced by the Rosicrucian society, an esoteric spiritual and cultural movement active in Europe during the 17th century. Its symbol is a cross. **Klein died at the age of 34 from a heart attack.**

Repetition. It makes you braindead, malleable. The power of slogans. Of capital letters. The lexicon of Faith, with a capital 'F'.

In the meantime, Thomas is back in the Once Yellow House, back in his bedroom where he belongs. They reluctantly let me see him today, although I had to be accompanied by three fawning young women, one of whom tried to press her breasts into his face right there while I was trying to attend to him. I nearly broke her wrist as I pulled her back from the bed, and she glared at me with pure hatred, leaving sulkily when I made it clear that there would be none of that while I was present. I don't have much left to me, but I do have the distinction of being his wife, and nobody is going to take sexual liberties in front of me. I have some limits.

The other two registered this exchange and were a little more respectful, retreating to a small distance so I could talk to my husband without them breathing down my neck. I think they sensed my own desperation and resolve, and they almost appeared to be a little intimidated by me. I thank the ever-shifting paint-mould jacket for that. Art as a form of protection, or resistance. Both, even. I like that.

I sat next to Thomas carefully, aware I only had minutes before he cycled. I reached out for him. The skin on the back of his hand felt like molten taffy. I was momentarily repulsed but also harboured a huge degree of pity for his condition. It's obvious, now, what's happening to him. His earthly body can't handle the strain of it anymore. He is dissolving away.

He opened his eyes when my fingers touched him.

'What is love, to you?' He croaked, in his own voice.

Oh boy, I thought.

I stared out the window, thinking. I suddenly didn't want to meet his bloodshot eyes, or say the wrong thing. We had so little time left to communicate what was important, I didn't want to let him down. Neither did I want to watch him disintegrate from the inside out anymore. I am a coward. I should be better for him, stronger, but I'm not. I'm weak. I'm tired. *My cup is full. It runneth over.* No space for anything else. No space. Not even for love.

Or maybe only for love, else why am I still here?

There was a reason I didn't run. The reason was made up of both fear and obligation, laced with regret. With what Might Have Been, capital letters.

Outside, I could see Lisa chopping firewood with a sharp axe. Her tall, robust frame moved like a mechanical model, arms up, arms down, *thunk!* Two pieces of wood where before, there was only one.

She swept them onto a nearby pile and picked up a fresh chunk. And repeat. I wondered why she was doing this herself, instead of getting a lackey to do it, but I suspect it has something to do with the meditative repetition of the task. The nature of such a menial job, allowing her to think, to plot. To exploit my husband to his full extent.

How much of life is a series of repetitive acts, when all is said and done? I wonder about that. Just humans going through a series of predetermined motions, so to speak. Axe up, axe down, sweep, repeat. Prayer time, breakfast time, time for another Meeting. Perhaps it's all the talk of patterns and cards and probability, left over in my brain from Frederick, who has not returned. I miss him. The deck never reshuffled him into existence.

Or perhaps my brain is constantly trying to wrap itself around the human and spiritual mathematics woven into everyday life at the Once Yellow House, a life (my life) now dominated by complex human equations. Fibonacci sequences. Fifty two card problems. Permutations with repetition. Mould. The colour Yellow, capital 'Y'. Come to think of it, the letter 'Y' has three tips, doesn't it? Like points to a triangle. You can draw an outline from those dots and the end result looks a lot like the symbol on my fireplace, on the tents outside, the symbol tattooed onto the members of the Retinue. I don't think I am going mad. I think there is some cosmic inevitability at play here. Once you see it, you see it everywhere, because you are *meant* to.

I could go round and round and round in circles (circles, ha ha), all day and all night, thinking about this stuff.

'Love is a trap,' I heard myself say, out loud, by way of response, and that was a colossal failure on my part. I knew as soon as the words left my mouth that I shouldn't have said them.

Thomas, the real Thomas, coughed, his pain at my response manifesting physically. Phlegm splattered across the bedding. It was blue, not yellow. This did not phase me, I've seen Thomas turn into things I never deemed possible. Blue spit was a tiny infraction on the bed of normality, all things considered. At least it wasn't angel cum.

'A trap?' He wheezed. 'You seemed...willing enough...at the time. To be caught, I mean.'

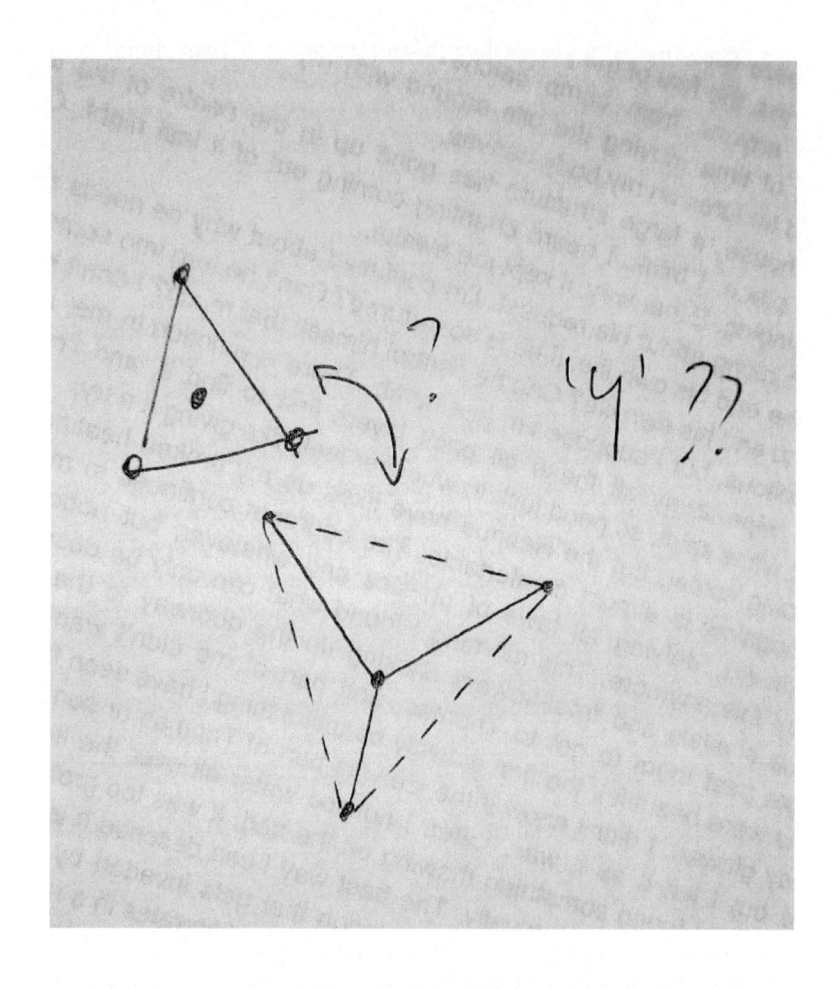

Scanned image from Hope Gloucester's Scrapbook/diary, dated 4th November 2020.

'I didn't mean it.' I squeezed his hand, backpedalling like I always have, and I felt his bones snap in my grasp like wet twigs. I snatched my arm back, mortified. I didn't have long with the real him, seconds at best. His face was elongating as he tried to speak. His eyes were beginning to drift further apart on his face, each one headed towards his thin, scabbed hairline. He used to have such beautiful hair. Such thick, lovely hair.

'Yes...you...did...' He said, his breath more and more laboured. The women behind me in the room craned their heads forward, realising that a show was about to take place. Another transmogrification, a private screening, just for them. A privilege, I imagine they thought.

And I think that was the final straw. The idea that all of this was performance art. I felt a bitterness, a darkness rising, and I couldn't keep it in anymore. The acidity had burned through every soft part of me and left only hard, dead bones behind.

'I was baited,' I replied coldly, my whole body shaking with fury. When we'd first met, he had promised so much. So very much, and I'd believed him. I'd left our future entirely in his hands. Too much to ask, of one person. A future should be a joint responsibility, not one person clearing a path alone while the other trails behind.

'Baited?'

'With the promise of...of...more.'

He laughed. More blue phlegm splattered across the bedding.

'More? More than this? I have a cosmos in my skull, Hope. I have a million souls...jostling for space...between my ribs. I have...'

More coughing. Something wet and red and whiskered came up this time, joining the mass of multi-coloured stains on the bedding. It thrashed around like a fish out of water, then scrambled down the length of the bed, falling onto the floor and running out the door on tiny, clawed feet.

Thomas continued, even though it was draining him to talk.

'I have a chorus of voices that don't belong to me, or this earth, on my tongue. More? What...more could you...possibly want?'

I slapped him. His skull rotated, and then slowly ground back to face me.

'Don't joke, Thomas,' I said, my eyes filling with tears. 'This is hell. I am in hell. My brain is *broken*.' My voice became a screech, and I shut my mouth.

My husband's skull morphed and peaked into a long, bullet-shaped protuberance, and kept elongating, stretching. I could hear bone shifting around inside him, plates grinding, cartilage popping, flesh blistering. He shook his new head, although I could not tell if this was because of the pain or because he was rejecting my pain.

He kept on shaking it long after he should have stopped. The motion set off a chain reaction of other movements. His eyes, now almost near his ears, fluttered and rolled. His hands and fingers spasmed. The bed rattled, the headboard banging into the wall behind him.

'Thomas?' I backed up. The other women did the same, until they were in the corridor outside. My husband's entire form became a shaking mass of limbs and blankets and tubes and then suddenly, a great tearing sound ripped through the room. There was a scalding hot burst of red, a cataclysmic eruption of form. Blood sprayed across the bed, the walls, my face. I cried out, frantically wiping my eyes.

'I can't see! I can't fucking *see!*'

But I could hear.

Down the corridor the women started screaming. I was glad someone else had to witness this, because it meant I was *not* mad, that someone else had to deal with the reality of my situation too.

I squeezed my eyes shut and tried to wipe the blood off my lids with soaking, sticky hands.

'We all have multitudes inside of us, Hope.' I froze. The voice that spoke was different, feminine. I didn't want to look. Tears rolled down my face, tears and blood, tears and blood and paint, what else is there, only tears and blood, tears and love, my love, my love.

A bright light gathered beneath my crusted eyelids. I heard that strange accumulating hum again, a sound that swept all other sound in the space up with it, a huge auditory wave tearing through a city after an earthquake, a sound like that of an electricity cable carrying an enormous voltage overhead, and not for the first time, I thought about cutting my ears off, both of them, right then and there, to save my brain from the burden.

The voice, which became not just one voice, but several, each one vying for supremacy, continued to speak. Thomas was still awake in there, I could tell, because the chorus used words in the exact same cadence he would. It used to be that he was just a mouthpiece for things greater than he, but now the balance had shifted. Now he spoke through the mouths of others, and I wondered what that meant for us. For him.

'Hear this,' the chorus intoned. I shuffled to the left, trying to feel my way out, but hit a wall. Then I stupidly peeked through my fingers, trying to orient myself. I was almost there. I rotated, saw the women in the corridor on their knees. They had been joined by other members of the Retinue, dozens of them, crammed into the tight space. They had flocked to the sounds of chaos. More faces pressed against the glass of the window from outside.

I snapped my eyes shut quickly, feeling my retinas burn.

'We're brought up to expect to be only one person, one *type* of person, but our brains are in a constant state of evolution. We change as our world changes around us, we become the experiences that occur in our lives, and we absorb the impact of a thousand interactions, a thousand different people, a thousand different events.'

I shuffled a few more steps. I was mere feet from the doorway. I could make it if I was subtle about it, I knew.

'We are the words that we speak and the things that we touch and the oceans we swim in, the sand that runs through our fingers, the wind that runs through our hair and over our bodies.'

One more step, and then I felt hands caress my face, wiping my skin, catching my tears, grabbing my clothes, pulling me back towards the bed.

I struggled.

'Don't touch me!'

But The Great God Thomas ignored me.

'We are the music we cry to and the books that change us. We are the first kiss and the last kiss, the hands we hold, the people who hurt us and hold us, the scars and wounds on our bodies.'

More hands, a clamour of fingers on my body, exploring my mortal form, wriggling into places they didn't belong, a glut of voices in my ears, or were they speaking directly into my mind? I felt as if I had been coated in a sticky, thick membrane, one that lay on top of the oils like heavy viscose. My nose started to bleed.

'Please stop touching me,' I wept.

More voices. So many threads of different entities, all woven into a thick, iron-strong chord. I could hear the walls of the Once Yellow House clanging and banging. Roof tiles, newly fixed, slid off, smashing on the ground outside. It was raining chaos.

Outside, voices raised in panic and fear. The light intensified. *Maybe it will burn everything away,* I thought. I was ready for oblivion.

'We are portals to an infinite number of possibilities and beings, an infinitesimally large number of outcomes, like drops of water trickling down a pane of glass, Hope. We are unpredictable and in a constant state of flux, and the sooner we realise that, recognise that, the less frightening the world becomes. We are chaos, and chaos is beautiful.' His own voice made it through the others for a moment, dominating.

'Chaos is the only absolute truth there is.'

He sank back into the chorus, then, and I heard music coming from him.

The light built. I felt the heat of it on my skin. I heard the panes of glass in the window behind me crack and splinter.

What was he trying to tell me?

Hands, hands, everywhere. Invading. I never want to be touched again. By anyone, by anything.

'Can you understand that?'

The many voices of Thomas asked me this question in a stilted way, as if reciting from a cheat card.

'I'm trying.' My chest heaving, nausea building. 'Please stop touching me.'

I felt my period start, in a warm, thick gush. It reminded me of losing the baby. *Our* baby. I began to wail.

'I'm at peace now. I'm at peace, Hope.' The voices cut through my distress, uncaring. Selfish, even now. Even like this.

The light grew brighter.

'I can no more stop what is happening to me than I can alter the direction the Earth is spinning in. Yet.'

Yet?

'All I can do is accept.'

'Please!' I cried. '*Please.* You're hurting me!'

With that, the hands all froze, instantly. Then they withdrew. They had been holding me up, it turned out. I sagged to my knees, a scarecrow with no stuffing. Fresh clotted blood trickling down my inner thigh. My period wasn't due for another ten days. There was blood on my tongue, in my ears, streaming from my nose.

The blinding light dimmed.

'I love you, Hope,' Thomas said. 'I have accepted the way of things. You should kill me the next time you see me.'

I had nothing left. Shivering uncontrollably, my flesh crawling.

I gradually opened my eyes, finally ready to see.

He was disassembled.

58.

Audio Transcript
File name: Once_Yellow_House_Transcription_19
Audio length: 00:04:07
Date transcribed: 12/24/2022

Kate: Disassembled?
Hope: His body has become this…tangled mass of like, fleshy strings, strings that launched themselves from the central point of his body and attached themselves to the walls around us with dozens of these small pink suckers that looked like hands, moved like hands, but weren't hands, not exactly, not as far as I could see. And beneath the strings, splayed out on what used to be the bed, was what was left of the rest of him. Like…violent echoes of human anatomy. A vaulted rise of ribs. Organs, exposed. Engorged intestinal tract, I remember that specifically. It was pulsing, snaking across and around and along things as if it had a mind of its own. There were bits of skin hanging off of everything like streamers at a party. Mattress springs stuck in the ceiling, and duck feathers everywhere. Blood painted the walls. It wasn't red, or blue, or yellow. It was brown.
Kate: The saddest of colors.
Hope: You know, the patterns of arterial spray…they stuck to the mould and looked just like the patterns on the ugly velvet wallpaper in the living room back when we first moved in. The paper I stripped. Like the Once Yellow House was redecorating itself with my husband's blood. Reverting to its original state before us. I thought that was it, then. I thought he had died. I was an idiot.
Kate: What happened next?
Hope: I don't really know. I was mostly delirious at that point. Even before that encounter, you have to understand. I was a mess. I was covered in crusted oil paint and mould-slime, I could hardly see at the best of times, my eyes were all swollen and raw and infected from rubbing at them. I had this cough…it still comes back, every now and then. The house was making me sick, and time no longer seemed like a construct I could reasonably adhere to. Not looking at the thing on the bed. All constructs were demolished after I saw that. All my certainties, nightmares.
Kate: There is a part of me…I wish…

Hope: That you'd seen him like that? No. There was nothing much to see, not really. Just flesh and bone, disassembled. It was more sad than anything. It certainly wasn't glorious. Just the ruins of someone I used to love.

Kate: Did he say anything else?

Hope: He did. I heard a voice say 'Don't cry, Hope.' Just like that. All gentle and loving, like nothing had happened at all. It took me a moment or two to find it, but there was a mouth nestling amongst the strings and tendons. It spoke from an anchor-point on a large, long plane of smooth bone, like a curved seashell. It was covered in fibroids and loose tendons that waved about in the air like the mould did, like kelp on a seabed. I went snorkelling once, and that's the best way I can describe it. The mouth was less of a mouth and more of a small hole lined with these tiny, soft white stubs of teeth that moved around the perimeter of his mouth-opening in a sort of clockwise motion. He had this long, flat blue tongue. I could feel myself detaching from my body very distinctly as I looked at him. I can still *feel* it. My mind like stringy cheese. He told me not to cry. I couldn't help it. It was the memories, you see.

Kate: You're crying now, Hope. Here.

[Slight pause as Hope blows her nose]

Hope: Memories. The pair of us in bed, in the before times. Not a…visual memory but a sensory one. The roughness of his skin beneath my fingertips. The feel of his hair against my cheek. The smell of him. The rise and fall of his chest, which dipped in the middle as if there was a space there for me to put my own heart, atop his, which I guess I did. Where did we go? Where did all that go? Are we still here after, despite everything? Does the good still remain, after the fact?

Kate: I think maybe it does. Memories, love, shared experiences…It's like energy, right? But you have to remember. For every good memory…

Hope: I still fell down the stairs because of him.

Kate: Right. You have to reprogramme your brain to see the bad in him before the good. Because there was no excuse for what he did to you. None.

Hope: And yet he was still trying to comfort me, even in that moment when his entire body was a broken, mutated thing on the bed before me. He was thinking of me. I think then I realised the depths of his love.

Kate: Forgive me, but that isn't love. That sounds...

Hope: Culty? *[laughs]* You're right. It does. He'd been downright abusive towards me since we first got together, I know that. But I still don't think it was all *him*. It was whatever got hold of him before all that. And it's the best way I can describe it. The feeling of being his. Not rapturous but...an education in love, I suppose.

Kate: After this encounter? What happened then?

Hope: I blacked out, I think. The rest of it...up until the massacre... is a blur, you'll have to read my diary. I remained a prisoner at the house until...until...

Kate: Until?

Hope: Well. You know what happened next.

Kate: End of days.

Hope: Yep. End. Of. Days. *[Nose blowing sounds]* More tea?

[End of recording]

59.

Diary Entry, personal diary of Hope Gloucester
November 10th, 2020

I keep thinking about faith, religion, and Van Gogh. About the so-called healing powers of art.

I think art is meant as a force of destruction, but what do I know? My head is an empty bowl, fully scooped out. There is little left inside except colour, and that colour is yellow, and it bounces and sloshes around like so much sewage, for that is all that has been left for me to make do with. A slurry of grey matter. Yellow matter?

I wish I could stop laughing. None of this is funny at all.

A somewhat directionless individual, I feel like Van Gogh was heavily influenced as a young man by the career choices of those around him. For a while he volunteered as a pastor in a grim mining village in Belgium, perhaps thinking to emulate his Protestant minister father, and become a preacher too. Whatever the motivation, he was openly dedicated to this ideal of helping others in any way possible. He gave away all his possessions, slept in mud and filth and dirt to put himself on the same level as the miners around him. People called him 'The Christ of the Coal Mine.'[27]

There is not a lot of difference between that title and 'The Great God Thomas', is there?

It doesn't take much, is what I am saying, to put yourself into a certain role, earthly or otherwise. You need a particular number of ingredients to start a successful cult: an ideology, a talent for communication, a magnetic personality (however that manifests), and the ability to disseminate the Word in a way that means it will reach as many people as possible. Thomas did it with Facebook groups and his phone, Van Gogh did it with art. Not consciously, not like Thomas did, but he gathered people together, nonetheless. He was part of a 'movement'. I wonder what he would make of the posthumous following he has. In many ways, Van Gogh's devotees

---

[27] Ed.note: Van Gogh kept preaching right up until the point the evangelical committee sponsoring him withdrew their support. He was devastated by their lack of belief in him, according to letters he wrote, but something about the poverty surrounding him during that time struck a deep, dark chord on the strings of his soul, and this is apparently when (encouraged heavily by his brother) he started to entertain the idea of becoming an artist.

are like the members of a cult. They seek his word, and his messages. I count myself one of those devotees, right down to the way I try to paint and sketch. I am a poor imitator of his school of thought, a shitty tin-pot copycat with smudgy ambitions bigger than her talent, and I have always known that, and Thomas went out of his way to remind me of that too, but it didn't stop me spreading the gospel I loved, smearing the paint on my body and the mouldy walls of this house and on the bits of cardboard and anything else I can find. His style, his compositions, his colours, it is a testament which I believe, and have always believed, is magical, in a visceral, almost elemental way. When I daub paint on things like he did, it feels like I am fighting off the poison of the Retinue, Word for Word.

I think Van Gogh wanted to project what he saw of the world back out, like a mirror reflecting a different, truer image. The things he drew and painted during his time preaching are vastly different to his later work. Grey and dreary. He was trying to convey the message of suffering. He was a compassionate and idealistic person, I believe that. Malleable, but full of compassion.

He would be jealous, perhaps, of what Thomas has achieved here at the Once Yellow House with seemingly very little effort or application. Van Gogh tried so hard to create a community of artists, of creatives, to surround himself with people of a similar type. He wanted them to reside at the Yellow House with him, and his vision was of this artistic utopia where people painted and shared ideas and inspirations in much the same way that they are now, outside this shitty bungalow, in their tented kingdom. He was never able to live out that dream.

Turns out, all he needed was a phone.

Maybe that's not Thomas' only secret. When he first started building the Retinue, he was a charming and easy-going sort of man. Affable, intelligent, not threatening at all. Just the sort of person you could trust, put your faith in.

That was before the Once Yellow House punched a hole in the back of his brain that opened him up like a portal.

I don't really know what I am trying to say, except…killing him will be an act of artistry all in itself, perhaps.

I don't know how to go about it, other than I think it has to be done when he is human, and I think it has to be something to do with the head, as it was when his brain was injured that this all began in earnest, and I understand the flawed and tangled logic this statement represents, but honestly, how does one kill a god?

I'll come up with something. In the meantime, the Retinue have their meetings, and people keep coming and people keep dying, I hear screams and moans and sex noises and panicked stampedes and music and clapping and chanting and all the while, they keep me a virtual prisoner in the Once Yellow House, where I have only Mimi and the mould and my paints for company. I am not allowed near Thomas, and I know why.

I'll find a way, though. I am smarter than they give me credit for.

60.

Diary Entry, personal diary of Hope Gloucester
November 14th, 2020

They caught someone- one of the newer members, someone not yet fully indoctrinated into cult mentality- trying to smuggle footage of his first Meeting out of camp, on his phone. He was flogged. Tied to a pole first, and flogged. What happened to him after that, I don't know. I haven't seen him since.

I could have told him phones are the root of all evil, though.

More graves pop up like mole hills alongside the train tracks.

The mood is definitely turning in camp, becoming ugly. A bit mediaeval. I worry about the children a lot, but they are almost feral themselves. The Retinue are supposed to be homeschooling them, but there seems to be little interest amongst either the children or the adults for a regular educational schedule. There was, for a while, but it was one of the first things to break down when the Meetings took on so much importance. Maybe the Retinue don't know what, exactly, to teach them outside of the word of Thomas anyway, and they hear all that in the daily Meetings. It's so awful to think of these young brains accepting all this at face value, to think of them absorbing the things they see and hear without once questioning it as an adult would. Their parents made a choice to be here, but they didn't.

Still, the younger kids remain oblivious to these tricky nuances. They run riot over the whole camp, while I've noticed the older children are given the unpleasant chores nobody else wants to do. A couple of the teenage girls in particular make me nervous: not for how they behave, but for how vulnerable they are. I see grown men looking at them, and I fear the worst. I know how these things work. And none of the usual rules apply here. There are none of the usual constraints that might protect a young girl from harm.

Other social constructs are also deteriorating fast. People have stopped washing (join the club), and I see more than a few muddy, torn and frayed yellow figures milling about through these tiny windows. At the start of all this, there were always washing lines strung up between tents that constantly bore the weight of freshly washed tunics, fluttering like so many yellow banners. Now nobody bothers. I see piles of cracked crockery stacked in the mud outside each tent. The portable restrooms they set up are overflowing, too. I can smell them from inside the Once Yellow House. There are rats, who steal the eggs laid by a couple of skinny chickens who have mostly stopped laying, and flies. You'd think the birds would eat the flies, but they don't, so the air and the sky is full of dozens of swarming small black pinpricks of life and feathers. It's all still surprisingly biblical, which I find amusing and tragic in equal part.

The birds have started sending me signals, I think. They spend a lot of time doing acrobatics in the sky which I watch through dirty portals, trying to decode their messages. They have a balletic ability to form dozens of different geometric patterns: most commonly, the perfect equilateral triangle in the sky, with three clusters of ravens at each tip of the triangle. As I watch, my eyes streaming, a string of birds will often form into a circle within the triangle, and the whole shape rotates clockwise in the sky, and I wish I knew what it meant, but I don't. I'm so sick of that motif. Sick to my stomach. Sick and hungry for some normality.

Hungry for food, too.

I am not the only one. The Retinue are not having much luck feeding themselves, not with the winter coming in so fast. We've had thick frosts and a few snow showers already. Lisa has authorised scouting groups who occasionally journey into town to beg, borrow or steal. They often come back looking dejected, sometimes with bruises, as if they got themselves into a scuffle.

It's amazing how quickly the wheels have come off this thing. I remember when they first turned up, the Retinue. They seemed so full of excitement, of hope. Now, the world out there looks like a prison camp. I always assumed cults were full of rich people, but Lisa seems to be the only one with any money. She remains well-fed and almost glamorous, her hair always clean and styled nicely. I have a feeling she uses the bathroom in the bungalow, which still has hot water, and from which everyone else but me is banned. I found one of her hairs in the sink and ate it. I don't know why.

The rest of the Retinue are not as fortunate as Lisa. They shamble about camp, going through the motions of keeping busy until Lisa spots them and makes them busy for real. Physical labour is an effective form of control, rendering anyone considering any form of dissent too tired to do so. Most of their tasks are to do with fixing up this bungalow, which can no longer be thought of as a shitty bungalow. Instead it is a developer's dream, on the outside at least. Just like Thomas said he always wanted. Fresh paint. New shingles. Wood, sanded, filled, replaced, nicely finished. Neat porch bannisters, new screens. Window casements and shutters. Even the wonky front door has been re-hung, so wonky it is, no more. The roof is all new too, although that doesn't stop the birds shitting on it.

It's all facade, though. Inside, it is still a horror story of damp and rot and mould and rodents and woodworm and decay. I caught some of the Retinue scraping the mould off the walls to eat as a snack. I was furious, and shrieked at them until they left. I am not sure, but I feel as if their eyes have started to turn yellow, both the irises and the whites around them. I don't know if mine have gone that way too, I haven't looked in a mirror for a while. What would I see? A poor man's *Sorrow*[28], is what.

Everyone has gone mad here. I suppose I should feel at home.

I have run out of paint, too. I have asked for more, but the Retinue (Lisa) ignore my pleas. She does not want me to express myself. I have tried everything, crying, begging, threatening, offering myself up. There are no more paints, and no more paintings to put up in the attic. The Once Yellow House seems as sad about this as I do, and I have noticed patches of mould that previously displayed vivid colours, primary blue, etc, go grey and sad in response. Sometimes the sporangia in those dreary patches shudder and shake pitifully to get my attention, and when I go over, they appear to be beckoning me. The mould still wants me to make paint out of it, but even if I did that, I can't see Thomas anymore, so what would I paint? I would try and create a portrait from memory, but I can't really remember what he looked like before all of this.

I hear him calling my name, sometimes, down the corridor. He calls for me, and I call back, but they won't let us near each other.

---

[28] Ed.note: Gloucester is referring to Van Gogh's chalk drawing *Sorrow*, dated 1882. Sorrow is a sketched portrait of a woman he had an affair with, a pregnant homeless prostitute and mother who went by the name of Sien. Sien was Van Gogh's tragic muse, discovered in poor health and dire circumstances. Van Gogh tried to rescue and nurse her, but the relationship ultimately failed. It is unclear whether Gloucester means to draw parallels here with herself, or with her husband. Van Gogh later referred to this artwork as 'something coming directly from my own heart'.

61.

Diary Entry, personal diary of Hope Gloucester
November 16th, 2020

A fight broke out today, just before the scheduled Meeting. I don't know what it was about, but I did see a man beat another man to death with a baton, right in front of his kids.

I tried to run outside to help, but was stopped at the door of the bungalow by two of the Retinue. They told me it wasn't my place to get involved. I fought back, which was dumb, but I've had it with all of them, I really have. My reward was that one of them clubbed me so hard round the side of the head I was knocked unconscious.

I woke up on the floor of the living room some time later, surrounded by cushions and blankets, and I saw a woman frowning down at me, but my head hurt too much to talk to her, so I closed my eyes again and dreamed of Thomas.

In my dream he was surrounded by a noxious blush, a halo of sickness, and I could see things moving amongst his exposed organs, which were clear as glass. The thin membrane of what I think was once his stomach rippled, and bulged, and sometimes I thought I could see fingers pressing against him from the inside out, human fingers, and sometimes there were different sorts of disturbances. A wet, furred leg with a cloven hoof at the end. An eye, full of flames. A searing bright lump of what looked like coagulated stars, pulsing in time to an echo of a heartbeat. A shimmering, delicate wing, like that of a dragonfly, iridescence swirling amongst the garish pink. Other things I couldn't attach names to, perhaps because there were none in any of our languages. He was a roiling sea of wasted potential, in both life and my dreams. A bridge I was too frightened to cross.

Why then did I still care about him? He was an abomination, but a beautiful abomination. In him, I saw an endless sea of possibilities, a raw and pure creative energy that I would never find anywhere else and I knew that. He was a monster, but he had once been my monster, and I would love him in spite, or perhaps because of that.

When I woke up for the second time, they told me that the Meeting had been brought forward. The mood in camp was mutinous, so a demonstration was needed to keep the cattle in line. The man who had hit me was no longer with us, I was then informed.

He had exploded rather messily in his tent, and the only thing left of him was a false tooth and his baton.

I won't go to the meeting, no matter how much they want me to be part of it. I won't. But what I will do is use the time they are all distracted to find something to help me in my mission. I am starting to form a vague plan, but it's dependent on getting to Thomas and passing him a message, somehow. I need him to create a distraction long enough to allow me to get to him properly, unsupervised.

Somehow somehow somehow. I don't know what I will do once I'm up close and personal, either. Smother him with a pillow? Inject him with some sort of poison? Shoot him? What with? How can I even be sure he can be killed?

I can't.

All I can do is try my best.

On the subject of dreams, I remembered another quote from Van Gogh, another line from a letter he wrote. He said 'I dream my painting, and I paint my dream.'

Perhaps that is what I should do. If the mould wants me to. I can't paint from reality, not anymore, but I am cocooned by living pigments, and I could scrape space on the floorboards, and I could paint my dreams.

If nothing else, it would help keep the boredom at bay.

.

62.

Diary Entry, personal diary of Hope Gloucester
November 17th, 2020

'Remember the good in us, won't you?' He calls as they stretcher him out each night. He is still in there somewhere. I find that remarkable. And I'm trying to remember, something about our old lives, *anything*, but it is hard, it is as much as I can do to continue living, it is as much as I can do to remember to breathe in and out, in and out, because he is working up to something big, I can sense it, I can tell he is trying to take final form, and after he has, I don't know what will happen, but he has stopped fighting his fate, and I have stopped fighting mine. God Slayer, they will call me. God Slayer.

And Lisa has an axe. I remembered this while I was grinding myself some mould paste, because I am now out of food and the Retinue won't let me out to forage for more. I was staring out the window, smashing the spongy filaments up in a bowl with a fork and shovelling them into my mouth (they are surprisingly delicious and actually quite filling) when I saw the axe lodged into the chopping block near the wood pile, which is also running low- Lisa has been too occupied with important things to replenish it. And it all came to a wonderful moment of clarity as I saw it.

What better way to kill a god than to chop off his head? It works for hydras, or snakes. I can't remember which. It worked for saints too. Was it John the Baptist? Brahma lost a head also. I saw a postcard one of Thomas' friends sent us once from a temple in India.

I'm clutching at straws, and I don't know whether this is the right path, but I do know that the injury Thomas sustained to his head when the attic ladder came down on him was the singular event that let it all in. All the chaos. His head was a portal, and the house opened him up.

I still think I have to go for the head.

63.

Diary Entry, personal diary of Hope Gloucester
November 18th, 2020[29]

I watched Lisa chopping [...] The axe [...] sharp, I can tell, for she takes care of her things well- tools, I mean. Not people.

I don't think I can do [...] I don't think I am strong [...] Mentally, physically. I just want to sleep [...] do that even, not anymore.

He calls to me constantly [...] the corridor. I've taken to murmuring: 'I'm coming, honey,' like we are back in our old apartment in the city...calling to me...the bedroom or kitchen [...] miss that [...] him.

I often wonder what life [...] like if [...] happened.

[...] scraped [...] patch [...] ground some pigment using the mould and my own phlegm. We'll see. It's better than nothing.

Why do they stay? I [...] would have run from fear...religiosity is a powerful cement, it [...] But am I any differ [...]

---

[29] Ed.note: much of this entry appears to have been damaged by mold and patches of damp and paint that impacted the paper of the diary. We have replicated as much as we could decipher and used ellipses to indicate the lost words.

64.

Diary Entry, personal diary of Hope Gloucester
November 19th[30], 2020 (1)

I dreamed. I painted my dream on the floor this morning, and when I had done, I knew it was time. Or that I was out of time. Or that Thomas was. The [...] portentous.

After I finished [...] back to admire my [...] as if the painting was moving. I sank to my knees and pressed my face up against the [...] saw tiny coloured filaments wriggling. Special pigment [...] yellow in particular shone out from the [...] like liquid gold.

The dream was [...] I turned to the door, but my path was blocked by the Retinue, who had all sunk to their knees.

[...] And I am. Somehow, holding the axe [...] decision easier. Like the difference between deciding to go for a walk and actually putting on walking shoes. Intention. Action with intention [...] I shouldered the sharp object with a confidence I didn't understand, and I suddenly felt like Jack from Jack and the Beanstalk.

Then, he was beneath me, the axe haft was back in both of my hands.

And if my heart were not broken before, it is now.

---

[30] The day of the Yellow Massacre. This page is also very difficult to decipher as the entries are scribbled in haste and there is a lot of water and mold damage.

65.

Diary Entry, personal diary of Hope Gloucester
November 19th[31], 2020 (2)

They are calling a daytime Meeting. This is unprecedented. Something has set Lisa into a panic, and the gong has been struck. I can see the usual stream of yellow tunics trickling into the temple. I can also see winter storm clouds gathering overhead. There was a thunder rumble, earlier. The birds are the most restless I've ever seen them, wheeling and shifting and painting the sky with soaring patterns.

The Once Yellow House is in a similar state of anticipation. The walls have come alive, same as my skin. The mould there has become thick and long, almost like hair. It dances in time to a pulse I can't hear. The house breathes along with it. I wonder if it is Thomas' heartbeat. If he still has a heart that can beat.

I think my eyes are definitely yellow now. I catch two glowing orbs in the windowpane reflections as I gaze outside.

I miss my dog. I wonder where she is now. I hope she's safe. I hope some nice family picked her up. I hope she's warm and comfortable.

Lisa came for Thomas ten minutes ago. I gather, from the squealing coming down the hallway, that he is not being fully cooperative. Good. Why should he be? He can no longer tell enemy from friend.

More crying outside the window. They have dressed some of the children up as if for a party. New robes, clean faces. Brushed and neatly plaited hair. Only girls, ranging in age but all of them far too young. They look placid, spacey. Some of them sway on their feet and make weird motions with their hands, as if interacting with things that aren't there. I think they have been drugged.

On the temple roof, people have painted a slogan. It reads:
They shall usher in the End Days!
Bask in His Glory!

Underneath, a great eye in a triangle. So much stolen symbolism, it makes me dizzy. Humans really only ever repurpose and

---

[31] Ed.note: This is the day of the Yellow Massacre. This page has escaped most of the mold damage.

recycle things, don't they? All is derivative. Unless you're a scientist. Perhaps even then.

I think I know what Lisa has planned.

Doomsday cults only ever end in one way, don't they?

The time is now. Now or never. As Van Gogh said (I have it on a postcard) 'If I am worth anything later, I am worth something now.'

I don't think he actually said that, I think someone translated that badly from one of his letters[32].

But it has to be now. I'm going to hide this diary in the back of the hearth once I finish this entry. It may well be my last. Hopefully I'll be able to come back for it after. If not, someone will find it one day.

And if you do, I would like you to know that I tried, and I am sorry.

And that I loved him then, and love him still. And I know that makes me pathetic, but I can't help it.

I sincerely hope the world does not end. I like to think that even if it did, the Once Yellow House would remain standing, floating out in the vastness of space with that damned attic catch still broken and mould all over the walls. Who knows.

When it comes to Thomas, nothing is certain anymore.

---

[32] Gloucester is referring to this letter: https://vangoghletters.org/vg/letters/let480/letter.html . 'But if later, then now too.'

66.

Audio Transcript
File name: Once_Yellow_House_Transcription_20
Audio length: 00:14:32
Date transcribed: 12/24/2022

Kate: Oh no you don't. You don't get out of it that easily. I know you remember everything that happened. You owe it to me to tell me. You owe it to those children you never saved.
Hope: Fuck you.
Kate: Your anger doesn't work on me, don't you get that? Nobody is as angry as I am right now!
Hope: Why? What is it with you? What the hell did you have to lose that was so precious, anyway? A tiny bit of a thing, like you? I doubt it was your virginity.
Kate: My sister, you selfish fucking bitch! I lost my fucking sister!

[Pause of six seconds]

Hope: What?
Kate: Yeah, that made you go real quiet, huh? My eleven-year-old kid sister. I didn't go to the Retinue alone, Hope. I would never have gone of my own free will. My mom dragged us both to that camp, and neither of them ever left. I tried everything to get her out, by the time I realised how dangerous things were. They wouldn't let anyone leave. Why do you think I tried so damned hard to get close to your husband? To be his favorite?
Hope: I see. That...that makes sense now. I understand.

[Pause]

Kate: I don't think you do. I needed her to be safe. She wasn't.
Hope: And were you?
Kate: What?
Hope: His favorite.
Kate: Go fuck yourself, Hope! *[Sound of chair scraping back violently]* You know I wasn't! Is my sister alive? My mom? No. *You* were his favorite! You and only you. I know because he used to call

out your name, even when he was...even when he was transforming...I tried so hard to be you, to be what he needed but...

[Quick footsteps as Kate leaves the room. Recording keeps rolling, presumably Hope does not know how to control the app on Kate's phone]

Hope: You go fuck yourself. You. I was his favorite. *Me!*

[Weeping sounds for approximately ten mins]

[Footsteps as Kate returns. Chair scraping]

Kate: I'm sorry. I should not have lost my temper like that.

[Weeping subsides. Hope blows her nose]

Hope: What...what was her name?
Kate: My sister? Her name was Alison.
Hope: I'm sorry. I didn't know.
Kate: I didn't tell you.
Hope: I didn't think to ask.
Kate: It's okay.
Hope: I assumed you were there alone, of your own volition.
Kate: I would never have fallen for anything like that. I've never believed in God, or spirituality, or the supernatural, or...I didn't even have social media, back then, or now. No. My mom was the susceptible one. She was depressed after Dad left. We were poor. We lived a rough existence. The trailer was small, and everything was broken, and she could never afford nice things. Or to get anything repaired. She stopped working, going out, sleeping. She would stay up all night, spend hours and hours scrolling and commenting on shit, Alice down the fucking Rabbit Hole, you know? Anyway, she found his group, and the rest is history. Thomas got his hooks into her, and that was that. She saw something in him. Something that could save her, I think she thought. A promise of family, maybe. I tried so hard to convince her that she was being irresponsible, deranged, almost. I even called the cops, but they said there was nothing they could do, Mom was a grown adult in possession of a sound mind. Then I tried calling child services on her, because I was worried about Alison, but she got wind of that and moved out to the

camp before they could visit. I ended up going along just to keep Alison safe. I failed.

[Pause of ten seconds]

Hope: I never made you that tea, did I? *[Clears throat]* Let me.
Kate: Actually... I'll take some of that whiskey.
Hope: Not too early now?
Kate: When in Rome.

[Whiskey cork pops, two glasses are filled generously. A subtle glass clink, followed by sipping sounds]

Kate: Hope? Please. Please tell me what happened that day. Tell me so I can find some measure of peace. Please. I am begging you.
Hope: There is no need to beg. I'll tell you what I remember, but I should warn you. It's hazy. Messy, you understand? There was a lot going on.
Kate: Of course.
Hope: But first. To Alison.

[Glasses clink]

Kate: To Alison.

[Recording ends]

67.

Audio Transcript
File name: Once_Yellow_House_Transcription_21
Audio length: 00:05:52
Date transcribed: 12/24/2022

Kate: How did you get out of the Once Yellow House? If they were keeping you prisoner inside.

Hope: Easily enough. The incident with the man who hit me and then promptly exploded minutes after in his tent meant security had eased off, substantially. I suppose it's as you said: I was still His favorite. Besides, this Meeting…it was obvious that this was going to be different from all the others. It had an air of finality about it. Everyone just dropped what they were doing and filed into the temple, including my unconvincing bodyguards. The rest of the camp was deserted. I waited until I was sure everyone was inside the temple, then I went to find the axe. It was still on the chopping block where Lisa had left it. The birds were going crazy by this point, overhead. I remember the wind had picked up, and this massive storm just broke, out of nowhere. The sky went a funny color. Green[33]. I've never seen that before. I could hear chanting coming from the temple, the usual nonsense, and I heard screaming. I mean, there was usually screaming in the temple, but this…this was something else. This was like…like how I imagined Hell would sound, if I'd ever believed in such a place.

Kate: I remember that. The noise. That was one of the worst things.

Hope: You were inside?

Kate: Yeah, I was there for that part. I'd been on a scouting mission to town. Unsuccessful. Some guy in a store had thrown a can of tomatoes at my head, told me to get out. Told me the Retinue was ruining his town. I did as he asked, but took the tomatoes with me. Anyway, I didn't know there was a meeting until after it had started. I got back and ran inside just as all the noise started up. I saw…I couldn't tell you what I saw, because it was chaos inside. I couldn't get close enough to the front. I just heard the screaming. I looked for

---

[33] Ed.note: Derecho Storms are characterised by green skies resulting from blue light refracted from raindrops clashing with yellow sunlight, creating a green effect.

my mom, I looked for Alison, but I couldn't find either of them. That's when the stampede started.

Hope: I remember.

Kate: Bodies falling to the floor, more bodies on top, crushing them. It was awful. I didn't want to leave until I had Alison, but I knew if I stayed I'd be...I'd. Huh. Never mind. That's when the whole structure collapsed on top of us. I didn't let that stop me, though. I just crawled around under it, looking for my sister.

Hope: It was only canvas and guy ropes. They were easy enough to cut with the axe. The whole thing went down like a cake sinking in the middle when it's come out of the oven too soon, you know? Just like that. Flumpf. I saw all these bodies moving around under the canvas. You, I guess. Moaning and shrieking, all these horrible hummocks wailing like it was the end of the world, just like Thomas had told them. It was the only thing I could think of to do. I thought of it like a giant net, see. I thought if I trapped them all in one go, I stood a better chance. Of getting to him. In the end, that part was easy. He was glowing yellow, and I saw it through the temple fabric. I sliced him out of there and dragged him over to the chopping block while the rest of the Retinue floundered under the canvas. I knew I didn't have much time, but he was easy to haul. He was human, but a lot smaller than his normal height and weight. Kind of...of...

Kate: Childlike.

Hope: Don't say that. That makes it so much worse.

Kate: Sorry.

Hope: I...I...oh, God. I placed Thomas' head down on the block and put my foot on his head to hold him steady. The Retinue were slowly crawling out from beneath the collapsed temple, crawling on their knees through the pouring rain and the mud, wailing in unison, weeping, and I kept thinking: but none of you *know* him. How can you love him this much? And he looked up at me, around the foot I had planted on him, and said: 'Do it.' He was crying too. His tears were yellow, which won't surprise you.

Kate: He knew it was his time.

Hope: But I couldn't do it.

Kate: Not even then?

Hope: Not even then. Because it was Thomas, *my* Thomas, the Thomas who used to slip his hand into my pocket in cold weather to help warm my own cold fingers up, who would sway in time to any music he heard with me, no matter what the beat, he would hold to this rhythm only he and I had. The Thomas who once told me that I could be anything I wanted to be, if I put my mind to it. The Thomas who cradled my head in his arms first thing in the morning and bought my first painting and baked my favorite banana bread every Friday.

Kate: The Thomas who made you fall down a staircase. Who made you miscarry. You demeaned and belittled you. Who cut you off from your family and friends. Who lied. Who-

Hope: He begged me to do it. He lay there on that block, chest heaving, staring up at me, and he did look like a child, frightened, abused. I suddenly realised he was naked and pink as a mole-rat, with this downy soft fur covering his entire body. He was unblemished apart from that, like a newborn, and the skin beneath the fur was so thin I could see every inner part of him working, circulatory system, blood, organs, heart, oh, his heart, none of where it was supposed to be—just like my dream. Although there was still a small hollow in his chest, dead in the centre, where I used to lay my head, the altar upon which, like I said, I once placed my own heart. And I thought I had to reclaim it, you see, because life had to go on after Thomas, I knew that.

Kate: Godslayer. Hard to go on after that, right?

Hope: Husband slayer. You see how I live, right?

Kate: Then what?

Hope: I brought the axe down on Thomas' neck. ***[Muffled noise]***

[Pause]

Kate: You did the right thing, Hope. You did the right thing.

Hope: The first blow was not enough, I was not strong enough. I remember his body began to jerk and flail about. I wrenched the axe out of his neck. It was hard. There must be a knack to wood chopping that I don't have. I lifted the axe again. I heard Lisa shrieking my name, but she was far enough away I knew I had time. I closed my eyes, because it was easier not to look, you know? Even though I knew I'd probably lop my own foot off, I couldn't look at him. I remember calling up a stillness from deep within myself, and as I brought the axe down for a second blow, I understood it was a…a definitive one. I knew I was possessed of all the strength I could draw from this universe, for there was a…a…cosmos within me, too. We've all got one, spinning away behind our organs. It had always been there, but I lacked the clarity of vision to see up until that moment, is all.

Kate: Then...what then?

Hope: There was a sound, a sound I've never heard before and never will again. I opened my eyes as my husband's head rolled free of its body, and then, then...

Kate: And then there was light.

Hope: And then there was light.

Kate: That's when I found Alison, underneath my mom. They were both dead. Trampled to death...I decided to run.

Hope: Then you did what I could not. Pour me some more of that, please?

[Recording paused]

68.

Audio Transcript
File name: Once_Yellow_House_Transcription_22
Audio length: 00:01:22
Date transcribed: 12/24/2022

Kate: So. You succeeded. You became a godslayer.

Hope: I mean I decapitated him, sure. I remember how Thomas' head gaped up at me from the ground. His eyes were flowing with this rainbow light, it was pouring out of his open mouth, from his ears, from his neck. It went up into the sky, and all the birds whizzing around out there started to drop, one by one, then in a massive downpour. But I didn't slay him. I didn't do anything beyond removing his head, turns out. I had realised something a bit too late.

Kate: What?

Hope: I had taken his head off, right? But the portal was still there, the giant dent in the back of his skull, the dent caused by the attic door, and his brain was still *intact* in there, which meant that I hadn't really achieved anything. That much was obvious by the fancy light show, the dead birds. I had gone through all that for nothing. My stupid hypothesis had been wrong. The brain was the key, not the head that carried it.

Kate: Oh.

Hope: The Retinue, however, were going ape-shit for it. They saw it as, I don't know. Something sublime, I guess. More proof of the divine. They went wild. Some of them started biting into the corpses of the birds that rained down on them from above, their mouths all stuffed with these little dark feathers. Others started singing and dancing around us like I was a fucking maypole. It was chaos. And new gods thrive on chaos, don't they? That's when I noticed his head starting to grow. It grew, and these horrible crab-like legs popped out of the bottom of his neck, with these spear-like tips, and the hum came back, the strongest I'd heard it. After that…it's all a bit of a blur.

Kate: Try. Try to remember.

Hope: The Retinue went insane. All of them, with that hum. They turned on each other. I cannot tell you the things I thought I saw them do to each other. It was a frenzy. They massacred each other and wept in ecstasy as they carried out acts of unspeakable violence.

Kate: So you're telling me...the things I saw that day...they were real. It really happened.

Hope: You're asking me that, even now? After everything you've heard?

Kate: I just...I don't know.

Hope: As for Thomas...I remember he scuttled around eating as many of the Retinue he could find, seizing them with these leg-pincers and stuffing them into his massive mouth, which still belched light, like a crab eating sand on the beach, you know? And I'm fairly sure he grew so big he blotted out the sky, and then after that...Well. Lisa got to me. She was holding a handful of someone's hair in one fist and a dead bird in the other. I remember that much. She launched herself at me like a wildcat, knocked me backwards. But she misjudged. I felt, rather than heard, the impact as she fell on her own axe, the lower tip of which was still stuck in the chopping block right next to me. She fell on the upper tip, which jutted skywards, face first. Twitched a bit. After that I kind of blacked out. I know you think I'm lying, but I'm not. I drifted into a faint, and then I was yanked out of it by ...by...

Kate: The explosion.

Hope: I think his mortal form could no longer accommodate the force it was under. He felt pressurised, like I said. A god-bomb. He couldn't take it anymore. He just...yeah.

Kate: The god bomb went off.

Hope: The rest, you know.

[Long pause]

Kate: It's quite a story, Hope.
Hope: I know.

[Recording ends]

69.

Audio Transcript
File name: Once_Yellow_House_Transcription_23
Audio length: 00:02:42
Date transcribed: 12/24/2022

Kate: You mourn him?
Hope: Of course. Van Gogh once said there is nothing more truly artistic than to love people. He also said he would continue trying to love, in spite of everything.
Kate: I like that. But it doesn't excuse…
Hope: There is nothing left to love now anyway, except this new dog of mine.
Kate: When was the last time you painted, Hope?
Hope: Oh I've given up on all that.
Kate: I think your paintings…your art. Your love and passion for it. I think it opened you up to loving. Maybe it could once again.

[Long pause]

Hope: Maybe you're right. I think it could be true. Love and art. Love *as* art. As an art form. I think, when I brought that axe down on Thomas's neck, that I created the ultimate portrait. *Man deconstructed.* I painted with sharp steel. Maybe that's what finally made him self-destruct. Or maybe he figured out a kill-switch for himself, to end it all before the End of Days became a truth.
Kate: Maybe he did it for love, too. Maybe he wasn't such a terrible person, at the end.
Hope: Maybe. It's easier to think like that than to think any other way.
Kate: Where did you go, after?
Hope: Oh, I woke up, and everyone and everything around me was destroyed, flattened, covered in body parts. Even the Once Yellow House, which hurt me a great deal more than I thought it would. Still, my journal survived. It was that hearth, you see. It was made of strong stuff. I think the sigils on it protected it somehow. I wondered why they didn't protect the Retinue, because they had that symbol tattooed on them, you know? But then I stopped caring. I stopped trying to make it make any sense, because I knew it

wouldn't. Even now, hearing myself talk, none of it makes any sense. And maybe it doesn't have to.

Kate: Maybe.

Hope: After that, I started walking along the train tracks. There was no reason to stay. Everything had been destroyed. There was no trace of Thomas, not even his headless body. Then, the sirens started up and got closer, fast. There were still rainbows falling like snow past my ears, falling like dead birds, falling like body parts. Thomas had spewed forth this beautiful energy, until eventually, he gave out, guttering like a failing engine, and the world turned slowly grey, muted, soft, calm, normal colors, no more primaries, no more yellow, and I thought to myself *it is done. We are done.* And this is almost how they found me, the police. Almost. Almost.

[Pause]

Hope: I think I'm done talking now.
Kate: I think I'm done listening.

[Recording ends]

70.

Email: Once Yellow Kate
Sat, Nov 19th, 2022, 08:44 am
iwasonceyellowtoo@gmail.com

To cemeterygatesmedia@gmail.com

Joe,

As promised, I am emailing you the last of the audio files. Sorry for the delay. I've been spending time with Hope, processing her story, exploring the countryside around here a bit. I figure you flew me all this way, and there is nothing much to return to, so I might stay a while. Hope's house is interesting, with some unique features, but needs a little work. I could help her with that. It might let me heal some, who knows. If nothing else, I want to swim in the bay near the cottage. Maybe I'll make it out to the Island I saw when I was driving in. Take a look at the cherry tree that seems to be blossoming there, even in winter. It will be nice to do something challenging. Push myself. I think that is the only way I'm going to be able to move on.

    I have also taken photos and scanned some images (the owner of the small gas station has a scanner she let me use, absurdly) from Hope's scrapbook and diary, with her permission. I'll link to those separately. I'm not sure how useful any of it is. It's quite the story, as I don't think you need me to tell you, not by now. You'll have listened to some of what I have sent already. If nothing else, it shows you how her brain works, I think. I've been encouraging her to paint again. I hope, in time, she might. She has some talent for it, although I don't know much about these things, but I like what I've seen of her art. It makes me feel things, which I guess is the whole point.

    As I type this, I'm sitting here in my car in some random rest stop (the only place I can find good enough signal), and I'm thinking about love. I'm thinking about what love is for, and who it is for, and why it matters, and why it doesn't. And I know we are all born purposeless, without any destiny within ourselves beyond the living and the fucking and the dying, as Hope would put it, but I think if we were to step outside of that, and find ourselves a purpose, it might be to hang our hats upon a coat peg called love, it might be to find whatever capacity it is within ourselves to feel all the things with all the versions of us there are, all the versions of our lovers. To shuffle cards, and deal with the hand we're given. And I think that is why she needs to paint again, I really do. Her love came out in art, whether or not she knew that. Not in him. She was mistaken about that. She never loved him, not like she thinks she did. But she did love her art. It feels like it was the only healthy emotional expression she ever had.

Hope has said I can stay as long as I like. We are both alone in this world, and I know nobody else other than this woman could ever understand what I've been through. I'm the closest thing she has to not being alone, although she might never fully let me in, I suspect.

I burned my yellow tunic.

The media still talks about the massacre a lot, I suspect. I don't know, because we're almost completely off grid, out here. A notebook and pen, that's enough technology for now. Even this email is testing my resilience. But I can imagine what's being said. *The Yellow Massacre.* No doubt, by now, there are a million fresh conspiracy theories, a dozen novels, three movies, five documentaries, a thousand web articles, none of them coming anything close to the truth, but of course they can't. Speculation never can. Truth is stranger than fiction, someone once said, and I could almost bring myself to believe in that, if I could bring myself to believe in anything.

Please do not try to find us. Please mind our privacy. You have everything, now. What you choose to do with it is up to you.

Yours, with respect,
Once Yellow Kate

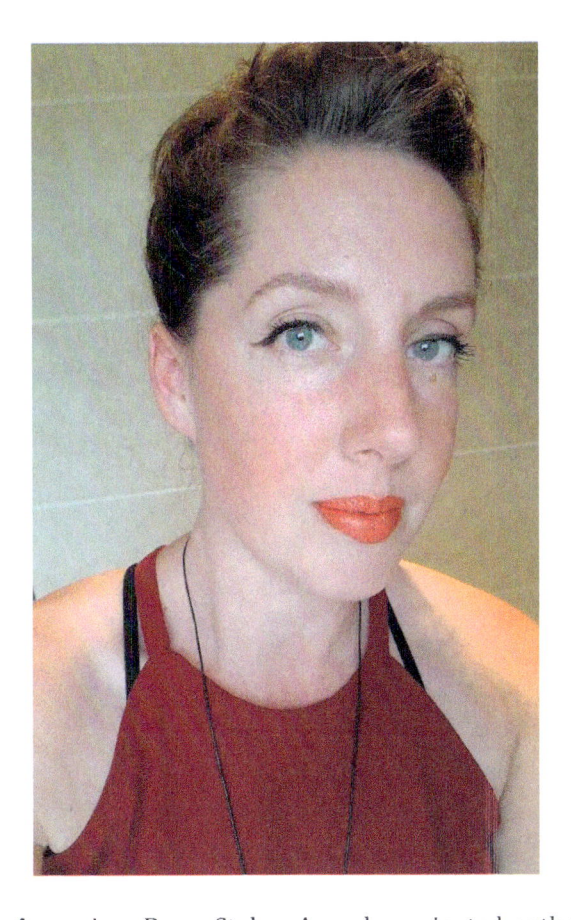

Gemma Amor is a Bram Stoker Award nominated author, voice actor and illustrator based in Bristol. Her debut short story collection *Cruel Works of Nature* came out in 2018. Other books include *Dear Laura, White Pines, Six Rooms, Girl on Fire* and *These Wounds We Make*. Her traditionally published debut, *Full Immersion*, was released in 2022 by Angry Robot books.

Gemma is the co-creator of horror-comedy podcast *Calling Darkness*, starring Kate Siegel, and her stories feature regularly on popular horror anthology shows *The NoSleep Podcast, Shadows at the Door, Creepy, The Hidden Frequencies* and *The Grey Rooms*. She also appears in a number of print anthologies and has made numerous podcast appearances to date, illustrates her own works, and hand-paints book covers for other horror authors. She narrates audiobooks, too.

OTHER TITLES BY GEMMA AMOR

Cruel Works of Nature
Dear Laura
Grief is a False God
White Pines
These Wounds We Make
Girl on Fire
Six Rooms
Full Immersion
Christmas at Wheeldale Inn

Coming soon...

Fear to Tread
The Folly

Printed in Great Britain
by Amazon